WHO SHALL LIVE

CAROLYN GEDULD

Black Rose Writing | Texas

ISBN: 978-1-68433-780-4
PUBLISHED BY BLACK ROSE WRITING
www.blackrosewriting.com

Printed in the United States of America
Suggested Retail Price (SRP) $19.95

Who Shall Live is printed in Book Antiqua

*As a planet-friendly publisher, Black Rose Writing does its best to eliminate unnecessary waste to reduce paper usage and energy costs, while never compromising the reading experience. As a result, the final word count vs. page count may not meet common expectations.

For my sons
Marcus Geduld and Daniel Geduld

GRATEFUL ACKNOWLEDGEMENT
IS MADE TO THE FOLLOWING
FOR PREVIOUSLY PUBLISHED CHAPTERS:

Infected. Vol.1: Tales to Read At Home. "Who By Plague." Spring, 2020. Pp. 73-83.

The Blue Nib. Online. "Who By Wild Beast." May 30, 2020. https://thebluenib.com/who-by-wild-beast-short-fiction-by-by-carolyn-geduld/ (Earlier version)

The Writers and Readers Magazine. "Who By Earthquake." May/June 2020. Pp. 81-82

Red Coyote. "Who Shall Wander." University of South Dakota. May, 2020.

Backchannels. "Who Shall Be Uplifted" July 2020 https://www.backchannelsjournal.net/edition-no-5-2020

Writers in Lockdown. "Who Shall Profit." July, 2020. Pp: 197-204.

Bookends Review. Online. "Who By Stoning" 9/11/20 (Earlier version.)

The Medley. "Who By Sword" https://themedley.in/issue5/fiction/who-by-sword/

ACKNOWLEDGEMENTS

In gratitude to the following for their support and encouragement:
Richard Balaban, Olivia Benowitz, Rabbi Brian Besser, Julie Bloom, Doreen Cole, Ryan Cole, Daniel Geduld, Marcus Geduld, Audrey Heller, Jackie Olenick, Leo Olenick, Renate Peters, Heather Rayl, Christina Ryan, Sue Swartz, Michael Taft, and the Black Rose Writing team.

WHO SHALL LIVE

LET US SPEAK OF THE AWESOMENESS

Who shall live and who shall die,
Who shall reach the end of his days and who shall not,
Who shall perish by water and who by fire,
Who by sword and who by wild beast,
Who by famine and who by thirst,
Who by earthquake and who by plague,
Who by strangulation and who by stoning,
Who shall be settled and who shall wander,
Who shall be sane and who shall be insane,
Who shall be serene and who shall be tormented,
Who shall be impoverished and who shall profit,
Who shall be humiliated and who shall be uplifted.
But repentance, prayer and righteousness remove
the severity of the decree.
–Unetaneh Tokef—8th Century Jewish Poem

CHAPTER 1
WHO SHALL BE SETTLED

Three months after Joe died in 1999 in a drunk-driving accident, followed by the autopsy, the funeral, the drug screen report, the casseroles from friends and neighbors, and the many condolence cards, Edith said the words to herself:

I am not a wife. I am a widow.

She gazed into her vanity mirror. Her complexion appeared darker while her shoulder-length hair looked grayer and coarser. Her hand grabbed the scissors and cut several inches off the back and sides. Who cared if it stuck out? Who cared if she didn't wear make-up, or if she didn't bathe? She was a *widow*.

There was nothing to look forward to, nowhere to go, no events on her calendar. Invitations to parties and dinners had dropped off. Couples didn't want "third-wheels" around. She climbed back into bed even though she had dressed for the day. Until now, she had been a *wife*. She had been a *wife* for thirty-seven years. Who was she if she was not a *wife?*

At eight, there was banging at the front door. With a sigh, Edith arose. It was Deborah, her daughter, carrying a flailing ball of fury, Edith's granddaughter, Eva. Deborah set the screaming child down on the floor.

"I'll be right back with her things. I hope you remembered. No daycare today. Staff training. It's been a hell of a morning, as you can see. What happened to your hair?"

As Eva thrashed and shrieked, Deborah bolted to the car and returned with a large, unicorn-decorated bag, setting it just inside the door.

"Sorry, Mom. I'm late. Gotta go." She rushed away as Eva screamed. Edith watched her rage.

I am not a wife. Am I a mother? A Bubbe? A grandmother?

She gave up on the child and returned to bed. After several minutes, there was quiet. Edith dozed. When she opened her eyes, Eva was standing next to her, thumb in her mouth, staring at her. She had been a winsome baby who turned into a sullen toddler. She hadn't outgrown her bad temper now that she was a snarled-hair four-year-old. Anything she didn't wish to do—change clothes, brush teeth, take a nap—led to a tantrum. Deborah waited for her to be old enough for medication.

"I want cereal, Bubbe." She spat her demand at her grandmother.

Edith got up and went to the kitchen. Eva climbed into a booster chair at the table. Edith put a bowl of Cheerios and milk before her.

"Not that kind!" Eva flung the bowl across the room. "Captain Crunch!"

Without cleaning up the mess, Edith returned to bed again, leaving Eva wailing in her seat. Edith recalled all her years as a *wife* doing whatever her husband wanted. If he demanded beer, she brought him one from the refrigerator. When he told her to quit her job, she quit. She had spent her entire marriage avoiding conflict, fearful that Joe, who easily angered, might strike her or leave her. No more. She was finished with that, now that she was no longer a *wife*.

When Eva came into the bedroom again, she was naked.

"No clothes." She gave Edith a defiant look.

Edith didn't care. She turned her back on Eva. Silence persisted for several seconds until Eva made her way around the bed to face her grandmother.

"Is Zaba a ghost?"

"Maybe."

She supposed she should have said something more reassuring to the child. Instead, she lay there, closing her eyes. Another brief spell of silence came next. Then Eva erupted again.

"I'm cold. I'm hungry. I want my Mommy," she wailed.

When Edith didn't respond, Eva grew louder.

"Mommy… Mommy…," she screamed.

The bed shook, as if the child pounded on it. When increasing her volume didn't work, Eva settled into incessant crying that seemed more anguished than insistent. Edith had to do something. The noise wasn't tolerable. She got up. With Eva following, she walked to the combination kitchen and family room. What did any of it have to do with her? Joe wanted this house, with two plaid recliners, a massive charcoal leather sofa, a TV that swept across the entire wall, and a kitchen island with an imbedded grill.

If Joe was a ghost, he could stay and haunt the place. It made no difference to Edith. She never wanted to live there. Grabbing her purse, she flung open the front door and headed out toward her car.

"Wait for me, Bubbe."

Edith sat in the driver's seat until Eva opened the back door and hoisted the unicorn bag, which she had dragged with her, onto the floor. Then she climbed into the car seat.

"Buckle me in!"

Edith began driving. She had no particular destination in mind. First, she drove along the main street, noting the stores and establishments frequented by Joe. *His* dry cleaners, *his* gym, *his* favorite Jewish deli, *his* liquor store. The only one of hers was the supermarket, and most of the items that would up in the cart were for Joe. *His* Pringles. *His* T-Bone.

She didn't care to be there anymore. It wasn't *her* town. While Eva sniffled and grumbled in the back, Edith drove past the synagogue—*Joe's* synagogue—on the road to the outskirts. The houses were getting further apart. She passed farms, noting the cattle lazing beneath the shade trees. A sign directed traffic to the state forest. For no particular reason, she turned.

"I'm hungry."

"Look for a snack in your unicorn bag." Deborah may have packed one.

Through the rear-view mirror, she saw Eva climb out of the car seat. There were rustling sounds.

"Animal crackers. Juice. Here's a sweater, Bubbe. Can I put it on?"

"Yes."

"I'm staying on the floor. I don't want to be in the car seat."

"Okay."

She wasn't about to fight the child and provoke another tantrum. They came to an unattended guardhouse at the entrance to the forest. Edith drove through without stopping. Ahead was a paved road, with pines and tall, leafy trees forming a green canopy overhead. She took a deep, relaxing breath. Something within her that had been frozen for years thawed. Eva busied herself eating her snack. Now that there was tranquility, Edith kept driving, mile after mile further away from all that was Joe's. Never had she been beyond the picnic area near the guard house in the days when she and Joe took Deborah and Ben on family outings. Joe feared poison ivy and snakes. He preferred to sit in a shelter and drink beer while she tossed a frisbee to the children nearby.

It occurred to Edith that she should find an unpaved road. It would be more remote from town. As soon as she spied a logging trail, she turned onto it. The car jerked along the rutted lane. Deep, herring-bone tire tracks from log-heavy trailers led the way. The bumpy ride stirred up Eva again.

"My tummy hurts, Bubbe," she cried.

She parked the car in a clearing as far from the logging trail as she could. It would not be easy to find. She left behind her purse and useless cellphone and pushed into the thicket.

"Bubbe! Wait for me."

She waited until Eva caught up. All the child wore was a sweater, but at least there were still shoes on her feet. She carried the unicorn bag, which she must have emptied at some point. Edith started walking again, with Eva following and complaining.

"I'm tired. Carry me."

Edith forged ahead, paying no attention to the complaints. Soon Eva was crying from fatigue. She had never walked that far.

"I have to potty, Bubbe."

"Go ahead."

"But there's no bathroom."

"Go where you are." Edith waited without looking back. Then she started again without turning to see if the child had finished.

"My Mommy won't like it when I tell her you made me go potty on the ground."

Edith said nothing. She had no idea where they were headed. She kept going, one step in front of the other, with Eva close behind. It must have been mid-afternoon when she spotted something among some thick vines that made her pause. When she parted the growth with care to avoid scratching her arms, she found a hut hidden beneath. She had to go around to the other side to find the entrance. The inside was no bigger than a large closet. One grimy window, covered on the outside by leaves, provided a dull light. A chair, an old wood stove, and a couple of mats were the only furnishings. Edith rolled out the mats beside each other on the floor. There were no pillows or blankets. On a shelf above the door, she discovered matches, a paring knife, candles, a frying pan, and a tin of lard.

"I don't like it here, Bubbe. It's *icky*." Tears slid down her cheeks.

"You can leave, but if you stay, this is your bed, and that one is mine." Edith pointed at the two mats.

"I want my Mommy."

"If you are staying, you can lie down and nap."

"I'm cold."

That sounded reasonable to Edith. She left and came back with an armful of pine needles and leaves. When Eva curled up with her bag, Edith covered them with her haul. The child fell asleep right away. Edith sat on the chair. She looked around, feeling pleased. It was a good dwelling for a *widow*.

An old book lay on the windowsill. Edith picked it up and blew the dust off the cover. "Roots in the Woods" was its title. It was filled with illustrations of plants with edible and medicinal roots, along with recipes. There were cures for rashes and coughs. Several pages described soups made from such wild food sources as dandelions, berries, acorns, and nutritious leaves.

Edith had a vision. She would settle in the hut with the child. They would learn how to make what they needed from what the forest offered. Whatever the forest couldn't provide, they would do without.

She was a *widow*. Everyone expected that her life would revolve around volunteering at the synagogue. Instead, she would live the way widows often lived before civilization turned them into second-class women. She would become skilled at healing and casting spells.

As for the child, Edith knew she broke the law. She hummed the tune her mother used to hum.

Que sera, sera. What will be will be.

One day, she might be discovered. A price would be paid for the kidnapping, unless, when Edith heard the authorities calling out to her, or saw the thick beam of their flashlights streamed through the window, she slipped out of the hut's door and moved deeper into the forest to evade them.

If Eva had followed her, Edith would figure out a way for both to keep hidden from all that belonged to the world of Joe.

CHAPTER 2
WHO BY FIRE

Edith sat in the chair for the entire time the child napped. Its cane bottom sagged. The wicker needed tightening.

Edith did not know how to tighten wicker. She did not know how to make a fire in the stove. She did not know where to find water or how she was going to make a meal. Everything that was easy in town was hard now. Back in her house, Joe put anything broken at the curb for garbage collection. If the house wasn't warm, he turned up the dial on the thermostat. There were large and small kitchen appliances for cooking the ingredients purchased at the supermarket.

Her ancestors came from towns, from Jewish communities near synagogues. In Europe, they had been peddlers. In America, they owned grocery stores and haberdasheries. Later, they were educated and became accountants, like Joe, or dentists. No one farmed or subsisted in underdeveloped areas.

Like most of the people in her circle, Edith spent much of her time indoors. Besides planting a few tulip bulbs and zinnias in the front yard and an occasional trip to the park, she only had glimpses of nature while dashing from parking lots to malls, gyms, or the library. Before quitting, she worked as an administrative assistant in the English Department at the same university where Deborah taught, in an office with windows facing other academic buildings.

Yet, here she was, on the run, having abducted a child, in the middle of the woods, where she belonged for the first time in her life, and feeling at peace. The forest called her. She heard it when she still lived back in town, wondering who she had become since Joe's death.

Then the forest led her to the little hut, to her new home, her real home. She closed her eyes and breathed in the scent of pine and ash.

"I want my Mommy."

It was Eva, awake and standing next to her, still naked except for a sweater and shoes. She stamped an insistent foot, signaling the onset of a tantrum. Edith had to take control of the child, the old-fashioned way. Grabbing "Roots of the Woods," she used it to give Eva a sharp swat on her bare bottom.

Eva gasped. Her parents never struck her. Her back arched, and her startled hands flew outward from her sides.

"You hurt me, Bubbe." Fat tears rolled down her cheeks. She buried her face in Edith's lap, sobbing.

"I won't hurt you if you're good." She rubbed the child's back.

I am a widow. Who is this child to me?

The book remained in her hand. She opened it and found an instruction manual for someone like her, a novice with no survival skills. The contents varied more than they seemed to when she scanned it earlier. The first chapter concerned a way to build a smokeless fire in a wood stove. This was important. Black smoke rising from the chimney pipe could alert authorities looking for her hideout, or it could attract curious hikers.

Eva bolted up, looking at her grandmother with furious eyes, rubbing her bottom.

"I want to go home."

"Go right ahead." Edith did not stop reading.

"You take me."

Edith closed the book, keeping a finger on the page she was up to.

"I'm not taking you home. This is home now. This is where we are staying."

"I'm cold. Take me home to get my clothes."

"You're the one who wanted to be naked."

Edith opened the book to the place saved by her finger. She had been reading how to start a fire. But her finger must have skipped to another chapter, further along. "How to Make Clothing with Woodland Materials." The book read her mind.

"I'll find clothing for you. But first, I have to light the stove to keep us warm."

She flipped back to the beginning of the book. "For a top down construction, place a layer of seasoned logs in the stove's bottom, then kindling, with crushed newspaper on top of the pile."

She would have to go outside and find these things. How would she know if a log was seasoned? The words appeared. She must have missed them.

"Seasoned logs are dark and cracked on the ends."

The logs would have to fit in the stove. She would need an axe. Something in a dark corner of the tiny hut distracted her. Stacked against the wall were several tools. An axe. A shovel. A poker. A stack of newspaper. Had they been there all along without her noticing them?

Eva's crying with more strident now.

"I want my Mommy."

Her fierce tone turned to panic. She scanned the hut wild-eyed, as if she might see her mother where Edith saw tools. Edith's heart softened. She took the child in her arms. What was she doing? Why didn't she just take the child back where she belonged? Maybe she would, but not today. Maybe tomorrow. Eva wept against her grandmother's chest for several minutes before shoving herself away.

"You're bad! You hurt me! When I see Mommy, I'm telling on you."

Without answering, Edith got up and left the hut, carrying the axe. Eva followed, crying and grumbling. Edith remembered circling the hut when she first saw its vine covered exterior. But when she looked in the back again, a rick of wood was stacked a few feet away. Perhaps a former occupant had taken the trouble?

"Here. You carry this." She handed the child a small log.

"I don't want to." Eva turned, refusing to take it.

"Have you heard the story of the Little Red Hen?"

"No."

"When the other animals wouldn't help, she didn't give them any bread. If you won't carry the log, you won't get dinner."

Edith chose a larger log, lay it on the ground away from Eva, then gave it several inexpert chops with the axe. She picked up the pieces and returned to the hut. Eva marched behind her without her log.

"I'm going back out to get kindling. Are you going to bring in the log or go to bed hungry?"

"I hate you, Bubbe."

"I don't like you, either."

Eva trailed her outside, crying all the while, and brought in the log, dumping it on the floor inside the door.

Edith set the kindling next to the stove.

"Put the log next to the kindling, please."

"No!"

"You don't get dinner unless you finish the job. Your job is to carry in the log and put it beside the stove."

After opening the damper, Edith stacked the wood, kindling, and crumpled newspaper the way the book instructed. She lit the paper, biting her lip, and waited. The log caught on the first try. Beginner's luck? The area warmed. Edith sighed. The book warned that the stove would need additional fuel every two or three hours through the night to keep going.

Meanwhile, Eva gave her log angry kicks, moving it toward the stove to the spot shown by her grandmother.

"Thank you. Now that you have done your job, you get to eat."

"I'm hungry."

Food. How could she feed the child? She flipped through the pages of "Roots of the Woods." The book had several sections on edible plants and berries. But it was too late for foraging. She had promised her granddaughter food for carrying the log. There had to be a follow-through, or the lesson would be lost.

As much as she could, she paced around the hut, as desperate thoughts whirled in her head. Eva spread herself on the floor, scissoring her legs whenever her grandmother walked by. Edith risked falling over the child or stepping on her if she continued her agitated movements. She stood still, looking at all the walls. That was when she noticed the cabinet above the shelf. Had it always been there? Was she so taken with the contents of the shelf—the knife, frying pan, candles, and matches—that she never looked above it?

The cabinet was within her reach. She hesitated. What if mice or some larger animal nested there? Stepping over Eva's legs, she seized the axe. She needed something to defend herself and the child. After taking three deep breaths to work up her nerve and raising the weapon, she flung open one of the two doors.

Nothing dangerous sheltered inside. Instead, staples in bright boxes and jars were stowed there, looking as fresh as if bought just days ago. There were two shelves—flour, sugar, dry milk, oil, rice, beans, tuna, yeast packets, baking powder, salt, oatmeal, coffee on the upper one and a pot with a lid, two tin dishes, two spoons, two tin cups, soap on the lower. She could cobble together a meal, if she found water.

She went in search of water, taking the reluctant child with her. A five-gallon container appeared as if by magic in the same corner as the tools. It struck her as strange that, just as the tools looked new, the plastic jug seemed to be unused as well. There was even an unopened box of water purifier tablets next to it.

Outside, she heard the creek before she saw it, not ten yards from the hut. It was shallow enough for her to allow Eva to wade in, although she would have to be dried without a towel. Edith filled the jug, then took off her own turtleneck for the shivering child. At least that solved the problem of a bath for her. Next time she would bring the soap.

The next uproar was over the meal. Eva had to sit on her grandmother's lap or on the floor, since the hut lacked a second chair. At home, Eva had a booster seat for either the kitchen table on ordinary nights or the dining room table when there were guests. In the kitchen, the tv was tuned to the Cartoon Channel.

With her lower lip stuck out, Eva chose the floor. But the absence of cartoons brought fresh tears. Edith also missed a television. She liked to watch Anderson Cooper on CNN with her evening meal and The Today Show with breakfast. It was her habit to flip through Netflix offerings before falling asleep, then waking at three a.m. to find some unfamiliar movie playing. But a habit wasn't a need.

She paid no attention to Eva's tears while placing a dish of beans, rice, and tuna on the child's crossed legs.

Eva roared. "I don't like this food. It's yucky. I want chicken nuggets."

"There are no chicken nuggets and no tv. If you don't want your food, I'll eat it."

"Noooooo!"

Eva raised her dish to sling it, but Edith grabbed it first.

"They'll be none of that." She ate a spoonful of Eva's rice.

"Gimme!"

Edith handed the dish back. Eva ate slowly, one bean or grain of rice at a time, with a comical look of repulsion on her face. Edith ate her own meal with her back turned to the girl.

It reminded her of her own childhood in New York. Her mother didn't have a job until she and her sister enrolled in high school. Instead, her mother worked night and day to keep their apartment in immaculate condition. On Fridays, before *Shabbat* services, she scrubbed her daughters with rough washcloths and pulled their hair into painfully tight braids.

Edith married Joe to get out from under her mother's insistence on scoured perfection. He took her to live in his hometown in Indiana. But the spirit of her mother still watched her, demanding gleaming spotlessness. Whenever Edith left cups unwashed in the sink or allowed a crease in the bedspread, she heard her mother's voice.

"Edith. Come back here, and do it right."

Although she vowed to be different, Edith wound up using the same tone with her children. Now that she was a *widow* living in a primitive hut in the woods, the voice that haunted her for so many years faded. There was no sink, no bedspread, no vacuum, no dust rag, no washcloth, no hairbrush. The child was a handful. Edith had to discipline her. It would take time. But the hard work of surviving would not be frivolous, just to look good for others or for the sake of a reputation.

The stove needed more wood. It would take a minute or two to take the log Eva had brought in back outside the door and chop it into pieces. The child still ate tiny amounts. If Edith interrupted her, there might be another struggle, but she had to take the chance. She sat down on the floor opposite Eva.

"I can't watch you every minute. The stove is dangerous. It's very hot. If you touch it, it will burn you. Do you know what a burn is? No? Remember how it hurt when I smacked your bottom? A burn hurts much, much, much more than that. A hundred times more. You must never touch the stove."

She stared at the child, barely more than a toddler, trying to see understanding in her face, perhaps a look of fear. Eva looked at her with the same disgusted expression she had for unfamiliar food.

Edith rose with a sigh.

"I'll be right outside getting the log ready. Don't touch the stove."

The terrible shriek came as soon as Edith had both feet out the door. She rushed back in. Eva held a bright red hand up for her to see. Food was scattered across the floor. In her defiance, the child laid her hand on the stove on purpose.

While Eva wailed, Edith poured some water from the jug over her palm. She leafed through the book. The page on cures for burns popped up. It directed her to a plant she had noticed growing just beyond the door. She ran out, picked some leaves, then plastered her screaming granddaughter's hand with them. She sat on the chair, drawing the child onto her lap.

If Eva's hand blistered, she would have to return to town with her for medical treatment. She faced arrest and a long prison sentence for kidnapping. There were no mitigating circumstances, no excuse. She couldn't explain her sudden understanding of her *widow*hood, how she was no longer a person. Well, she was a person, but like someone without a country or someone who had lost her identity. She no longer belonged in her house or her town. She belonged in the forest. Eva just came along. Who could make sense of that?

The child's racking sobs eased. After a few heaves, she quieted, resting against her grandmother. Her eyelids drooped. The thumb of her uninjured hand was in her mouth. Edith peeked under the leaves. The skin no longer flamed. It was a reddish-pink. By the morning, there would be no signs of the burn.

Their first day in the forest ended.

CHAPTER 3
WHO BY EARTHQUAKE

Her tremors began six weeks after the child disappeared.

Deborah reached for her morning tea. The next thing she knew, the mug hit the floor and shattered. Runnels of liquid skittered in all directions across the floor. She noticed her right hand shaking. Her fingers refused to peel paper towels off the holder or grip the larger shards. She used her left hand to clean up the mess.

She and Josh, her husband, had an appointment to meet with Detective Williams for an update. Her mother, Edith, had disappeared with their four-year-old daughter, Eva. The question was whether her mother took Eva or whether someone abducted both Edith and Eva. An Amber Alert, search parties, and posters displaying the missing girl and the girl's grandmother yielded nothing. They hadn't been found.

Although the investigation continued, the original hourly updates had trickled down to once every three or four days. Soon, it would decrease to weekly, then monthly. The odds of children turning up diminished rapidly if they weren't found within twenty-four hours. Deborah understood this. Josh wavered between hopefulness and despair. Every sentence he said started with a "maybe."

"Maybe the Detective Williams will have news?" At least he was out of bed and getting dressed. He had bad days and very bad days. "Maybe your mother took her to the wrong day care, and one of the teachers drove both of them somewhere?"

"Maybe."

They discussed the possibilities many times with each other and with Detective Williams. The only established facts were that Deborah left Eva at her mother's house at 8:30 a.m. because the daycare was closed for staff training. When she returned from work at 5:20 p.m., the front door was wide open, the car was not in the carport, and both her mother and daughter were missing.

At the police station, Detective Williams went over the same facts. No witnesses. No sighting of the car. No credit card purchases or bank withdrawals. No anonymous tips. No clues.

"I don't want you to think the investigation is slowing down. I'm working every minute to bring Eva and your mother home." His restless fingers twirled a pen.

"Maybe our Rabbi can ask our congregation if anyone knows anything?" Josh tilted forward in his chair until a dark strand of hair fell across his forehead. His eyebrows arched, as if just voicing his question had already generated a lead.

"If anything comes of it, I'll look into it." This is what Detective Williams always said.

By the time they returned to the car, Josh was deflated and weeping. Deborah would have to drive. She worried about steering, but the tremor was gone, and she held the steering wheel without a problem. Sleep deprivation or stress must have caused the issue with her hand. There had been plenty of both, *Lord knows*.

Six months ago, her father, an alcoholic prone to road rage, died in a drunk-driving accident. Then her mother and daughter were kidnapped, or worse. She shuddered. Josh fell apart and took Family Leave from his law firm. She forced herself to resume teaching at the university. Someone needed to bring in money to pay the bills. Someone needed to keep functioning. While Josh soaked the pillow with tears, Deborah jumped out of bed when the alarm sounded, showered, dressed, taught classes, graded papers, shopped, cooked, and answered Detective Williams' questions.

From the sideways glances the detective gave her, Deborah feared that not falling apart made her a "person of interest." She dared not allow herself to cry or she wouldn't be able to stop. That made her an unnatural mother and an unnatural woman in the view of the police and the media. They described her as "dry-eyed," "cold," and "formidable." Josh was "distraught" and "devastated," as everyone expected a father of a missing child to be. The media interviews helped generate publicity, but her stiff response to questions made her look suspicious.

Am I paying the price? For not being what they want?

Eva wasn't an easy child. The colicky infant who wailed day and night graduated into the "terrible twos." These continued to the "terrible fours." She needed a good shaking, if it were safe or permissible. Instead, Deborah sometimes dreamed of running away. Whenever she reached the end of her rope with the child's tantrums, she offloaded Eva to her mother. Now she felt guilty. If she kept her daughter with her, there would have been no disappearance. Her child would still demand to see cartoons and howl if she didn't get her way—in her own house with her parents.

On the morning of the disappearance, Deborah thought, "I'm going to be late for classes. Let Mom deal with the kid. Wasn't she the one who couldn't wait for grandchildren? Who pestered me to get married?" Her mother seemed to go numb when she became a widow. It was a big change, now that her father was dead, but it was natural that her mother would be grieving or depressed. Deborah worried.

Now, six weeks after, with no sign of her mother or daughter, the tremor that caused Deborah problems in the morning returned in the afternoon.

"Can you see my hand shaking?" She extended her arm, allowing Josh to examine her hand.

"I don't know. Maybe a little," he said.

"It shook so bad this morning I dropped my tea."

"Huh." He turned toward the bedroom. The police update wore him out. Her problem was one more thing he couldn't handle.

She followed him.

"I don't know if something's wrong. Since this morning, my hand's been shaking on and off. In fact, my entire arm vibrates."

"You probably pinched a nerve. If it's still a problem tomorrow, go to the clinic." He was already sitting on the bed, removing his shoes.

The next day, she had classes to teach. There was no time for the clinic.

"I'm leaving now," she shouted to Josh. He didn't answer. It aggravated her when he stayed in bed, wearing ear plugs. She went to pick up her briefcase, trying to make her fingers of her right hand clutch the handles. After several attempts, she gave up and used her left hand. She steered the car with her useless hand in her lap.

During the drive, the question she asked herself the day before about her daughter's disappearance returned.

Am I paying the price? For not loving others the way they want?

She couldn't say she ever loved Josh. She married him because he loved her. Now he was a millstone. She couldn't say she loved her father. His rages frightened her. And her mother, who enabled her father's drinking and bullying? She considered her contemptuous.

But Eva's absence left a lump in Deborah's chest. Eva was her daughter, flesh of her flesh. It hurt to inhale. She took shallow breaths. In private, she agonized about her daughter, whether she was alive or dead, hurt or safe, held in sexual slavery by a pedophile or taken by her mother to who-knows-where. She wanted relief from the daily battles with Eva, who defied her at every turn. Now she would give anything to have her difficult daughter back.

The wrenching sensation called "love" began with a jolt when she first looked into the infant's eyes soon after her birth. The thought of never finding Eva, never seeing her again, made the tremor climb to her throat. Her tongue twitched.

She entered the classroom, keeping her right hand down at her side. After laying out her notes on the dais, which she couldn't read because of visual shuddering, she began her lecture.

"Today, we'll... we'll... review... review... today, we'll..."

She couldn't say more. Her voice was tremulous. The words caught in her spasming throat and either repeated themselves or remained stuck. All that came out of her mouth was a halting half-sentence. Even her lips fluttered when she tried to form words. She raised her shaking hand to show that she needed a minute to compose herself. The students stared at her with wide, alarmed eyes.

One of them must have called 911. EMTs burst through the door, and, in front of the students, many of whom stood craning their necks, sat her down to take her vitals. She tried to protest.

"I'm… fine… fine… It's…"

"Don't worry about talking, Professor. We'll be taking you to the ER. The stretcher will be here any second. Don't try to stand." The EMT, a young man, took her pulse and then recorded the number on his iPad. He asked her to nod her head "yes" or "no" to the questions he read. The first one was whether she used recreational drugs that day.

After a long wait in the ER, Josh appeared. It disturbed her not having her mother there. The lose of Eva was so horrible she often forgot her mother was also missing. Meanwhile, she endured many tests, MRIs, and blood work. Each one came back negative. Yet, although she felt the tremors spreading, a neurologist found nothing wrong. He discharged her without a diagnosis or treatment, writing her off as imagining her condition. A therapist was recommended. Deborah shook her head "no."

Although only a few days passed since the tremors began, Deborah was already trapped in a body that shook constantly, impeding her ability to walk, use her hands, or speak with any clarity. Even if her daughter returned, a doubtful prospect after so much time had elapsed, the shaking was too severe for Deborah to take care of her.

It must be punishment for all my wrongdoing. Failing to love Josh or tolerate his sorrow. Criticizing her mother's hard choices. Her frustrations with Eva.

Back home, her condition confined her to a chair. Walking to the bathroom was an ordeal, requiring her to hold on to the walls and furniture. Sometimes she fell. Josh rallied. She didn't know if he believed she was ill, but her helplessness forced him to find strength. Although he still pined for Eva, he became the functional one in the marriage. He returned to his law practice. Deborah refused to let him hire aides, as if she were an old woman.

"Maybe I'm the victim of some obscure disease that has no name. Maybe it is psychiatric." These were the thoughts she couldn't say out loud.

In her head, she picked up Josh's habit of starting sentences with 'maybe.' Both the disappearances and now her illness were mysteries. For no reason any medical professional gave, if they gave any, her health continued to decline. In time, other symptoms appeared: migraines, insomnia, rashes, nausea. She lost weight. The shaking was the hardest symptom to bear.

With difficulty, she used the remote to turn on the tv. The media became interested again in the mother of the missing child who appeared to be faking illness. There she was on the local news on tv, being loaded into an ambulance.

"Sources tell us that there is increasing speculation among the investigators that Eva's mother murdered her daughter. She might be using her 'shaking disease' as an alibi," the anchor said.

She was being blamed for something she didn't do—committing a double murder of the two family members she should have protected. People would think her a monster.

Detective Williams showed up at the house with more questions.

"We need to go over the timeline once more. Do you still remember the last time you saw Eva as being at 8:30 on the morning she disappeared?"

She stuttered the answer.

After the detective left, she wondered if he planned to arrest her. The thought of being carted off to prison frightened her. Punishment might be coming. The idea was terrifying.

Suddenly, she recalled a time she was punished when she was Eva's age. Somehow, she annoyed her father. What she did to enrage him was unknowable. It could have been anything. His massive hands gripped her shoulders hard enough to leave purple thumb prints. He lifted her high off her feet. Held inches from her father's face, she saw his huge clenched teeth and his blazing eyes up close. He began shaking her with force. His steaming exhalations and spittle wet her cheeks with each forward thrust. Her head slammed against the wall when jolted backward. He growled a single word with each shake.

Don't. You. Ever. Do. That. Again. Or. You. Will. Pay.

When he finished, she lay on the floor, too dizzy and stunned to move. Her mother used her pleading voice with her father. He brushed her aside with a flick of his hand, returning to his game on ESPN. At her bedtime, Deborah lay her spinning head on the pillow. Through the sleepless night, she fantasized about living in the woods with winged unicorns and fairies—those kind creatures who gently float children to the treetops where they are protected .

Her daughter was still gone. Deborah would sit in her chair for the rest of her dwindling days, staring out the window at the shuddering view, waiting for the girl to run up the walkway to the house. If Deborah had to slither like a snake to get to the door, then hoist herself up until she reached the knob, if she had to turn the knob with her chattering teeth, she would spend the last of her limited energy on opening it and letting Eva in.

CHAPTER 4
WHO BY STONING

About two years later, without a clock or calendar, with a cell phone lying without charge in her abandoned car, without a laptop or other device, Edith guessed the date and time. She learned to use the sun and moon to calculate both. She estimated that Eva passed her sixth birthday.

The "terrible twos," which extended to the "terrible fours," eased. Eva was still headstrong and willful. That seemed to be her character. She had inherited part of her temperament from Joe. Grandmother and granddaughter still clashed, but even at six, the child understood the fundamentals of survival. No cooperation, no food. No unity, no water. No teamwork, no heat. One day, Edith wouldn't have the stamina to do it all by herself. She had to train Eva early. If she could carry kindling, a quart of water, a sack of wild raspberries, it would create the work ethic necessary to survive in the forest.

The first winter, they were cold and miserable, stuck in the tiny cabin for days at a time, while the wind lashed through cracks in the walls. The chill turned Eva into a red-eyed, blue-fingered demon, crying, spewing fury, pummeling and kicking her grandmother, even beating her head on the floor. Edith took solace in "Roots of the Woods." It included a chapter on child-raising in the forest, even covering parenting issues during periods of confinement in a dwelling.

Although she used some techniques described with Deborah and Ben, she had the advantages of tv, day care, playdates, toys, and—on the rare occasions when he was in the mood to deal with them—Joe.

She didn't have imagination back then. Now, as the book suggested, she made up songs and stories to entertain Eva. She crafted simple toys from sticks and pieces of vine. She made clay from flour, salt, and oil and shaped crude letters and numbers from twigs in order to teach the child counting and the alphabet.

When spring came, she read and re-read the chapter on simple ways to tan hides. She had already learned to set traps to catch rabbits and other small mammals. Their meat wasn't Kosher. It would have horrified her mother, who had kept a double set of dishes and shopped at a Kosher butcher. But keeping Kosher was impossible in the forest.

In town, she killed nothing larger than an ant. Now it became necessary to kill game for the child to be provided with a source of protein. Whatever she needed somehow appeared in the hut or close by outside. Barrels and pickling salt to preserve meat for winter. Tools and ammonia alum for tanning hides in the warmer weather.

Tanning was the most labor-intensive job Edith had to master. Her plan involved using cured hides to cover the walls, ceiling, and floor of the hut for insulation. She caught and killed rabbits and squirrels, cooked their meat, and tanned their pelts. She learned to make use of everything, even their brains, which softened leather in the tanning process.

Hauling water, heating it on the wood stove for bathing and laundering, making more soap when the bar she found in the cabinet ran out, were some of her tasks. She didn't mind. She had chosen a primitive life-style, even if she had to rub her red, cracked hands with animal fat and use liniments mentioned in the book on her aching muscles.

She had to wonder. Why had she picked the forest when she could have gone to another house, another town, a farm, California, Maine? She frowned. They all smacked of the world of Joe, without room for a *widow*. But the child. Why kidnap her? It would have been possible to wait for Deborah to return before fleeing. But waiting didn't seem possible, at the time. If she stayed in Joe's house one more minute, she thought she would die.

It seemed unreasonable, now. But what was done was done.

Without realizing it, she was humming a tune, the same one her mother sang while cleaning. Since coming to the forest, she often found herself humming it. Throughout her childhood, Edith heard that song. When she was an adolescent, it played one day on the radio. It was a shock to discover her mother hadn't made it up.

Que sera, sera. Whatever will be will be.

As her mother sang it, the words seemed to circulate in her bloodstream.

Que sera. All of her mother's family gone in the Holocaust.

Que sera. Her marriage to Joe.

Que sera. Harassing bosses in her jobs.

Que sera. Joe's death.

And now, *Que sera.* What was done was done. The kidnapping of Eva.

She didn't seem to have control over anything that happened to her. Free will? She reacted to the things that others, like Joe, made happen. She allowed a four-year-old child to decide to follow her, which was plain wrong. Children must be guided, not permitted to make choices that could be dangerous. *Que sera* created a mess. Returning Eva now would mean getting stuck in the world of Joe again. When she considered taking her granddaughter back, her feet planted themselves to the floor of the hut. Every day, she awoke thinking she should return her to town. As soon as she arose from her mat, her legs refused to lift. They rooted themselves to the earth until she was as immobile as the surrounding trees.

"I'll take Eva back tomorrow," she'd tell herself, releasing her legs as soon as she decided to stay in the forest one more day.

But in order to keep Eva even for a day, Edith had to distort her thoughts, until she imagined she did what no one had done for her — protected Eva from the world of Joe.

Meanwhile, she had to clothe the child and herself. She didn't have patience for sewing pelts. Against her better judgement, she left her granddaughter by herself in the hut, with reminders not to touch the stove, and snuck into campsites at dawn to steal what campers left unguarded. She only needed one change of clothing for herself, but Eva was rough on clothes, requiring several outfits. Because Edith feared getting caught, she made several excursions, stealing a single shirt or one pair of pants at a time. She hoped campers would think they just mislaid the garments.

It came as no surprise when Eva objected to anything her grandmother brought her.

"I don't like that shirt. It had a truck picture on it. It's for a boy. I don't want to wear boy clothes."

"Then don't wear anything." Edith knew how to handle the child's defiance, the part of her that was like Joe.

"I hate it." She huffed before yanking it over her head.

When Eva wasn't helping with tasks, Edith instructed her to stay nearby. But the child wandered when her grandmother wasn't watching. She had grown into a sturdy girl, whose dark hair was woven into a braid once it was long enough to unsnarl. Her bold dark eyes glinted with curiosity. She wanted to explore, but remained within calling distance of the hut, often returning with an insect or geode or nut that interested her, asking Edith to look it up in the book. Sometimes she roamed further away.

Edith suspected that the child hunted for other people, perhaps her mother and father. If Edith heard hikers approaching, she grabbed the girl and pulled her into the hut. Sometimes, she put a hand over her mouth to keep her from calling out. Eva could be a danger to her. Although she never asked to go back to town, she might accompany a stranger who offered to take her. Then Eva would be back in the oppressive world of Joe, and Edith might be dragged back with her.

There were several close calls. Twice, she found her in campgrounds, playing with a gaggle of other children. The adults didn't realize she wasn't the child of just another camper, Edith called to her, walked away with her and pretended they were set up at a more distant site.

There were also times when Edith found her talking to adult backpackers.

"Where's your Mommy?" They shaded their eyes with their hands while looking up and down the trail for parents. Edith would run up, all smiles.

"There you are. I hope she didn't bother you. We're having a picnic over there." She gestured vaguely to an unseen picnic area, then hurried the protesting girl away.

She didn't know how to explain the reasons for their isolation to the child. It reminded her of the excuses her mother gave her for vigorous cleaning.

"In case someone comes in the house and sees." Her mother wiped the molding or dusted high shelves while saying this.

"What stranger is going to go into the bedrooms? The F.B.I.? Nazis?"

"If you can't figure it out, I won't explain."

That would end the discussion.

Her dilemma with Eva was that the usual reason for a child not talking to strangers, that they might kidnap her, didn't apply. In this case, the reason was that they might rescue her from a kidnapper. It was better to just insist on obedience, like her mother did.

"Don't talk to anyone in the camps or on the trails. Don't let anyone see you."

The child was too young to know that her grandmother had abducted her, and that she was probably the subject of an Amber Alert. There might be yellowing posters of her in store windows in town. There might be media coverage on the anniversaries of her disappearance.

On this date two years ago, four-year-old Eva vanished with her grandmother Edith. Neither has been seen or heard from since. Authorities continue to investigate.

On a warm spring day, Eva had her most serious and deadly episode of wandering off. The lush, cedar tree canopy, the green undergrowth, the creeks, the ravines, the wildflowers and birds surrounding the hut delighted her. She kept running back to her grandmother, telling her about her discoveries.

"I saw a new part of the creek. Little wiggling things swam in there." She was breathless. Before Edith responded, she ran off again. The girl's chattering grew fainter. Edith had a strange foreboding that something bad was about to happen. She had been having a growing number of premonitions. This time, there was an unsteadiness beneath her feet. The ground shivered. Her sensitivity to the forest was growing.

"Eva! Where are you?" She had been trimming the vine that grew over the sole window of the hut. There would be no daylight if she didn't cut it back.

"I'm here." She sounded far off, up the hill.

Edith, feeling increasing uneasiness, followed her. When the trees thinned, she saw her in the distance on the trail, a small figure yards ahead, sure-footedly climbing steep ridges. She wasn't alone. An adult man and a boy of her size hiked with her. The two kids scampered ahead of the man. Edith's admiration conflicted with annoyance. Children were so nimble, their movements so fluid. The man, who might have been the boy's father, climbed like she did, steadily, but with little grace.

She should take the girl on hikes, maybe overnight ones. They might find caves to investigate and other abandoned huts. Joe had taken her to the Mammoth Cave of Kentucky, before they married. She navigated the narrow passages and low ceilings without having to squeeze through or bend over. Joe wasn't happy contorting himself. They wound up in a large chamber. The lights were turned off. It was so dark that space seemed to expand, becoming infinite. The children on the tour screamed. She held onto Joe. Then the lights were turned back on. There might be better caves in this part of the forest. Edith would see if "Roots of The Woods" mentioned any.

Eva and the boy approached the vista on the top of the hill. The tree-lined trail widened to a clearing. From there, miles of forest were visible. The limestone outcroppings were becoming more magnificent. The children kept stopping to try to scale them. It gave Edith a chance to catch up. The man didn't realize Edith was behind him. He stayed focused on his son and on his footing.

The ground seemed to shiver again. Edith knew it was an ominous sign. Ahead, the boy had reached the top.

"I beat both of you!" He yelled down to Eva and his father, grinning.

Edith was thirty feet from the top. The man and Eva were almost there.

"Eva! It's me. Come down here right now."

Eva turned an irritated face toward her grandmother. The man looked from Eva to her and back again.

"Aren't you…?" Was he guessing they were the two who had disappeared?

"Eva! Right now!"

The child responded to the urgency in her grandmother's tone. She ran down to her. Both turned to watch the man reach the summit. Standing next to the boy, he looked back at them with a puzzled expression. His head cocked. His mouth opened.

But before he could say what Edith suspected he would say, a sinkhole suddenly opened. There was no warning. The two vanished, as if a rope tied to their feet yanked them downward. It obliterated the hilltop. Boulders toppled into the newly formed cavern with a great crashing noise. It was over in seconds. Thick limestone dust obscured the change in the landscape. Edith and Eva, safe on the trail below, coughed and choked, wiping at their tearing eyes, unsure of what happened.

"Bubbe! Where's the boy?"

Eva flew back up the hill. Edith rushed after her. The ground still shook. Fissures opened, one under Eva's feet. As the child toppled, Edith managed to grab her ankle with her left hand. She fell to the ground and seized a stout branch with her right hand. Eva's shoe, stolen from a campsite, dropped into the chasm as Edith's left hand slid against it. The child's helpless foot was exposed, as Edith maintained a tight grip on her ankle. With one hand on the branch and the other around Eva's ankle, without the strength to drag the dangling child up, with no one around to help, Edith knew she could only depend on the mercy of the forest.

Que sera.

Overhead, the indifferent sky was a cloudless blue, and the sun continued to shine undaunted. Birds chirped across the vastness to others of the same species. Deer ate the greenery without concern. Only the bats, whose dwelling had been disrupted, flew about, disoriented, crazed by the light and the absence of a landing place.

CHAPTER 5
WHO SHALL BE UPLIFTED

"Wait, Professor! Can we talk a minute?"

It was Ben. The Ethics Committee meeting had just adjourned. Aaron didn't want Ben, a tragic graduate student, to engage him in some sort of disagreeable conversation. Ben's mother and niece had gone missing. Then his sister, who was on the faculty, developed a serious medical condition.

It was more important for Aaron to finish his quarterly faculty report, which was late, as usual. The report devoted a large space for listing of any forthcoming book or article. It would humiliate him if the space was left blank. During the past decade, he typed the same title into every report: "Similarities in Pronouns in Proto-Linguistic Meta-Families."

Although he hadn't written a word, it wasn't a lie, exactly. As a linguistic historian who studied the origins of language, he knew "forthcoming publication" could mean thinking about doing the research, then banging out three hundred tiresome pages on his keyboard.

He had ten years left until retirement. Could he get away with another forty faculty reports with the same title? The Chair, who was an opportunist from the lower ranks, might summon him. The younger man or woman would look up from the report, straight at him, not yet through the top half of bifocals worn by most of the middle-aged faculty.

"I notice you've had the same entry for several reports. Do you actually have a publisher?"

"I'm in conversation with a couple of presses. There's a snag over advances. It should be straightened out next semester."

This was a slight exaggeration. Aaron had queried two or three presses about his unwritten manuscript. He never received a response.

"No news is good news," he told himself.

After he helped Ben gain admission to graduate school as a favor to Ben's sister, she manipulated the Promotion and Tenure Committee into promoting Aaron to Associate Professor. It wasn't a merit promotion. He had published nothing. It was, at bottom, a "pity" promotion, a way the university expressed compassion to the mother of the missing girl. No second tragedy boosted him to Full Professor. He would need to write a damned book.

How unfair it was! When was there time for anything but teaching the new undergraduate courses the Chair unjustly assigned him every semester? Never mind the hours of class preparation and grading, advising students, and serving on numerous committees. Was he expected to give up eating and sleeping to write, for God's sake?

He focused on these injustices between presentations at the 2018 Linguistic Historians Conference. Since the Chair didn't appreciate him enough to award him a travel stipend, he would have to drive home each night to avoid the cost of the hotel. His only expenses would be gas and meals, plus the hefty conference fee.

The conference occupied several rooms in a convention center. While waiting for the keynote address, delivered by that phony from Harvard, who would no doubt bow to fashion by denigrating the work of the great Jeff Greenberg and the Russian linguists, Aaron wandered into the Dealer's Room.

He perused the booths from various academic presses displaying their publications. Then he spied one hidden in a corner for a company called Academic Ghostwriters. It shocked him to see a familiar face manning the table. Larry Anderson, of all people, still youthful, with thick blond hair that mocked Aaron's near baldness.

He slinked away before Anderson spotted him, recalling the day the Chair assigned him to the Ethics Committee, much against his will. He was already overloaded with assignments. Such was the destiny of faculty like him, called "deadwood" behind their backs for failure to publish. Anderson's case was the first one he heard. Aaron voted with the Committee to find him guilty of plagiarizing, resulting in the denial of tenure and dismissal from the university. It was amazing that Anderson put up a vigorous defense while never denying the transgression.

"Since when is being influenced conflated with stealing? Knowledge is built brick by brick, with each new insight built upon the preceding bricks." Anderson's fists clenched. Aaron slouched in his chair, fearing that the accused was planning to strike Committee members.

He might still be angry. Aaron had been one of those who destroyed his career. It would be best to avoid him.

Listening to derivative conference papers all day had been exhausting. A single drink before driving home wouldn't hurt. He found a bar a short walk from the conference center. He didn't wish to join the other academics, who might ask what he was researching, only to sneer at him for not giving a credible response.

He found a comfortable establishment, dark, soothing, urbane. The bar was made of polished mahogany wood. Light classical music played. He slid into a maroon leather booth and ordered. The other customers looked like business men and women, judging by their well-fitted suits and briefcases. He glanced around.

To his horror, he noticed Larry Anderson at a nearby table, reading the menu. He considered leaving, but a quick exit might attract Anderson's attention. It was safer to remain seated, keeping his head down. But Anderson spotted him anyway. He smiled, eyebrows arched in a friendly manner. He raised his glass, then ordered an expensive scotch for Aaron, who wondered why Anderson wasn't driving a cab or digging ditches. Wasn't that supposed to be the outcome of losing tenure? Instead, the former faculty member was in an upscale bar, attending an event for reputable academics.

Anderson joined him in the booth without being invited. Aaron thought it best to bring up the ethics investigation right away, to see how things stood.

"The Committee only found one of the sources I borrowed, Professor. In those days, I could be a little careless."

This surprised Aaron. Anderson took pride in being able to plagiarize without being detected.

"Didn't the loss of tenure affect you?" He starred at Anderson's suit. It looked custom-tailored. Not off the rack, like Aaron's.

"You may not realize it, but you did me a great favor by voting to kick me out. I'm making several times the income I might have made with a university career, and I am doing my favorite activity—researching and writing about linguistic history." He picked up the table's menu. "Allow me to thank you by ordering some appetizers."

"Does your success have something to do with the booth you manned, Academic Ghostwriters? Are you a ghostwriter?"

"Yes and no. I'm substituting for a friend at the booth. I'm a freelance ghostwriter. Those employed by Academic Ghostwriters may be knowledgeable enough to tackle student papers or parts of dissertations, but they aren't capable of original book-length scholarship." He spoke as if they were old friends or amicable colleagues. "Call me Larry, Professor."

"Do you mean you have written academic books for faculty?"

Anderson leaned forward, replying in a hushed tone. "You'd be surprised how many at the conference I have helped along the way."

Aaron thought Anderson had to be exaggerating. Such deception couldn't be widespread. "What about the key-note speaker?"

Anderson put his finger to his lips.

"But he's at Harvard!" Aaron sipped his second drink. Perhaps it was his third. It might not be wise to drive for a while.

"Are you staying at the conference center tonight?"

"No. I'm driving home, since it's so close."

Anderson twirled his drink, seeming to mull something over.

"Look. This might be forward of me. I feel I owe you. There are two beds in my room. Why don't you bunk with me tonight? That way we can keep talking. It helps me to hear the latest ideas in the field. I planned to attend the sessions, but that's out the window now that I'm in charge of the booth. You can give me the run down on those you attended."

"Well… "

"It's win-win. You get a room; I get to pick your brain."

They stayed several hours longer, drinking, eating appetizers, talking about linguistics. Soon Aaron was telling Anderson everything. His promotion to Associate without having published. His desire to make Full Professor before retirement. The pile of obligations leaving no time for research.

"That's the main reason academics hire me. It's not that they don't have ideas. What they don't have is time. If they weren't so overloaded, they would be quite capable of producing solid manuscripts themselves."

"I guess you have a point, but…"

"I'm just a transcriber. That's all. I take the theories of my customers, worked out over years, and put them in a form that benefits the field." He motioned to the server to bring the check.

"I'm not sure that's ethical."

Anderson smiled. "How long were you on the Ethics Committee? It's so small-minded. Tasked with finding plagiarism. As if borrowing a sentence or two from a colleague is the moral equivalent of sexual misconduct or hate speech."

"We handle those cases, too."

The server arrived with the check. Anderson put his credit card on the little tray.

"The problem with plagiarism is the likelihood of getting caught. The victim will come across the plagiarized material if it's published. Especially in a small field like linguistics history. The plagiarist could be fired, even sued."

"Isn't it just as risky to hire someone like you? Academic Ghostwriters is openly advertising at the conference. It will alert academics on promotions and tenure committees. They will be on the look-out for ghostwritten publications."

"And if they are? How would they find out? You would supply the ideas. You would read each draft of the manuscript. It would be your own work that I type out."

The two men started walking back to the hotel. Aaron staggered, not used to heavy drinking.

"Better let me hold your arm, Professor. You don't want to lose your balance." Anderson gripped him. Aaron leaned into the ghostwriter, relying on his support.

"Are you expensive?" Somewhere, a clock chimed twice. Two A.M. Very late for Aaron.

"That depends on several factors. How much research is necessary. How soon you need the manuscript. It's length. That sort of thing."

That was the last thing Aaron remembered. He awoke in a bed in the hotel room, in his underwear. His clothing was folded over a chair. The other bed didn't look slept in. A handwritten note lay on it next to a business card.

Sorry — something came up. I had to leave. The room is paid for. I've treated you to breakfast downstairs. Just give them the room number. It was good to catch up. I'm leaving you my card in case you need to get in touch. Larry

The next day, Aaron attended the conference after having several cups of coffee and aspirin for a headache. He ran into academics he knew in graduate school as well as from his own department.

"What are you working on these days?" This was a common question.

"I'm planning to give a paper myself at next year's conference, now that my book is almost ready for publication." It might be true, or almost true.

Back in his office on campus after the conference, Aaron made sure the business card was in his jacket pocket, as he turned Anderson's words over in his mind. Was ghostwritten work unethical or another way of representing ideas? He knew the Ethics Committee would find it problematic, but would they consider all the factors? As Anderson said, lack of time created the need for a ghostwriter. Whose fault was that?

Furthermore, the old way of researching, writing, and publishing had changed. Everything was digitalized nowadays. Research resources that used to require travel to distant libraries were available on line. Editing apps approached computer ghostwriting. No one considered them unethical.

"Yes, but… it just doesn't feel right." He kept fingering the card.

He went to the cafeteria for a quick bite. His open computer on the table signaled that the lunch eater did not wish to be disturbed. Yet, someone often approached him carrying a tray, a graduate student asking to join him. The last one who interrupted his lunch was Ben. He hadn't seen him since the Conference.

"I'm afraid I only have a few minutes. Is there something you wish to discuss?" Aaron had asked him.

He swallowed a lump of turkey sandwich, thinking, "Just what I need."

"No. Well, maybe." The tall, husky student had hunched, burdened shoulders. He sat and kept stirring the bowl of soup on his tray without raising the spoon to his lips.

"I know the Committee only deals with academic cases."

Aaron waited, biting into his sandwich. It was dry, lacking enough mayonnaise. He chewed with caution, fearing he might choke on the overcooked turkey. With a strange mixture of pleasure and distress, he imagined Ben clutching him in a Heimlich maneuver.

"…but, what if you have a problem that isn't exactly academic?"

With the image of being administered abdominal thrusts floating into his mind, Aaron listened to Ben with increasing interest.

"What do you mean?"

"I hope I am not out of line if I ask your opinion as one who has adjudicated ethical cases. It's just that… I wonder if you know… where one goes to find guidance for grief issues?"

Ben pushed his soup aside and stared straight at Aaron, his rounding shoulders pushing his head forward, leaning his muscular arms on the table. These would be the arms forcing the meat from Aaron's throat, if he swallowed the wrong way.

"To a therapist or a rabbi, I suppose." The mat of dark hairs on the young man's arms distracted Aaron.

"Yes. Of course. The thing is… my mother and my niece, Eva. They've been missing three years now. I'm afraid I'm losing my sister

Deborah, too. She's all the family I have left. My brother-in-law Josh is even more depressed than me."

Aaron couldn't think of any words of comfort. He nodded, waiting for Ben to continue.

"I'm having trouble writing my thesis. I can't concentrate. All I can do is wonder where my mother is. And poor Eva."

Aaron pushed his sandwich aside, near to the tray of unfinished soup. Tears formed on Ben's lower lashes.

"This may be crazy thinking. If they're dead, it's my fault for not offering to baby-sit the day they disappeared. I should've taken Eva to the zoo. Maybe it would've saved her. Why didn't I take her to the zoo like a good uncle?"

Ben's sadness and guilt awakened a moment of sadness in Aaron. He avoided feelings by focusing on academics. The personal problems of students never interested him. Linguistics interested him. The price he paid for the pleasures of reading article abstracts and attending conferences was teaching young people.

The sight of Ben's arms aroused both desire and protectiveness. He placed a sympathetic hand on Ben's wrist, wondering if his gesture meant he was gay or just a professor expressing compassion for a student. He didn' t want to be gay! Quickly, he removed his hand. His mind shifted to a more acceptable fatherly mode. He spoke to Ben as a parent would.

"What happened to your family is not your fault. It was fate. If you had taken you niece to the zoo, a bus might have hit her. Your mother, wherever she is, and your sister would want you to finish your degree. That's what you should be doing."

Ben listened, then nodded. He folded his arms against his chest, shielding his heart.

Later, as he walked across campus, Aaron fingered Anderson's card again. He thought he might call the ghostwriter to find out what he charged for a full-length academic manuscript. Just to enquire. There were many things to consider. He imagined the two of them having pleasant conversations about linguistic theory. Developing ideas. Weekly meetings. The manuscript taking shape. Promotions. The respect of his colleagues.

And beyond that, talking to Anderson about Ben and his family, about who undressed him the night they shared a room, and about how the muscular arms of a sad young man had forced some compassionate words from the depths of Aaron's throat.

CHAPTER 6
WHO BY STRANGULATION

In the months since Edith found the strength to heft her granddaughter from the precipice at the top of the hill to solid ground, their relationship changed. Eva was no longer as defiant. The seven-year-old became less confrontational, but she craved new experiences, especially with other people.

Nearly losing the girl scared Edith. The birth of Eva had thrilled her. She spilled tears of joy when she held the tiny bundle in the delivery room. Her first grandchild! She expected to have more. Deborah and Josh might conceive a second child in time, and although Ben was still a student and single, he, too, might have a family in the future.

She pictured *Shabbat* dinners and *Seders* — extra leaves in the table, platters of food covering every inch, the good silverware, candlesticks passed down from her own grandparents, matzo ball soup, brisket, roast chicken, Hebrew prayers, laughter, and several children sitting on books to reach their plates.

Her delight in her granddaughter continued through her infancy and babyhood. The tininess of her, little pearl fingernails, a fluff of dark curls, eager dark eyes, enchanted Edith. She bought onesies stamped with "I Love Bubbe" and newborn dresses decorated with tiny pink roses. She attended the milestones, videoing on her phone — first tottering steps, first words, first birthday cake.

When had it changed?

As the girl hung over the abyss, screaming, "Bubbe! Bubbe!" and Edith's shoulder ripped out of its socket, she snapped into the terror, the awesome responsibility, the instinctual force, of protecting a small child. A moment before, she could have dropped her without remorse. The child could stay, the child could go. When she wandered off, Edith worried about strangers finding her, contacting the rangers, getting caught. She took care of Eva, stiffly, by the book, fed her, clothed her, treated her burns and bruises, the way she took care of the wood stove. Her mind turned on her own internal state, the unwinding from all that was *Joe*. It took years. Meanwhile, the child strived for scraps of her grandmother's attention by whatever means.

At one time, Edith was a normal woman, enjoying her children and the new baby. Her greatest pleasure was her family, but they weren't her only pleasure. She enjoyed folk music, tv, novels, magazines, theatre, movies, restaurants. Then, when Eva was about two, her feelings snuffed out. What remained was a shell of who she used to be.

It was Joe. His drinking reached a tipping point, and they both plunged into a marital sinkhole. She met him in her senior year in high school. He was older, already graduated, taking college courses and working in construction. He owned a late-model Ford, which he used to take her on dates. It seemed sophisticated when he took a flask from a coat pocket, unscrewed the cap and swallowed before kissing her. In those days, she didn't mind his alcohol breath.

Drinking was just what Joe did. It didn't register that, over the years, his consumption increased. He had a temper. The children were victims of his periodic lashings-out when they annoyed him. After Deborah and Ben became adults and moved away, Joe's new boss harassed him. He reacted by drinking more. He came home late from work, often staggering in past dinner time, in a foul mood.

By the time Eva was a toddler, rage consumed him. Edith watched her step. If she didn't do what he wanted as soon as he wanted it, he bellowed with fury, roaring and cursing at her.

Anything might set him off. She heard a low growl, an animal sound, and smelled a pungent gamey odor, even from another part of the house. There would be a sinister padding on the hardwood floors, as he drew closer, hunting her, sniffing her out. She flattened herself against the nearest wall, digging at the wallpaper with her fingernails, fearing the firing beats of her heart would draw him to her. Or she ran to the bedroom and crouched quivering in the closet.

When he reached the room's doorway, his hands soldered into fists.

She learned to choke off all sensations. When Joe cooled down, she might be curled up on the floor. Within minutes, she stood and resumed her routine. If she passed a mirror, any cuts or bruises surprised her. It violated her self-imposed rule not to remember what happened.She called Joe into the kitchen for dinner in the normal way. They ate together, chatting about the day's happenings, leaving out Joe's rage spell. Whatever irritated him was in the past, over. They moved on. Joe acknowledged to others, in Edith's presence, that he might have a small "anger problem." It was almost a boast. Anger was a manly problem. Edith didn't disagree.

She was proud that a manly man chose her. Drinking and anger problems went along with masculinity, in her view. Her mother understood. Real men were just that way. The woman's job was to keep men from becoming frustrated. This wasn't modern thinking. Edith supported the Women's Movement when it came to legislation. She objected to spouse abuse when it happened to other women.

If Deborah or Ben asked if Joe hurt her, she denied it. She fell. She braked the car hard and her head hit the windshield. She tripped on the stairs. One time, she went to the Emergency Room to have a deep cut on the back of her head stitched. The physician noted the red marks on her throat.

"How did you get these?" He turned her head left and right, peering at her neck.

"I don't know." Her voice rasped.

"Did someone choke you?"

"No. I don't think so."

"I can see the imprint of fingers. You've been choked. How about I call the police?"

"No! There's no need."

"What I suspect happened to you is very dangerous. People who are choked can suffocate, even after the choking stops. Airways can spasm closed."

After the doctor left the exam room, a woman entered with pamphlets in her hand. Her badge said "Social Worker."

"May I call you Edith?"

"Yes."

"In case you need them." The Social Worker handed Edith the pamphlets for a domestic abuse hotline and for a women's shelter. Edith tossed them in the trash before driving home. Joe mustn't find them or to learn of her trip to the emergency room. He was in bed, sleeping it off, not aware she left the house. When she returned, she tied a scarf around her head and another around her neck. There wouldn't be any questions.

She worked harder to make Joe happy, suppressing her own needs. She didn't ask for anything. If he disappeared, she didn't ask where he'd been. If his pants were rumpled and soiled, she took them to the cleaners. She made his favorite food. Whatever happened in the past wouldn't happen again.

That was when Joe was alive, before Edith escaped to the forest. Now she sat on the trail just below the sinkhole, hugging the child, her granddaughter, feeling terror, feeling joy, feeling feelings. Eva was crying and choking from the dust, hugging her grandmother. Edith lifted the child's face and looked into her eyes.

"You're alright. Bubbe will make sure you will always be alright. From now on, Bubbe will keep you safe."

Hikers and rangers raced up the hill.

"Hey, Lady. Are you okay?"

A man with a badge checked on her and Eva. He helped them down the trail, carrying Eva. Edith clung to him, sobbing, stopping every few minutes when her knees buckled. When they reached the trailhead parking lot, she said she would wait there with the child for her husband. He was probably frantic with worry, looking for them, she said. The man nodded, then took off again to see who else needed rescuing.

Although her left arm would be useless until healed, it surprised Edith to feel pain again. It had been years since she felt it. Taking Eva's hand with her right one, she slipped back to the hut before anyone else spotted them. There, she sat Eva on her lap and inspected her, moving each of her limbs. No bones were broken. She would wash her in the creek to find any scrapes.

"Bubbe, do you think that boy is dead?"

"The one you talked to before the sinkhole happened?"

"Yeah."

"I think so."

"If he isn't dead, the dust will make him cough."

"It would."

"I coughed. That's because I didn't die."

"No. You didn't die. I'm not going to let you die."

"You're not?"

Such a sad question. The child wasn't sure. Edith felt something else she hadn't experienced in a long time. Shame. It corkscrewed through her. While Eva dangled in the chasm, she didn't know if her grandmother would pull her up or drop her. What a horrible doubt for a child. She had to make it up to her.

And what of Deborah and Ben? In the three years since she left town for the forest, she never thought of them. She erased them from her mind. In a vague way, she remembered her children. But her maternal instinct vanished.

What had she put them through? Ben, her youngest, in his mid-twenties, still reeling from his father's death and needing a mother more than ever, having to suffer from her disappearance along with that of his niece. Deborah and her husband Josh, experiencing the excruciating pain of the loss of a child because of her abduction of Eva. They must think their daughter is dead, perhaps murdered. And Deborah had no mother to comfort her, not knowing her own mother caused her grief.

She must undo her crime by returning the child right away. She should find a ranger and confess. But it might further damage the child to be torn from her arms by uniformed men, who would take her grandmother away in handcuffs.

It would be better to bring Eva back to town herself, if the child could manage the long walk. But what then? The child might not recognize Josh and Deborah. She might cling to her grandmother. Perhaps she could leave her with Rabbi Samuelson, although he was not warm with children. She imagined Eva screaming in terror as she left the synagogue.

"Bubbe! Bubbe! Don't leave me!"

Could she face the certainty of prison at her age, or would she be able to get back to the forest undetected?

At a loss, she opened "Book of Roots," her guide for over three years. For the first time, she noticed an inscription inside the front cover, written in cursive in ink.

"Keep her. She will have no one else."

The book's power extended beyond the forest. Its instruction was clear.

Edith hadn't seen her image since she left town. She remembered cutting her hair. Now it was long, covering her back, unshaped, with streaks of gray, twisted into a bun when others might see her. Her face had deep lines, she assumed.

She was becoming inseparable from the forest, part of it, like a deep-rooted vine-covered plant, no longer simply a *widow*. Maybe a female *dybbuk* or a *witch*. A *witch* of the forest, something not imagined in all of Judaism, raising a child who became more feral every day. They would stay in the hut. She would teach her granddaughter the secrets of the book. The book wasn't the *Torah*, God's gift to the Jews. "Roots of the Woods" was another type of gift. There was no author or date listed on the title pages. Whoever or whatever wrote it intended it for just for one reader — her.

CHAPTER 7
WHO BY WILD BEAST

Ben did not feel well. It occurred to him that he had not felt well for at least a week. Maybe more. He had a low-grade fever. It wasn't just his throbbing head stirring up his imagination. He was really sick.

The time on the digital bedside clock seemed to jump from six to nine. Had he fallen back to sleep? He had to leave his hotel room for the conference on the lower level. The first meeting had started. He wondered if he could make it to the elevator, much less to the keynote address by a well-regarded linguistic historian from Harvard. Linguistics wasn't Ben's field. He was a graduate student in Economics, but an overlap in his thesis topic between the two disciplines made it worthwhile to attend. His research investigated the ways a region's language had shaped its economy.

If he had a girlfriend, she could have accompanied him, bringing him tea and Tylenol, laying her cool hand on his forehead, and insisting he stay in bed. She could have recorded the more important sessions for him. Or she could have curled her soft warm body next to his in the bed, lulling him to the blessedness of sleep. But he didn't have a girlfriend. He had been too depressed to date after his mother and his niece disappeared.

That had happened three years before. It shocked him to realize that Eva would be seven, if she was alive. Every time the earth completed another circuit of the sun, whenever another class of students graduated in May or enrolled in the university in August, every *Rosh Hashanah*, every time the last page of the wall calendar was ripped off and replaced by a new calendar with a different National

Geographic wildlife photo on its cover, the world would be a year older, but Eva would still be four.

Four. An awful number. The weekdays before *erev Shabbat*, Friday night. The number of years he had left in graduate school. The years he had been an orphan, if someone murdered his mother.

Terrible sadness racked him for the first months after the disappearance, repeated whenever a new lead fizzled out. It now muted into a duller, constant ache. He no longer described himself as "mad with grief." Now he was "mad with loneliness." Especially while attending a conference where he knew no one except one faculty member from the Ethics Committee at his university. They spoke for a few minutes the day before.

The graduate students and professors he studied with and had beer with after classes occasionally wouldn't be here. No one would walk him back to his room if his fever spiked or get him medical attention. He was on his own. But the weakness and nausea were just symptoms of some temporary bug, a twenty-four-hour flu. He'd be fine the next day. Other conference attendees might be stuck in their rooms, or fighting to stay upright at the conference sessions, with the same contagious condition.

By the lunch break, he knew he wouldn't last through the long afternoon and evening of presentations. He staggered to the elevator and returned to his room and its freshly made bed.

After several hours of deep sleep, he woke up refreshed. His temperature was normal, and he was hungry for the first time in days. The hotel's pricey restaurant was unaffordable. Instead, he purchased several candy bars from a vending machine near the ice maker and made decaf in the coffee machine in his room. Rather than attend the evening sessions, he settled in for a night of Netflix. He should be healthy enough for the last day of the conference after another night's sleep.

But the next morning, the wooziness started again. He stared at his complimentary breakfast in the lobby cafe, wondering if a piece of dry toast would settle his stomach. A man carrying a tray approached his table. Ben recognized him from the Dealer's Room, staffed by academic publishers.

"Do you mind if I join you? This is the only table left."

The stranger set his tray down. Graduate students were expected to talk about their dissertations, hoping to procure a publisher's interest in a future book. Ben wasn't up to this kind of conversation.

"Larry Anderson. And your name, Professor?" The publisher took a seat.

"I'm just a graduate student. Not yet a professor." The sight of curdled eggs, muddy gravy, and pale doughy biscuits on the stranger's tray brought on a coughing fit.

"You okay, Professor?"

Shaking his head, Ben stood to leave. Anderson stuck a business card into Ben's conference packet.

Still coughing and unable to speak, Ben grabbed the packet and stumbled back to the elevator. He pushed the button for — was he on the eleventh floor? As soon as the ascent began, he vomited onto the floor. When the doors next opened, permitting a group of conference attendees to pile in, he rushed out.

He found himself in an antechamber, in front of three closed elevator doors. A large mirror covered the opposite wall, partly obscured by an urn containing a spray of metallic flowers. His reflection did not resemble him. The green-tinged face, the round-shouldered lankiness, the thinning hair: *is that me?* He needed to find his room, shower, and change clothes. He needed to sleep more. He needed to attend the presentations. Not daring to risk the elevator again, he located an emergency door. It led to a stairwell. After climbing one flight, his energy dwindled. Lightheaded, he sank down on the steps.

He might have dozed off. When he awoke, he noticed the card from the stranger in the cafe, lying on the floor, face up. It must have dropped out of his packet. He read it without touching it, although the lettering was hazy.

Larry Anderson. Academic Ghostwriter.

Not a publisher. A ghostwriter. The word "Ghost" floated above the rest of the card, shimmering in the half-light. As he stared, the word sharpened, while the other words and the card itself oozed into the general grayness of the area. While trying to comprehend what was happening, he heard a whimper. He forced himself to concentrate. Was an animal trapped, perhaps on another floor? After a few minutes, the sound changed. A child whimpered. Ben strained to listen.

Uncle Ben! Uncle Ben! Get me!

It was Eva! His niece called to him. She was in trouble, possibly hurt or lost. He sprang up, looking around. The voice circled his head, coming from several directions, both from the flights above and the flights below.

"Eva! I'm here. Where are you?"

I'm down here, Uncle. Get me. Hurry!

Ben looked over the railing. The stairs spiraled down for several flights. It was too dark to see the bottom. Perhaps there were several lower levels. Had his niece fallen, tumbling down several flights? An object three flights down caught his attention. He began the descent to see what it was.

"I'm coming. Stay where you are. I'll find you."

He reached for the object. It was a child's battered pink and white shoe, with its velcro straps undone and hanging open. He was sure it belonged to Eva. He remembered Deborah buying her just such a pair. If the girl had fallen to this floor, whichever floor it was, she couldn't be much further down. But when Eva next called, she didn't sound closer. If anything, she seemed more distant.

Uncle! Hurry! I'm hurt.

Ben rushed down the stairs with holding the shoe in a tight grip. Each level had a landing with a door to the hotel floor. The first two were unlocked. He pushed them open to see if Eva found her way out. But the third one and all subsequent ones were locked. This would make finding Eva easier. She couldn't wander off.

Ben raced downward, calling his niece's name. If he looked over the rail, the bottom remained invisible. As tired as he was, he kept going down the endless stairwell. Eva was down there, somewhere, calling for him. She was alive. Soon, they would be reunited. Ben wheezed from the exertion, but that didn't matter. Only finding Eva mattered. He would descend to the earth's core if it meant bringing the girl back. He clutched the shoe.

When he lost his footing, he did not realize at first what happened. The walls, stairs, and ceiling changed places. His head banged hard on each step. Something was wrong with the angle of his legs. The shoe was gone, dropped somewhere. As his consciousness faded, he heard Eva calling, quite near, but out of sight.

The blackness ended. Someone in a white jacket hung over him, shining a penlight into his eyes. The stranger said he was a doctor, that Ben was in a hospital, that he couldn't talk because he was on a ventilator to help him breathe.

"We'll do all we can to make you comfortable," the doctor said.

Ben thrashed. He tried to pull out the ventilator. He had to tell the doctor that Eva was in the stairwell. Someone had to find her. Maybe she was hurt.

"Just a little prick," someone said. Then it was black again.

When he awoke, he saw his mother, Edith, smiling in a chair near his bed. She held a plate of oatmeal cookies, nodding for him to take one. And there was his father, Joe, in his recliner, reading Sports Illustrated, with a beer in his hand, as usual. Near the door, Rabbi Samuelson intoned the *Mi Shebeirach* prayer for healing. Ben's brother-in-law, Josh, stood at the foot of his bed, texting rapidly with both thumbs. Deborah, his sister, sat on the other side of the bed, holding his hand. Her eyes were moist.

"Darling, you have the Powassan virus. It's from a deer tick," she said.

His father lowered the magazine and spoke in Ben's direction.

"Ticks. A nearly invisible enemy. They carry obscure diseases, like Lyme and Powassan. Makes your brain swell." He thumbed the pages of Sports Illustrated. "Your mistake was joining that manhunt for Eva. That's probably when ticks attacked you."

Ben remembered the phone call from Josh, the frantic search around his parents' neighborhood, the line-up of volunteers using flashlights to sweep the farmland surrounding the town. No, he had not tucked his pants into his socks or sprayed himself with DEET. He hadn't thought of it. His niece was missing.

"You're a dead duck, man," Josh said without looking up from his phone. He was a lawyer, always working overtime.

Ben turned his head toward Deborah. How kind she was. He saw her shaking. Parkinson's. Soon he would lose her, too. Tears leaked from his eyes. She wiped his face with the end of the blanket covering him. He wouldn't let go of her fluttering hand. Looking straight at her, he spoke with his gaze.

I love you, sister. I'm so sorry.

She gave him a warm smile. He knew she understood.

Another figure hovered just behind her. It was Eva, still four years old.

Uncle. I lost my shoe.

The shoe! Where was the shoe! Ben tore at the ventilator tube. He had to go back to the hotel to find Eva's shoe. Deborah yelled at him to stop. Josh yanked his hands away from the tubing.

"He's having a seizure," someone shouted. "Code blue."

"Don't forget. Pants tucked into socks," his father shouted as Ben raced out of the room and into the farmland after Eva. She ran just ahead, with only one shoe on. The sock on her other foot was decorated with the image of a mermaid. Ben squinted to see it whenever the arc of a volunteer's flashlight swooped by it.

"Wait for me," he shouted.

Catch me, Uncle. I'm right over here.

CHAPTER 8
WHO SHALL WANDER

Rabbi Samuelson found his old white Nikes in the back of his closet. He only wore brogues since being ordained a decade before—traditional rabbi shoes and rabbi clothes—dark suit, tie, long black coat, *kippa*. He wasn't one of the Reformed clergy who wore jeans to shortened services, skipping pages of liturgy in favor of crowd-pleasing sing-a-longs.

That he left to Isaac, his younger assistant, the more popular part-time rabbi, who did most of the pastoral work, consoling the sick and the grieving. Rabbi Samuelson wasn't comfortable with emotional outbursts. He didn't know what to do when someone wept in his office, other than point a stubby finger at the tissue box. He was a small, round man, whose trousers had to be hemmed and sleeves shortened. When he composed his weekly sermons, he used classic Jewish texts—the *Torah*, the *Talmud*, the *Mishnah*, and the *Tanakh*—that appealed to the older intellectuals in the congregation. The rest listened with glazed eyes.

Just the past Saturday, he had given one of his more accomplished talks on *Lech Lecha*, the chapter in the *Torah* in which God instructs Abraham.

Go from your land, from your birthplace and from your father's house, to the land which I will show you.

It reminded Rabbi Samuelson of leaving the comforts of his parents' home in Brooklyn, where his mother did everything for him, to take the position of rabbi in a synagogue in a university town in Indiana. He looked on a map to find it—a small municipality attached to a large campus, surrounded by state forest. The Rabbi seldom visited the forest. He was city bred, uneasy in nature, preferring libraries and synagogues, the known Jewish world over new and possibly dangerous non-Jewish experiences.

Yet, he made the unusual decision to venture alone into the state park. The year 5764 had been an unfortunate one for his congregation. Edith, a long-time member and recent widow, disappeared with her four-year-old granddaughter, Eva. Three years later, Deborah, the girl's mother, died of Parkinson's, soon after her brother, Ben, died of a tick-borne illness. An entire family wiped out within three years. The only one left was Deborah's husband, Josh, now a widower. The congregation was still in turmoil.

A year ago, two people resembling Edith and Eva were spotted when a sink-hole in the state forest claimed the lives of several hikers. Most likely, they were victims, too, although their bodies were never found. What they were doing in the forest all these years was anybody's guess.

Even if Rabbi Samuelson was stern on the surface, he had a heart. He considered himself as having as much *chesed*, loving kindness, as Isaac. He just didn't connect with the congregation the way Isaac did.

His particular concern was that *Kaddish*, the prayer for the dead, hadn't been recited for Edith and Eva. The girl's father refused to give up hope because no remains were recovered. Witnesses shown the Amber Alert photos were too uncertain to make an identification. Who knew? They might be alive, wandering around, living like animals in the forest or not in the forest at all. But a year had gone by since the collapse and four since their disappearance. It agitated the Rabbi when traditions weren't followed. This couldn't be permitted to continue.

He thought it might help if he saw the devastation for himself. Then he could talk to Josh more convincingly about the improbability of anyone surviving a fall into the hole or a winter in the wild. Josh might accept their death, even in the absence of proof. At least, that was Rabbi Samuelson's wish. He knew it was a long shot. But until Josh gave up hope, it was forbidden to recite the prayer for his deceased mother-in-law and daughter.

Just after lunch on a crisp November Friday, the Rabbi gave in to an impulse that had no logic or Jewish tradition to justify it. It was time to see the sinkhole for himself without further delay. From what he gathered from others, it took an hour to hike from the trail head to the sinkhole. The way back would be quicker because it was downhill. He had plenty of time to complete the task before *Shabbat* services began that evening after sunset.

After parking at the trail head, it comforted him to find that the foot path was covered with wood chips, easily visible across the meadow where the hike began. The Rabbi strolled through it, carrying a small bag containing a flashlight, a protein bar, and a bottle of water. The forest waited on the other side.

As soon as he entered it, he realized that conditions were more challenging than they had been in the meadow. A thick mat of damp fallen leaves covered the wood chips and the entire forest floor. He would have to rely on trail markers. At least these were easy to spot. Red arrows painted on trees and on posts pointed the way. Despite his misgivings, he marched ahead.

The strangeness of the forest was daunting. He worried that the greenery contained poison ivy or snakes. Copperheads were said to be dangerous. Enormous spiders waited in huge webs strung between trees. Yet, many of his congregants spoke of sensing God's presence in the state parks and other natural sites: oceans, deserts, mountains. This was pantheism, idol worship, not monotheism. He corrected them. God requires a *minyan*, a group of ten Jews, and the *Torah* to be said to be "present." No doubt Rabbi Isaac would be less stringent. Of course, the forest was beautiful in the sense that all of God's works are beautiful. It was part of God's creation, blessed by God Himself in the opening verses of Genesis. He wasn't incapable of appreciating beauty. He was just unaccustomed to it outside of art museums.

The trail did not go straight uphill. It went in an unexpected direction, downward into a ravine before angling upward. The red arrows pointed to a creek, and another was visible on the other side. Large stones scattered across the water provided footing. He stepped from stone to stone. Further along the trail, the arrows pointed back across the same creek again. He couldn't fathom why. Wouldn't it have been easier if both parts of the trail had been on the same side? Or if whoever was in charge had built bridges? This time, the stones were scattered wider apart. He tried to jump from one to another, but missed and wound up wading through cold water. At least he hadn't worn the brogues.

Now that his feet and the bottoms of his trousers had been soaked, the hike wasn't pleasant. He considered turning back. That involved re-crossing the creek twice. He kept going.

The arrows directed him upward in switchback fashion, reminding him of the child's game, Chutes and Ladders. It followed the contours of the hill, ascending to the right, then turning to ascend to the left. His thoughts drifted to Mt. Sinai, somewhere in the land of Israel. It wasn't a mountain like those in the Rockies or the Himalayas. Although no one knew its location, Mt. Sinai was supposed to be about the height of the hill he was climbing, without the forestation. No wonder Moses carried stone tablets up and down. He didn't have to grab branches to keep his balance. He had no creeks to cross. He didn't have to worry about turning his ankle on slippery wet leaves.

The Rabbi was out of breath. Although it would dirty his coat, he sat on a log. He was not used to physical exertion. Exercise had never appealed to him. He spent most of his life sitting in libraries, classrooms, and his office in the synagogue. Outdoors, he only walked to and from his parked car. It had been years since he had been outside for over ten minutes. He prided himself on loving books and the *Torah* in particular more than people, animals, flora or fauna. That was as it should be. The *Torah* was God's gift to the Jews. Perhaps he had betrayed his values by hiking. Maybe he should have gone with Isaac.

Why hadn't he? The younger man might be an accomplished hiker. He rode a bike to the synagogue. He claimed to be a vegetarian. Sustainable-types like Isaac seemed at home in the natural world. He could have asked Isaac to accompany him on this rash mission to the sink-hole. But although they were both rabbis, they had little in common. Rabbi Samuelson was glad to be spared awkward silences and strained conversation. Besides, he did not want Isaac to witness his physical clumsiness, the panicky way he grabbed at saplings to keep from falling, his chattering teeth from the chill of the creek, the slowness of his uncertain gait.

After eating the protein bar for energy, he rose and began the ascent again. A short while later, the trail ended at an orange traffic cone. A sign was posted.

No trespassing. Unstable area. Trail closed.

At the outer edge of the area containing the sinkhole, he paused. Several feet beyond the sign, yellow tape was strung between trees. Tangled brush and fallen logs lay ahead. Having hiked this far, he wasn't going to miss what he had come for. He hoisted himself upwards by grasping limbs. As he neared the hole, he became more cautious, testing the ground before taking each step as if it were thin ice on a pond. When he reached the yellow tape, he stooped under. The ragged rim of the hole was a few steps away. On the far side of the opening, he glimpsed a view of miles of forest and the wide cloudless sky.

With an abundance of caution, he sank to his hands and knees and crawled through the brush to the edge. His trousers would have to be dry cleaned after their dunk in the creek, anyway. It wasn't clear what he hoped to see. A vast pit of fire? A heap of boulders? The remains of the grandmother and granddaughter? The disappointing sight was of nothing but darkness. He fished his flashlight out of his bag. Its dim beam only revealed a very deep, black hole. The bottom wasn't visible. If anyone fell in, it would be difficult or impossible to climb out unaided.

Satisfied that he had the description he needed to advise Josh, he stood and pulled his phone out of his pocket to check the time. "No service." He frowned, at first not understanding what it meant. Never had he been anywhere without phone service. He should have known. It wasn't the only problem. No electricity, running water, bathrooms were provided in the middle of hiking trails in state parks. He guessed it was mid-afternoon. If he hurried, he would get back to his car before dark.

Except that because he had abandoned the trail, no red arrows directed the way. By retracing his steps, he should be able to find the orange cone and follow the arrows back to the trail head. Why hadn't a ranger been stationed at the sinkhole to help people? He would have to figure it out himself. He would descend until he found the creek, hoping the rest of the trail back would be obvious. But after thrashing his way through thick vegetation to get to the top, the path he made closed up again, like the giant fish that opened its jaws just long enough to spit out Jonah before clamping shut again.

He wedged himself through a random parting between trees, then began stumbling downward, hoping to pick up the trail, eventually. He tried to spot anything that looked familiar. All the trees looked the same. Any space wide enough for him to squeeze through was a likely path. Like a maze with false exits, a pathway might appear, then disappear, forcing him to go in another direction. The forest itself guided him, opening and closing routes, providing a convoluted map either into or out of the interior. He couldn't tell which.

As the light failed, he sat on a log, perhaps the same log he had sat on during his ascent up the hill. Who knew? He thought of Abraham, sent on a journey without knowing where he was going.

Go to the land which I shall show you.

He noticed a numbness, of a tingling in his arms and legs, while his heart thumped and squeezed in his chest. His breath was shallow and uneven. If he didn't find his way out soon, he'd spend the night in the forest. Already, there were the sounds of hoots and rustles he had not heard before. Night sounds. He stood up and glanced around for a path, a sign, a red arrow, anything that would point the way.

Then a movement flickered in the corner of his eye. Pivoting, he saw nothing. He took a few steps in that direction and waited. There it was again. A flicker off to his left.

"Hello. Who are you?" He called out. There was no answer.

The movement at the edge of his vision only appeared if he didn't look straight at it. Was it an animal, a bear or mountain lion, stalking him? He picked up a fallen branch, his only possible defense. Once darkness came, he would be helpless. This made the numbness spread. His hands shook, unable to keep a solid grip on the branch.

The wind picked up. Unless it was a whisper. He listened while holding his breath.

I shall show you.

His mood lifted. Someone was going to rescue him. He wasn't alone. Who could it be? Perhaps a ranger, another hiker, or even Isaac, who may have guessed where he went and that he needed help. He shouldn't be so hard on him, so jealous. It wasn't righteous. He would be friendlier in the future.

A flicker appeared again, on his right this time. It occurred to him that it was Edith, alive in the forest as Josh hoped. Of course it was. He could almost see the older congregant in his peripheral vision, with the child at her side.

"I'm coming," he called out. "Show me the way!"

CHAPTER 9
WHO BY THIRST

Eva was ten years old, and Edith neared sixty. Life in the primitive hut was demanding. She aged fast, while the child grew stronger, able to carry two or three logs from the woodpile, which seemed to replenish itself every autumn. They both hauled five gallons of water at a time from the creek. Together, they hung dripping laundry on low branches to dry. They scrubbed dirt off roots after they dug them up. They dragged the sleeping mats outside for airing and swept the earthen floor with a twig broom Edith fashioned.

But the restless child needed education and companionship. She knew the alphabet, but couldn't go further without a simple text. One day, she would inherit "Roots of the Woods." It would only be useful if Eva could read it. Edith needed to teach the girl. Opening the book at random, which she had done many times before when problems needed solving, she discovered an insert, about half the size of the regular pages. It slipped out of the binding. The print was large and illustrated. It was a child's reader. She gave it to her granddaughter.

It fascinated Eva. She learned to sound out the letters by herself. The story was about a family. Two parents, two grandparents—Bubbe and Saba, an uncle, and a little girl. They lived in the same town until the grandmother and the little girl moved to the forest. When she could, Eva read it aloud to her grandmother.

Edith thought it strange that although the child cried for her mother for days after they first arrived in the forest, she stopped very suddenly. After that, she never mentioned her parents or her uncle again. Edith waited in dread for the reader to provoke questions from the girl. Where are my parents? Why can't I see them?

Her memory of her life in town seemed to be obliterated. Even the concept of a family may have been meaningless to her. Edith cringed at the thought of her asking. Eva read the book often, then lapsed into an unusual silent spell for a talkative child. Edith waited. The heavy air in the hut swirled with unvoiced concerns.

Finally, Eva did ask about the one family member it was impossible for her to remember—her grandfather Joe, her Saba, who died when she was three. As often as Edith avoided answering, Eva insisted on knowing about him. What was he like? Was he dead?

What could Edith say about a husband she'd rather forget?

"Your Saba was a strong man. Sometimes, he would get angry."

"Why?"

"Do you remember when you used to get angry if you didn't like the food I made or if I found boys' clothes for you instead of girls' clothes? Your Saba got angry about the same things—anything he didn't like."

Eva's puzzled eyes would stray back to the reader. The mystery of family anger might be hidden within those pages.

Some things about Joe were secrets Edith wouldn't tell anyone, especially a young child. Among these were the facts shared with her by Detective Williams, assigned to Joe's case, put together from witnesses to his last hours. Eva's grandfather did not die from natural causes. The coroner ruled his death a suicide. His death certificate read "Cause of death: blunt head trauma."

Joe's co-workers and HR had been the first to give information about what happened in the early afternoon on the day he died. Like the biblical Joseph his parents named him after, Joe predicted seven lean years after seven fat years of rising sales at his company. Unlike the biblical Joseph, he hadn't saved a penny during the good times. Edith knew this.

A year after the agony of his own father's death, Joe told co-workers he had a feeling the company would force him out, and that would be the next blow. The office scuttlebutt suggested layoffs were probable. The entire industry was going through a slump, now that the Chinese were imposing tariffs to counter those imposed by the American administration. His company took a hit.

If a downturn happened, he was expendable, disposable, chopped-liver. A recent college graduate could replace a sixty-year-old worker for half his paycheck. It came as no surprise when HR offered him a meager severance package: three months' salary. Then, nothing. He would be the first worker thrown away like balled-up trash after decades of service. He admitted his productivity declined in recent months. What did the company expect? He had been in mourning for his father.

When he emptied his cubicle, all that remained to carry out were two small boxes plus his empty briefcase. He left behind the scrawny philodendron on top of the file cabinet. His embarrassed co-workers did not look up from their computers or even wave. They had survived the first layoff. A security agent accompanied him to the entrance of the building and held the door open for him. His dented 1994 Toyota waited in its usual place in the employee parking lot. The security agent told Detective Williams he watched while Joe pulled into the street and drove away.

Two blocks up the road, Joe found a space in front of Wednesdays, a gloomy little bar he patronized after work. It would be another loss. He enjoyed the transition time between work and home, often staying in the bar for an hour. The establishment was squeezed between a laundromat and a hair salon, with booths compacted into the narrow space behind the bar stools. Everything inside was black—the walls, the bar stool cushions, the booths, the bar itself. The dour bartender, interviewed by Detective Williams, was about the same age as Joe and wore a black apron over a black t-shirt.

"The usual two for the road." Joe took a seat at the bar. "It's my last day at work."

"Retiring?" The bartender passed him two shot glasses of amber liquid.

"Laid off."

On the flat-screen above the bar, an anchor and two guests discussed President George Bush in tones of outrage.

He's unfit for office.

His family covered up his drinking.

And if they did, so what? He's sober now.

With a backward tilt of his graying head, Joe downed the first whiskey. It would take the second to relax him. His reflection in the mirror behind the bar revealed his bloated face and double chin. He seemed to have gone to fat since the previous hour, when he was still employed.

He wondered aloud what he would tell Edith. He wondered how they would pay the bills. He wondered what he was going to do with himself. Who would hire him? HR refused to give references, and, if asked, would only state the number of years the company employed him. He was told he often smelled of alcohol and appeared to be drunk. If he volunteered to be drug tested and submitted to addictions treatment, he might avoid being laid off.

He refused. No doubt they would find an excuse to fire him, anyway. As if he couldn't hold his liquor. No, their motive had to be economic.

Another customer sitting at the bar a couple of seats away spoke to him.

"I heard you say you were laid off. That sucks, man." The speaker, a younger man, about thirty, had a sweep of thick blond hair across a high forehead. He remembered their entire conversation.

Joe finished his second whiskey.

"HR pretended they canned me for other reasons, but everyone knows it was a layoff. I was just the first one. The oldest."

"*Geez.* Which company?"

Joe told him.

"Oh, well. Them. Not surprising. There's no loyalty anymore. Take my Dad. His company came up with this diversity hoo-ha. They kicked him out and replaced him with a black woman. She unpacked her stuff in his office while he packed up his. At the same time."

The speaker held out his hand for Joe to shake.

"I'm Larry. Larry Anderson."

Joe leaned over to accept the younger man's hand.

"Allow me to buy you another of what you're having, Mister. Might as well celebrate."

As a rule, Joe stopped at two when he had to drive, but what the hell. He could handle three. He thanked Larry Anderson. A stranger with a head on his shoulders.

"Some people who are laid off 'go postal,' as they used to say. If it was me, I'd buy an AK-47. I'd take the elevator to the top floor and shoot every fucking person starting at the top and work my way down to the janitor in the basement. That's what I'd do. My dad should've done that. Shot himself in the head, instead."

It shook Joe to hear such talk. It had to be the alcohol speaking. But, as he told Larry Anderson, these companies robbed workers of everything when they kicked them out. Their income. Their dignity. Their reason to exist. If he didn't have a job, he'd be a burden to his wife. She'd be better off without him. Maybe she'd leave him. Then what?

On the tv, the talking heads continued.

Not fit for office.

Drank away his youth.

His company abused its power. What was it HR said? He had been insubordinate with his supervisor? He no longer dressed like a professional or took care of his hygiene? His clients reported him? It was a witch hunt. Total fabrication. Just an excuse to get rid of him without giving the real reason.

"Bartender. A drink for my young friend. On me. And another for me, too."

"Thanks, Mister. Don't let them get away with it. Sue the bastards."

"That would be too good for them." His words slurred. Something ground in his chest. Suddenly, he was mad, furious. Crazy mad. If he had a gun, he would drive right back and kill that HR son of a bitch. Even better, he would kill him with his bare hands. Wrap his fingers around his windpipe and wring his fucking neck!

"Take it easy." The bartender worried when a customer sounded off like that, he told the detective.

Joe drank the shot the bartender placed before him and threw two twenties on the bar. He stood to go.

"Keep the change."

"Leaving already? You okay?" The young man gave him a concerned look.

"I'm fine. More than fine." Perhaps he staggered a bit.

Edith speculated about the next bit, knowing how Joe thought. It seemed logical to the detective.

Back in his car, he sat awhile, thinking about his father. He angled the rearview mirror until he saw his own face reflected. He resembled his old man. If only he had been more understanding, knowing what his father went through. Now he lost a fucking job, too. He imagined telling his father what happened.

"They fired me, Dad. I say 'laid off.' HR called it 'terminated'." He blubbered.

Nazis, his father said.

"What should I do?"

The Final Solution.

"That's what he said. Something like that. The guy in the bar."

He was thirsty. A convenience store was a few blocks away. He could buy a six-pack. Why not? He wiped away his tears with his sleeve. Knowing he had a little too much, he drove under the speed limit. He reached the store without a problem and made his purchase. The cashier remembered him and watched him out the window.

In the car, Joe guzzled a can, throwing the empty into the passenger well. Edith knew how he ranted when he was drank. She imagined him thinking his co-workers smirked when the news reached them he had been "terminated." How righteous it would be if someone "exterminated" them. He should do as the young man in the bar suggested—buy a gun and mow them down. Let them smirk after that!

He pulled the tab on a second beer, promising he would sip it slowly. After taking a slug, he put the can in the cup holder and started driving. It was found later. It violated the open container law. If he got a ticket, big deal.

He dreaded the idea of driving home and facing Edith's questions. Instead, he went around the block a few times, scowling at the other drivers, the pedestrians walking their little yipping dogs, and the people wearing suits and carrying briefcases who moved purposefully across intersections.

Some turned to look at him, the one *unfit for office*. Were they sneering at him? He had been yelling profanities out the window, he realized. He had a right to freedom of speech. If he wanted to scream "fuck you" at everyone he saw, it was his business. Those who heard him would phone the information to the police.

He finished the second beer and threw the can out the window. He reached for a third. In a boiling rage, he drove back toward his office. Larry Anderson's words circled in his head — *shoot every fucking person.* Witnesses said that when he reached the building, he braked the car in the middle of the busy downtown street, the in the lane opposite the set of glass doors leading to the foyer. A line of impatient cars behind him honked. He paid no attention. It was time for the "final solution."

He waited for the light up ahead to turn red, so there would be no vehicles in the oncoming lane. As soon as it was clear, he jerked the steering wheel to the left and accelerated hard.

Detective Williams and Edith agreed. How satisfying it must have been to Joe when the Toyota jumped the curb and roared ahead. The last thing he would have seen was his determined face reflected in the shattering doors that shut him out two hours earlier.

CHAPTER 10
WHO BY FAMINE

The summer of 2016 was one of the driest on record. Not even "Roots of the Woods" provided the food Edith would need to keep her adolescent granddaughter nourished through the winter. Nearing her mid-sixties, Edith ate little herself. The various brews she made from foraged plants, following recipes in the book, sustained her.

But Eva consumed prodigious amounts to fuel her growing body. Pails full of nuts, berries, roots, and fruits of the forest. Fish, birds, rabbit, squirrels, and on occasion, deer meat left behind by hunters. Entire loaves of *challah* and *babka* baked by her grandmother.

When the time came to harvest, the barrels used for salting food and the holes dug beside the hut to store roots were only half-packed. The empty cabinet above the shelf that was replenished winter and summer with items not provided by the forest only contained table salt and a tiny amount of coffee. Every day, Edith opened the cabinet doors, hoping for more. There was nothing.

It was a desperate situation. If they were snowed in, they might starve. Edith couldn't let that happen without breaking her vow to protect Eva. The only solution was to send the girl back to the town to collect staples. It might require more than one trip.

First, she had to steal town clothes from the last of the campers. Eva couldn't show up wearing anything too worn. She would need a coat, hat, gloves, and boots, and a large bag to load with food. Edith took the risk of swiping what she needed for Eva without getting caught.

It astonished her how many useful items were left in camp grounds — unopened bags of chips, matches, sweatshirts, blankets. She took them back to the hut.

Eva had dim memories of civilization. Television. Phones that people carried with them. Trains.Her grandmother prepared her for her return to the town, without mentioning the possibility of running into her parents or uncle. She hoped that wouldn't happen.

"When you want to leave the forest, go beyond the picnic area to the guard house. Follow the road in the direction that the sun sets. If you leave early, you can reach town by nightfall."

"What should I do there?"

In town, her forest skills would not help her. Other people would also be a problem. Would they help or prevent her from finding food?

"You will figure it out." That is all her grandmother would say.

Edith took out the unicorn-decorated bag Eva had dragged with her when she and her grandmother began living in the hut. Items for the journey could be packed in it. A knife, bread, a jar of water, another empty bag for groceries. The long walk wouldn't be a problem. Eva had grown into a muscular girl, used to hauling, tree climbing, and lengthy hunts for food. She wound her dark hair into a tight braid to keep it from blowing in her face on the journey. It was important that her vision not be obscured with so many unknown experiences ahead.

Traffic was her first concern. She had seen cars moving at slow speeds along the paved forest road and service vehicles on the gravel roads. Once outside the forest, traffic sped by. She jumped on and off the shoulder, fearful of being hit. The passengers were the first people she saw outside of the campers and hikers she and her grandmother always tried to avoid.

"If they see you, there could be trouble," her grandmother had said.

Someone might report the girl to the authorities. Eva pictured uniformed men carrying her away as she thrashed and screamed, while her grandmother waited back in the hut, not knowing why her granddaughter didn't return. But Eva knew how to hide. She spent many hours spying on camping families, who amazed her. It was hard to understand why children complained about boredom, mosquitos, and missing their friends. Adults distributed lavish amounts of food from coolers. They dared to wear brightly colored clothing, never a good idea in the woods.

By late afternoon, the road took her past houses larger than the hut or the guardhouse. She picked corn and wild berries on the edges of fields. Dogs ran at her, barking. She didn't fear them, having often climbed trees when they were let off their leashes by pet owners on hikes.

The houses became closer together. It was sunset. She kept going. Her goal was to get to town by dark and find a hiding place for the night. She reached the outskirts. Her grandmother hadn't told her how light it would be. Lamps on poles along the streets, lights on and in houses, and vehicle headlights showed the way. When she reached the town center, stores were brighter than all the candles her grandmother lit. People were everywhere. Her ears hurt from the constant din.

Nothing was familiar. The determination that kept her going, one foot in front of the other, lifted. When it did, her teeth chattered. What if someone asked her what she was doing there? What if they told her to leave, that she didn't belong? But except for passing glances, no one paid her any attention. Spotting a dark space between two buildings, she hid there. It was paved and treeless, like the road. Objects she couldn't identify littered the ground. At least it was dark. She crouched down into a squat and peered at the activity on the street. As time passed, it became quieter.

A voice came from the darkness further in the narrow space.

"Hey, kid. You got any money?"

An older man with a beard, wearing clothing campers often wore—over-sized lumber-jack shirt, loose jeans, baseball cap—came closer. She took in his animal smell. If only her grandmother was there to tell her whether to stay or run. She didn't answer him. He looked her over.

"What's in that thing you got there?"

He reached out and grabbed the unicorn bag, dumping the contents on the ground. The jar of water shattered. Only the knife interested him.

"I'll take this."

He disappeared back into the darkness. She repacked the bag, shaking with fear. Dark alleys in town weren't safe. She had learned that lesson. On the street, lights revealed anything dangerous. The moon was high. It was the middle of night. No stars were visible. The shops had signs reading "Closed." Only a few people were around. She sat on the ground with her back to a building. Although she tried not to, she nodded off.

The next thing she knew, another male voice addressed her. Startled, she jumped up. Where was she? A man in a uniform grabbed her arm.

"Don't run. I'm Officer Sullivan. Are you in trouble?"

He was the second person to talk to her since leaving the forest and the first one to touch her. She cowered, trying to pull away.

"Whoa! I won't hurt you. Do you have any ID?" He kept his grip. "How old are you? Did you run away from home?"

In a panic, urine streamed down her leg, puddling on the sidewalk between her feet. With his free hand, the officer talked into some sort of phone.

"I'm bringing in a girl. Looks fifteen, sixteen. See if you can find clean clothes, medium size."

She wasn't strong enough to free herself. He led her to a car with the word "police" painted on its side. She had seen this kind of vehicle in the campgrounds after fights broke out. Sometimes, a camper was put into the back seat, as she was now.

"Don't worry. I'm just taking you to the station to get you something to eat. The social worker will find you a place so you won't be on the street. Sit tight. You'll be okay."

The car was warm. She didn't realize how cold she had been. Her grandmother feared the police. If Eva was under arrest, maybe it was better than the street. The police officer mentioned food. How hungry she was! She didn't know how to get a meal in the town. She hadn't thought that through.

At the station, they put her in a room with three folding chairs and a mental table. The police officer left. Another one came in with the kind of food campers ate—a cup with a brown fizzy drink, what they called coke, and a sandwich. She took cautious bites and sips. Then nothing happened for a while. With her arms on the table, she lay her head down and slept.

Her grandmother said, "Tell them your name."

A woman was asking, "Can you tell me your name?" She sat in a chair on the other side of the table. "I'm a social worker. My job is to reunite you with your family. If that's not possible, place you in a foster home."

Eva didn't know what a foster home was. A prison? A cage? The rangers sometimes trapped animals in cages and took them to the banding station. Her grandmother told her to stay away from there. Eva imagined she'd be banded if they caught her.

"I'm guessing you have been living on the street for a while. You look kind of rough. There's a shower in the back of the station, and I have some clean clothes for you. They aren't fancy."

She was taken to the shower room. The social worker promised to guard the door. Eva had used the camp shower when no one was there. She understood what to do. Still, it was a luxury, preferable to the creek where she and her grandmother bathed when it was warm enough. In the winter, there might be a pot of water heated on the wood stove.

Once out of the shower, she saw a shiny rectangle above the sink. It was a mirror. For the first time in twelve years, she looked at her reflection. She gaped. A stranger with dark eyes gaped back.

The clothing was cleaner than the camp clothing she had worn, but similar. Sweat shirt. Jeans. Socks. Underwear. Sneakers.

"I had to throw out the clothes you came in."

The social worker took her back to the room with the chairs and table. More food waited.

"Are you ready to tell me your name?"

Her tone was gentle, but Eva was too scared to say anything.

"I must put you in foster care if you don't tell me who you are."

Eva remained silent.

The social worker left the room. She returned with another man, who introduced himself as Detective Williams.

"Twelve years ago, a girl named Eva disappeared with her grandmother, Edith. I'm wondering if you are that girl. If you are, you'll want to see your father. He'll be here in a few minutes. Let's find out if he recognizes you. Then we'll do a DNA test to confirm. You must wonder about your mother."

"I'm so sorry, but your mother died." The social worker put a kind hand on Eva's arm.

Her father? Coming now? Her mother dead? Her unicorn bag was missing. They had taken it. Words boiled up from her throat.

"My bag! Get me my bag!" She was red faced, screaming. The detective and the social worker stared. Without warning, Eva bolted out the door. As she sprang for the exit, she heard shouts behind her.

"Wait! Grab that girl, someone."

She raced through the streets, not stopping until she reached a Walmart at the edge of town. There, she saw everything she had wished for when campers spoke about them. Wall-size tvs. Warm coats. Pillows. Clothing. Books. Refrigerators. Lamps.

And food. Lots of food. She threw boxes and jars into a bag she found on a shelf. No one stopped her. All the colors and bright lights made her head hurt. She wasn't ready for the town. A man said to be her father was coming for her. The detective, the social worker, even the man in the dark space between buildings took the little she had — her clothing, her knife, her unicorn bag.

When the grocery bag was full, she headed for the exit. Just as she reached the door, a man grabbed her arm.

"Did you forget to pay?" The man had a badge. It said "Security."

Just then, three boys around her age raced out with three skateboards.

"Hey!" The security man yelled, releasing Eva and taking off after them. Eva sprinted out the door, across the parking lot, and down the road to the forest. She would have to make her way by moonlight, lugging the heavy bag of food with her.

Later, when she thought about the awfulness of the trip to town, the only thing she remembered liking was the fizzy brown drink.

CHAPTER 11
WHO SHALL BE TORMENTED

Josh stood for the summation and faced the jury.

"Ladies and Gentlemen, have you seen any evidence that is *beyond a reasonable doubt*? Remember: it is not good enough just to think the defendant is guilty. You must think he is guilty *beyond a reasonable doubt*."

In the overheated courtroom, Josh took a handkerchief from his pocket and wiped his forehead. Even in November, the courtroom boiled. If the jury room wasn't cooler, twelve irritable jurors would squabble over the verdict. The judge's impatient lips pinched. The defendant, a heavy man, dripped sweat onto an ill-fitting suit.

After court, Josh inhaled the crisp air on the way to the parking garage. He had been too hot; now he was too cold, and the temperature wasn't the only thing lacking stability. He had an appointment with Detective Williams in the police department, which guaranteed another roller coaster ride.

Twelve years earlier, his four-year-old daughter Eva disappeared with her grandmother and was never found. A year later, his first wife Deborah died of rapid onset Parkinson's disease. He didn't remarry for several years. Meanwhile, every so often, Detective Williams called him in to identify a girl of the approximate age Eva would be. They had all been false alarms.

Josh's heart stopped with each new possibility. He wouldn't give up hope yet. The right girl had to be sixteen to be his missing daughter. Would he recognize her? Would she recognize him? How would he know *beyond a reasonable doubt* it was her? Of course, there would be a

DNA test. There would be a low probability of a false positive result. Mistakes occur.

But even if it was Eva, after so many years would she still be *the* Eva? She might be so changed, so damaged by whatever or whoever kidnapped her, there would be nothing left of the toddler he remembered. Maybe it would make no difference if Eva turned up because, in a sense, she would always be missing. Nothing made up for the lost childhood years.

At the police station, he was led to Detective Williams' cubicle. He sat in a chair opposite the detective, with a computer desk between them. The detective hadn't aged well. When they met on the day Eva and her grandmother went missing, the officer had been wiry and eager.

"Don't worry. I'm on it. I'll find her," the Detective said back then. He seemed ready to sprint out the door at a moment's notice to follow up on any lead.

He must have put on fifty pounds since then. Now, he sat heavily in his chair, looking at Josh with cynical eyes. All the false leads had wearied him, too.

"I've got good news and bad news," he said. "The good news is the girl we picked up last night I phoned you about looked about Eva's age. She refused to talk to us, so I'm guessing. The bad news is that, as I told you in my second phone call, she ran off before anyone could stop her. But we've got an APB on her and… here's what I didn't tell you, we've got video."

Josh studied the family photo on the desk. In it, the Detective, his wife, and their son stood together on skis against a snowy background. They looked happy. He sighed.

"You have video?" That was something, at least.

"Yes. There are two bits. One is from the interrogation room where the girl ate a meal while she was at the station. The social worker tried to talk to her there, before she bolted. The other is from a security system at Walmart. That's where she was last seen."

The Detective turned the monitor toward Josh. Neither spoke while the videos played.

"Anything?"

"Difficult to say." Josh's voice was flat.

"Hmm."

Both men knew the search would continue for the girl and her grandmother. Both knew finding them this late was a long shot, and that it was an even longer shot that the girl was Eva. Josh buttoned his coat to the top when he left. It had become chillier.

He drove the familiar route. At home, his second wife Leah waited in the kitchen. He appreciated her keeping some distance when he was in one of his moods.

"Was it...?"

He shook his head, not able to tolerate any conversation about it. But the sound of feet running down the hall from the bedroom area broke the silence.

"Daddy! Daddy!"

Dinah plowed into him, reaching up, jumping. He stood like a pole, unmoving. The child whipped around him, pulling at him, grabbing his leg. He didn't look down.

"Guess what, Daddy? I found a frog in the yard. It's dead. Flies are crawling all over it, and it's too yucky to touch. Mommy made me wash my hands, anyway." Her frenzied voice was high pitched, like a mosquito's buzz in his ear.

"Dinah! Daddy just got home. He has to change clothes. Let's let him do that while you help me set the table."

His younger daughter was a pretty blond-haired girl. She wasn't Eva.

At the time of his older daughter's disappearance, Josh underwent a severe depression. He barely got out of bed, barely ate, barely spoke. But when his deceased wife Deborah deteriorated, he rallied and returned to work. After her death and the sightings of the false Evas, he fell apart again. This became the pattern. Rise up, fall down. He married Leah during one of his up spells.

In the bedroom, as he changed out of his suit, all he wanted was to crawl into bed and sleep. He didn't care if he missed dinner, CNN Nightly News, or a glass of wine with his wife.

Then, the thoughts that had slowed to a crawl began racing.

"What if it is Eva? What am I doing here? I must find her." His agitated fingers fumbled with the button on his Levis.

"I'm going. I'll drive around. I might spot her," he told Leah.

"Daddy, take me with you. Please, Daddy. Daddy?"

Without answering the wailing child, he returned to the car. The girl who might be Eva was last seen in Walmart, so he headed there. At dusk, the sunset spewed a red glow across the menacing sky. Like an alarm. Climate change. Nothing was predictable anymore. The earth swung between extremes. Species disappeared. Girls disappeared. Here today, gone tomorrow.

While driving at as slow a speed as traffic permitted, he stared at pedestrians. Teenage girls in halters and cut-offs texted, laughing, arms joined. He asked himself the old question. Did Eva live somewhere in town, right under his nose? Would she be out walking with friends?

Whenever he asked Detective Williams, all he received was a shrug.

"Anything is possible."

After pulling into the Walmart parking lot, he rushed around the perimeter on foot. When he reached the back of the store, with its fenced dumpsters and loading docks, he saw a few employees on breaks, smoking outside.

"Did you see a girl? About sixteen?"

They shook their heads.

Beyond the back lot, there was nothing but fields and scattered houses. The Walmart was on the edge of town. He couldn't imagine Eva having a reason to go in that direction, by herself, in the cold.

He circled back to the entrance. The greeter grinned at him, or was it a grimace? He was a lawyer, not a shoplifter. But not a shopper, either. He was a desperate father looking for his daughter. Yet, he couldn't recall her, exactly. Photographs of her were more distinct than his memories. Despite that, she was his. He would know her when he saw her. Somehow.

Families escaping the weather filled the store. As he began walking up the aisle nearest the grocery section, he had an idea that might just be clutching at straws.

Walmart is open twenty-four hours every day. It might be possible for a girl to live in Walmart, undetected. She might sneak into the store room and find a place to sleep. She could steal food and whatever she needed. Eva might be right here, only an aisle away.

Just then, he heard a child's voice.

"Daddy! Daddy!"

A tiny girl, perhaps three or four, called him. Josh dashed toward her, but a man who had to be her real father reached her first and picked her up. He gave Josh a suspicious look. *Don't take this one. She isn't yours.* Josh backed away.

As he scuttled around the aisles faster, he heard children calling.

"Daddy!"

"Padre!"

"Papa!"

Each time, he ran toward the voice, forgetting that Eva was no longer a pre-schooler. None of these children could be her. Yet, as he thought he heard himself being called from different parts of the store, he kept changing direction, running toward them, not noticing the people he pushed aside, the items he knocked over, and the security guards closing in.

He fell. Blood spurted from his nose. Someone helped him up. He wiped his face with his sleeve. There wasn't any time to pinch his nose at the bridge. Let it bleed. He had to find his daughter.

Eva hid somewhere just around a corner, or in the next aisle, calling to him, teasing him, flitting away whenever he came too close. If he ran fast enough, he might catch her. As he sprinted through the store, he yelled to her.

"Eva! Stop! It's me! Your father!"

He paused to catch his breath. Blood still streamed from his nose. He sobbed, choking. The guards caught up with him. They offered to call an ambulance, unless he wanted to leave of his own accord. They escorted him, still calling his daughter's name, to the exit. As he left, someone laughed. Was Eva having fun at his expense?

He decided to wait in his car. The cold no longer bothered him. Many people parked there who weren't Walmart customers. Homeless people needing a place to spend the night. Owners of rvs.

Parents waiting to pick up their child, who had finished shopping and who had texted them for a ride home. Eventually, his daughter would come out of the store to find him.

It would be Eva *beyond a reasonable doubt.*

CHAPTER 12
WHO SHALL REACH
THE END OF HIS DAYS

When Rabbi Isaac was fourteen, his grandfather Abe lay dying. The family gathered around his hospital bed. The old man's eyes closed. His jaw slackened. Raspy breathing stopped for long seconds, then started again.

"It won't be long," the Hospice nurse said.

"What does that mean? Hours? Minutes?" Isaac's father, Marty, was the usual whirlwind of rapid speech and constant movement.

"I would say… If he doesn't rally, not over forty-eight hours."

"Can he still hear us?" Marty asked.

"You can talk to him. Hearing is the last sense to go." The nurse had dark sorrowful eyes. Her saddest duty was comforting families.

"Dad. If you only… a last word. It would mean so much. You never told me. I'm ready for you to tell me before you pass. There's not much time. Please, Dad. Dad?"

Marty pounded the bed with his fist. The nurse sprang up. She took a step forward.

Isaac's mother, Ruth, stepped between the nurse and her husband. She tried, as usual, to calm him. Isaac's grandmother, Nancy, held her hand to her chest. She thrived on illness, but her husband outdid her this time.

"Don't exhaust yourself, Marty. Would you like a Valium? I have extra."

Ruth dug into her purse. She had a large stash of supplies — protein bars, energy drinks, sweaters. Hospitals were chilly.

Even at this critical moment, the family fell into their familiar pattern. Abe would have been silent even if he were not in a near coma. When Marty wasn't pleading in his ear, he paced. Abe's unwillingness or inability to communicate agitated him. Nancy attracted attention to herself. Ruth was the peace-maker. Isaac's older sister, Leah, rushed in, late as usual. Isaac, the youngest, observed.

Abe was a Holocaust survivor. He had been in Treblinka from the age of eight until the liberation when he was fifteen. At the end of the Nazi era, he was the only one of his relatives left. He spent a year in a refugee camp before coming to America, where he lived with a distant cousin until he finished high school. He never talked about the war.

Marty wanted to know, *had* to know, about Abe's suffering, the entire story — how Abe endured, what happened to him in the camps, how he felt. But the more he badgered him, the more Abe withdrew. This struggle had been going on all of Isaac's life and, no doubt, for all of his father's life.

"Don't bother Abe," Ruth would always say to her husband. "The past is too painful to talk about."

"Sometimes I have the urge to shake him or choke him until he tells me."

"I made sponge cake. Have a piece. It will distract you."

Years earlier, right after Isaac's *bar mitzvah*, his grandfather took him aside. Abe was still spry. He invited the boy into his grandparent's tiny bedroom, in the back of the house, and closed the door. His grandfather sat in the only chair. Isaac leaned against the bed post.

"This is only for you to know," he told Isaac. His insistent blue eyes pierced the space between them. "There *vas* a round-up. *Ve vere* jammed into the back of a truck. For two hours, *ve* stood. There *vere* no seats, no *vater*. *Ve vere* taken deep into the forest. The truck stopped in front of a large pit. *Ve* had to line up at the edge and take off our clothing. Many dead people *vere* naked in the pit."

Abe stopped talking for several seconds. He held Issac's sleeve bunched in a tight grip. He hadn't finished.

"The guards told us to face the pit. They stood in back of us. Ve heard the clicks of their rifles being loaded. Then they shot. I vas pushed forward by the force of the bullet. I must have passed out. Vhen I awoke, it vas dawn, still dark. I vas under my father's body. He vas dead, and my mother vas dead, too. I climbed out. Mounds of dirt and lime stood vaiting for day light, vhen they would be shoveled into the pit, on top of the bodies. I vandered away. Of course, I vas found. A naked boy in the forest. They sent me to Treblinka."

Isaac didn't breath. Saliva collected in his throat, but he dared not swallow. Abe still gripped his sleeve. He stood and moved closer, standing directly in front of Isaac.

"Here is vhat to know. I vas shot. The bullet vent into me. It is still there, in my head. I died that night. I am dead. Vhat you see is a casing for a bullet. That is vhat I am. A casing for a bullet. Dead."

He held the boy's gaze for another moment, then he looked away, letting go of Isaac's sleeve.

"Go now," he said. "And don't tell anyone. Your grandfather has been dead for sixty-two years. It's a terrible thing to be dead, but continue to live."

In that moment, something inside Isaac's chest twisted, like a wet towel being wrung out. For his entire life, he never lost that sensation. The image of a boy being shot and falling into a pit carved itself into his brain. Sometimes, he pictured the boy from behind, as the guard would have seen him before pulling the trigger. Sometimes, his view narrowed to that of the boy, staring down into the pit. Mostly, he saw the scene from above, as if he climbed a tree and watched from a height.

If only he could have told Marty the secret. But his mother would not have allowed it. His father was too excitable.

"His blood pressure. We don't want your father to have a stroke."

This is what she would have said. That was another reason for Isaac to keep the secret to himself. He didn't want his father to die from a stroke. It was lonely to have such terrifying images and no one to talk to about them.

The secret bore a hole in Isaac's heart. His wound wasn't from a bullet. But he had to cope with the pain. Neither descending into silence like his grandfather nor spinning into a frenzy like his father seemed the right way. There was his mother to think of, already burdened by the needs of both men. He wouldn't wear her down further. The image of the boy buried under the dead bodies of his parents spurred him in a different direction.

He pretended to be optimistic and eager, the opposite of how he felt. It was an act. When he was alone, his imagination took over, mixing himself up with his grandfather, who climbed out of a pit. What if there were other Jewish children in the forest near Treblinka, still lost?. He would look for them one day. That is how he decided to become a rabbi, the kind who helped people find a pathway out of whatever "woods" — place of suffering — they were in.

In the seminary, he studied the binding of the biblical Isaac, almost sacrificed by his father, the biblical Abraham. He wondered if his inner pain was the same as the biblical Isaac's, while he waited to die. When God stopped Abraham from murdering Isaac, did Isaac feel like he died, anyway?

It's a terrible thing to be dead, but continue to live.

The years passed. His grandfather's words came to him often when he took the position of assistant rabbi in a small Indiana town. They left him with a strong impulse to visit the forest that surrounded the small community where his synagogue was located. One day, no longer able to withstand it, he drove to the nearest trailhead parking lot. Through the windshield, he saw a pleasant meadow filled with wildflowers. Beyond lay the forest, a mass of dense pines.

For a long while, he wondered if he should get out, cross the meadow, and peek into the forest. It was just American wilderness, he told himself, nothing like photos he had seen of the dark European woods near Treblinka. As he kept staring, the trees seemed to shimmer, stabilize, then shimmer again. What was happening? His lungs squeezed out air as he continued to sit, frozen in the driver's seat. Suddenly, the roof peeled away. A wind entered the vehicle, lifting him upwards, then floating him across the meadow. From tree-top level, his shoes dangled at the bottoms of his legs. Once in the forest, he was blown past ravines and creeks and rises, moving steadily upward, following the contours of a hill.

Without tapering, the wind ceased, leaving him hovering over a large sinkhole. He snatched at nearby branches to anchor himself. Looking down, he saw the horrifying sight his grandfather described. A pit filled with naked, intertwined bodies. The mounds of soil and lime. There was a sound of a motor approaching. It was a truck with an open bed, filled with people. There was a shout. *Schnell.* They jumped out, helping one another. *Schnell.* They moved to the edge of the pit. *Schnell.* They took off their clothing. A young boy stood naked between his parents.

The boy's confusion entered his own head. Where were they? What was going to happen? Why were his mama and papa crying?

As the boy reached for his father's hand, a violent thrust toppled him into the pit. Isaac felt it. A scream tore from his throat.

The vision ended. He still sat in his car, shaking and disoriented. Touching the back of his head, it amazed him to find hair, no blood, no hole. He looked in the rear-view mirror. There wasn't an exit wound on his face. He hadn't been shot. It was his grandfather, not him. Right?

In a state of uncertainty, he started the drive back to the town. If he was driving, he had to be alive. Yet, he felt hollow. The car drove itself. His hands lay limp in his lap. With an effort of will, he raised them to the steering wheel and held on.

It took awhile for him to regain control of his thoughts. He had no choice. His parents needed him. His sister Leah, too. And his congregation. But, of course, it was the friendly mask that they wanted. No one wanted the Isaac who screamed at the top of the trees.

By the time he returned to his apartment, his head cleared. The experience in the forest faded, and his grandfather's words lost their vividness, returning to their storehouse in the back of his mind. His head filled with the mundane, again. What to have for dinner. What book to read before bed.

But darkness remained below the surface, churning within, continuing to haunt him.

CHAPTER 13
WHO BY SWORD

The first time God talked to Roger, he was sitting in the detention hall in high school, doing nothing, not even thinking.

They caught Roger smoking weed, an infraction worse than cigarettes, but they didn't expel him. In those days, God was friendly. He understood that Roger tried to stop his restless thoughts from crashing together into jumbled cacophony. Maybe weed would work. It made you laid back, his friends said. Instead, it made him distrustful of his friends, who spied on him.

He stared at his geometry homework, with its incomprehensible "equilateral triangles," when he heard a voice coming from above, perhaps from one of the vents in the ceiling. At first, he assumed it was a teacher on the second floor, calling down to him. But then he realized it was God's voice, coming from heaven.

You are My beloved Son, in You I am well-pleased.

It made Roger think he might be Jesus. He should tell the others in detention. He stood up, so they would realize he had something important to say.

"Everyone. I'm Jesus. Jesus Christ. God told me."

About a dozen bored kids, most of them boys, served detention with him. They perked up. Something happened to break the monotony. The detention teacher, who maintained the silence rule while grading papers, looked up.

"You! Sit down now and be quiet." She pointed her red pen at Roger. It may have been the one used to write "F" on his quizzes and homework. He did not like that pen. Advancing to the desk, he snatched it and threw it on the floor. It made a satisfying crunch when he stomped on it.

When he told the teacher he might kill her, the result was the first of many commitments to the psych ward for evaluation. During the fifteen years since, he had cycled from the psych ward to rehab to jail to the streets. He didn't mind as long as he had the right to refuse treatment. If he took medication, God wouldn't speak to him. He wouldn't be Jesus anymore. That was out of the question.

Over the years, God became less friendly. When Roger transgressed by forgetting to praise Him or by touching himself, God would be stern.

Thou shalt obey all the commandments which I command thee this day.

Sometimes, for no reason Roger understood, God cursed him, calling him "fat" and "useless," words his father used. God suggested he jump off the roof of a parking garage. Since it was just a suggestion and not a command, Roger punished himself instead by making cuts on his body with a razor blade. Still, hearing God's angry voice was better than not hearing it at all. As long as God was present with him, he knew he existed instead of just imagining he did.

The last time they let him out of jail, he returned to his regular sleeping spot in an ally between a bar and a pizza restaurant. In the middle of the night, a young girl invaded his space and awakened him. She could have been an angel. But God told him the girl was a whore, and that he could take what he wanted from her. He could even rape her. But that wasn't what he wanted right then.

"Hey, kid. You got any money?" He moved toward her.

She had a purse decorated with unicorns. He grabbed it dumped the contents on the ground. An old scarf and a knife with a long blade fell out. He kept the knife, but let her have the rest back. The girl didn't protest. She must have known it was God's will. Otherwise he would have been forced to stab her.

After the girl ran off, he hid the knife behind a loose brick in the wall. Later the same night, a stranger disturbed him again when he tried to steal Roger's sleeping spot. An altercation followed, alerting the cops. He must have slugged the guy too hard because they arrested him for battery. That was unfair. The stranger wasn't even taken to the ER.

At the arraignment, he told the judge he was Jesus Christ.

"I'm only thirty-two. There can't be a trial until I'm thirty-three."

The judge asked him a question, but Roger couldn't concentrate on the answer because of the heat. There was something wrong with the temperature control in the courtroom. The ceiling fan made a panting noise like his father made before walloping him. It distracted him for several minutes. When his attention returned, the prosecutor and the court-appointed lawyer, named Josh Something-Or-Other, had approached the bench. The judge nodded and sent Roger to the psych ward for a "competency evaluation.".

There, the psych techs and nurses recognized him.

"Hi, Roger. Back again?"

They greeted him with cheerful voices. He explained to them that even if he looked like Roger, he wasn't Roger. He was Jesus. When they kept calling him by the wrong name, anyway, he turned the other cheek, like God wanted him to.

They know not what they do.

The psych ward had two wings. Roger was in the Medicaid wing. The cement block walls were painted an institutional green. Patients slept in hospital beds. Barred windows overlooked the parking lot. The windowless cigarette room had exhaust vents that were too weak to extract the smoke.

The other wing was for patients with insurance. Beds had bedspreads, like in a hotel. It overlooked an area with trees. Patients from both sides collected in the central area, in front of the nurses' station, separated by a screen.

He had been there several days when he saw Josh Something, the lawyer, on the other side of the screen. It was his fault Roger got stuck in the hospital. Because of him, the judge did not believe Roger. At first, he thought Josh Something was there on lawyer business. But the lawyer pounded on the locked exit door and yelled about needing to find Eva, his daughter. The techs led him away, as if he were just another patient.

Roger knew that Josh Something was there for God's purpose—to make sure Roger didn't sin. Unless the Devil sent Josh Something to the psych ward to provoke him. Roger's eyes narrowed. He saw whirling lights, green and red, as thoughts cascaded into his head. Josh Something was an abomination. The daughter he yelled about finding? She was an abomination, too.

But the next week, after the injection, Roger stopped thinking about Josh Something. He attended groups on the Medicaid side about dealing with stress and knowing the signs of a relapse. He stayed away from the screen, spending time in his room, sleeping, eating hospital food, staring out the window at nothing in particular.

Several months later, after completing his evaluation and his jail sentence, Roger returned to the streets. He violated parole by not attending therapy, stopping his medication, and drinking. Eventually, they would find him and return him to jail. Meanwhile, he reclaimed his sleeping spot in the ally and called himself Jesus again.

Josh Something re-entered his mind. He remembered how the lawyer had whispered lies about him to the judge. The lawyer had yelled insults at him in the psych ward. How he wished to get even. But God reminded him that vengeance was His.

I, the LORD, have drawn My sword out of its sheath. It will not return to its sheath again.

Roger's mind fell into in shambles, at first. Then it occurred to him that God meant that he, Roger, who was Jesus, was now the Sword of God. The Sword of God punishes for the sake of the Lord.

Roger had a new name. He told anyone who asked.

"I am the Sword of God."

He felt good, powerful, mighty, and furious at Josh Something. The lawyer who betrayed him, who betrayed Jesus. He had to find the lawyer.

He took the risk hanging around the exterior of the courthouse. Sooner or later, he was bound to spot Josh Something descending the wide steps of the limestone building. The Sword of God was patient. He could wait for as long as it would take.

It was hard to keep track of time. He didn't know if days or weeks passed before he saw the lawyer make his way from the court house to the parking garage. Roger followed him, noting that the lawyer's car was a newer model Prius. An arrogant car. The license plate was EVA16. That was easy for Roger to remember.

At the library, he used a computer to do a reverse license plate search. He discovered where Josh Something lived, in a suburb, far from the center of town. The bus would take him part way. Then he would have to walk. God would give him the strength. Zaps of energy prepared his legs for the journey.

First, he retrieved the knife from the ally and sharpened it with a stone. He tested it on his thumb, smiling at the blood bubbling from the slice.

He made a plan. God would keep his mind from the distractions that caused him to forget most plans. His focus was solid. His willpower, strong. A dollar was left over from his disability check. He used it for bus fare. At the end of the bus route, he began walking. He would reach the lawyer's house at dusk, when the lawyer was sure to be home from work. Roger would ring the doorbell with his left hand. The knife in his right hand would be raised, ready to plunge.

Josh Something might plead for his life and the lives of his family—anyone who lived in the suburbs had a family. He said something about a daughter in the psych ward. As if that would spare them. Roger would make him accept the truth—that he and his children must pay for his crime *to the fourth generation*, as it says the bible. If he asked what his crime was, Roger would tell him.

"You are a Jew lawyer. You tried to crucify Jesus."

The Sword of God would show no mercy.

CHAPTER 14
WHO SHALL NOT REACH THE END OF THEIR DAYS

Simon lived next door to a girl named Dinah who had been stabbed. Both were six-years-old at the time. On the night of the attack, he tried to piece together his Melissa and Douglas wooden train tracks. The circle was almost completed when he heard a shout from outside and rushed to the window. At first, he fogged the pane up with his tense breathing. He rubbed the window with his hand to clear it enough to see.

A man in a lumber-jack shirt stood very close to his playmate. Something shiny glinting in his hand rapidly jabbed into her. Then her father jumped out and struggled with the man. Dinah fell backward into the house. Her pink princess sparkle shoes and the bottom of her legs extended out onto the stoop. Her father slumped forward onto the steps. He lay unmoving, his legs at odd angles, looking broken. Neither he nor Dinah moved. Her hysterical mother ran in and out, shrieking and sobbing, while the strange man just stood there holding the glinting object down at his side. Soon after, several police cars, sirens blaring, came roaring into the cul-de-sac.

Eight years later, people still talked about what occurred that evening. Dinah's father, Josh, a prominent lawyer, was murdered trying to defend his daughter. The shocking crime occurred in a gated community far from the center of town. The attacker walked in on foot, avoiding the guard shack, and rang the doorbell of the lawyer's house. The girl answered. There was some confusion about what happened next. The attacker yelled something before stabbing the girl and her father with a long-bladed knife. It appeared he had a simmering hatred for the lawyer who was court-appointed to represent him after a previous arrest for battery. He wound up sentenced to life without parole for the crime.

Dinah, stabbed multiple times with the knife cruelly twisted during the last piercing, survived with severe heart damage. People said it was a miracle. She spent months in the ICU in a medically induced coma while Simon advanced from one grade at school to the next. During the years he played soccer and went on family vacations to Disney World and the beach, she endured multiple surgeries, infections, and ever-worsening kidney function. By the time he entered high school, she had been wait-listed for a heart transplant, but had been too ill the few times her turn came up. Yet, somehow, she lived.

She often sat on the stoop in a wheel chair waiting for medical transport or for a bit of sun, up to her nose in a quilt. While he grew taller, she didn't seem much bigger than she had when the attack happened. If she was outside when he got off the school bus, he would mumble "Hi," but she never answered. If he dared to peek, he would see her looking his way through the narrow gap between the quilt and her hat.

Whenever Simon thought about her, his skin seemed to constrict, as if he was being squeezed. Maybe he shouldn't be having fun if Dinah suffered. Maybe what happened to her was his fault, somehow. He should have screamed for his parents instead of watching helplessly.

At the time of the attack, even though he was the only witness, his parents wouldn't allow the police to question him. He couldn't remember much, anyway — just his steamy breath on the window and the princess sparkle shoes. After the attack, his parents tried to calm him by moving his bed from the window side to the far wall. For many years, he was afraid to look out. Even when the attacker went to prison, Simon still expected him to be standing on the stoop, with his head swiveled to stare up at the boy in the house next door. The attacker might linger there, or sneak up to Simon's bedroom, to stab him before he told anyone what he had seen.

He outgrew his fear by reminding himself that the man who murdered their neighbor and who almost killed his playmate was locked away forever. If he looked out the window, an uneasy tightening in his chest lingered—no longer the twisted-knife terror of childhood.

Once in high school, he didn't think as much about the attack. His mind filled with thoughts of finding a girlfriend. But whenever a girl tried to talk to him, the heat rising from his neck silenced him. He was one of those red-heads who blush. It was an agony to say anything to a girl. He turned crimson before he opened his mouth.

"Look at Simon. He's red as a beet," one of them might say. It hadn't happened yet, but it might.

It would be too much to bear from any girl in school. His thoughts turned to Dinah. She didn't count. She wasn't pretty, like the girls in his classes. Before the attack, they played together every day. He might be able to talk to her without the cringing shame he felt with regular girls. If he practiced with Dinah, it wouldn't matter as much if his face turned red, since she didn't go to his school or any school. Even if she laughed at him, no one would know.

On the other hand, what was there to say to her? I'm sorry you got stabbed? Why did he wait eight years to say that? Only a jerk would say such a stupid thing after all this time. She would look at him funny if he did.

But if he could ever say more than "Hi" to Dinah, he could to tell her he witnessed the stabbing, that it still haunted him.

"It scared me. It still sort of does when I think about what happened."

He imagined her saying words of comfort

"We were both scared, Simon."

He imagined her saying words that stung.

"You weren't the one who was stabbed, Simon. You weren't the one whose father was killed."

He imagined her sneering at him. He imagined her bursting into tears.

What he liked best was picturing her weeping. Then he could put his arm around her. Even kiss her. She might stop crying and smile at him. She would be his practice girlfriend. Until he found a real girlfriend at school.

For many days, he tried to work up the nerve to talk to Dinah. Even though there were several opportunities now that the weather warmed enough for her to sit outside more often, he still didn't dare approach her. He muttered "Hi" when he got off the bus, like he always had. Then he rushed right into his house.

In his room, he knocked his head on the wall, calling himself a "retard" and a "baby" for being too scared to say more than "Hi." He slapped his own face hard while looking in the mirror. At least the red mark wasn't a blush. He had to raise the stakes, to force himself to talk to her. There would have to be a painful consequence if he dashed into the house, as usual, or he would keep finding excuses to avoid her. He didn't want to ruin his chances for a girlfriend.

He went through several ideas for consequences. Break his phone? Shave his head? Destroy his Converse All Stars? But the phone was insured, his hair would grow back, and he had almost outgrown the All Stars, anyway. None seemed like enough.

His mind drifted back to the attack. What if the attacker rang his doorbell instead of Dinah's? The two houses looked alike. Anyone could mistake one for the other. If he answered, he would have been the one who got stabbed. Maybe that's what *should* have happened.

It was like an algebra problem. If $X = a$, did it also $= b$? He was bad at math, but it gave him an idea that would force his hand. If he didn't talk to Dinah, he would have to stab himself in the heart. It was talk to her or die. One or the other.

That night, he stole into the kitchen while his parents slept and found a knife with a long blade. He brought it to his room and lay it on his bed. He would sleep next to it, if sleep was possible, so he would see it when he woke. It would remind him — one or the other. The next day, right after school. No more waiting.

In his classes, dread and indecision made it impossible to concentrate on the assignments. There were girls in the school seated around him. Girls he would like to know. If he couldn't even talk to

Dinah, he would never talk to any of them. A loser like him might as well die.

One or the other.

On the bus home, he began trembling. The kid next to him noticed.

"What's up, man? You okay?"

"Fine! I'm fine." He blushed and perspired. Probably he stank. He pressed his arms tight against his sides to stop vapors from spreading. The kids around him did not seem to notice, unless they just hid their disgust.

When it was his stop, he stumbled up the aisle and out the door. As the bus drove off, he stood still for a minute, looking down at the grass, trying not to vomit. His stomach roiled. He had seen Dinah sitting outside as the bus pulled up. He knew she was watching him. When she was outside, she always watched him get off the bus.

The knife waited in his room. *One or the other.* Without looking up, he muttered his usual "Hi." She didn't say anything, as usual. Losing his nerve, he took a step toward his house. He would have to kill himself. He pictured the knife plunging into his skin, piercing his heart, the blood, the agonizing pain. Anything would be better. Terrified, he swiveled back toward her house and dragged himself to her stoop. He still kept his head down. Her white sneakers and socks between the front wheels of her wheelchair were all he saw. Quick bursts of air came from above. It was Dinah, breathing.

"Um. What happened to the princess sparkle shoes?" He choked out the words.

Why did such a brainless thing pop out of his mouth? Those shoes would be eight years old. What a dumb-ass. He should go and stab himself right now.

Somewhere, a crow cackled. A dog yelped in the distance.

"Do you... have any... weed?"

His eyes sprang up. He hadn't heard her say anything since before the attack. She had a thin childish voice, delivered between shallow breaths. Despite the warmth, she was wrapped in a quilt.

"What?"

"Weed... Can you get any?"

Now he gawked. Close-up, she was weirder than he remembered, uglier. She squinted at him through puffy lids. Her face was round, bloated, a white marshmallow of a face, with wispy hair sticking out from beneath her hat, feathered by the breeze.

"Um. No. I don't have any weed."

"How about… a cigarette? Get me… a cigarette."

There was an oxygen-tank attached to the back of her chair with a tube like a spaghetti strand up to her nose, splitting into a part for each nostril.

"I don't think you should…"

"Just get me… a cigarette."

"Yeah. Okay. Maybe. If I can."

"Hurry!"

He sprinted to his house. His parents were at work. He was the only one there. A cigarette. Where would he find a cigarette? His mother used to smoke. A pack might be hidden somewhere. In his parent's bedroom, he rifled through his mother's belongings. He hesitated to look in her underwear drawer, trying hard not to picture his mother in lacy undergarments, then closed his eyes and plunged ahead. There, buried in the back, a couple lay loose. He took them and ran back outside.

"A lighter… get a lighter." A woolen glove emerged from the quilt, grabbed the cigarettes, and withdrew back into its folds again.

This time, he searched the kitchen draws until he found the kind of lighter his mother used for something to do with cake decorations. It was the length of the knife, still lying on his bed. If he didn't finish his talk with Dinah, he knew what he had to do. One or the other.

"Turn off… the oxygen," she piped when he returned.

He found the valve and struggled to close it, guided by the directions she snapped at him. He fumbled until he got it right, while she held out the cigarettes.

"You have one…"

"But I never smoked."

"Light them both… And give one to me."

Using the lighter, he managed. She pointed to her mouth and parted her lips like a baby bird. He put one of the cigarettes in the tiny opening.

"I don't know how," he said.

She closed her eyes and inhaled. He did his best, but coughed and sputtered like he had when he learned to swim. At least she didn't laugh at him. She paid no attention. Smoke drifted around her head like a halo.

Back in his room, he lay on his bed, staring at the ceiling with the taste of tobacco in his mouth. He talked to a girl and smoked a cigarette. He hadn't been great, but he hadn't been too pathetic either. Mostly, it shocked him that Dinah wasn't more, well, like he thought a cripple would be—meek and grateful that a boy paid attention to her. Even a loser like him. That was the reason he wanted to practice with her in the first place. He thought she'd be easier than regular girls.

It was a relief not to have to stab himself. He didn't want to die. Now that he broke the ice, he figured he could speak to Dinah again. He would have to get more cigarettes from one of the older boys at school to make sure. A tiny prick of victory eased his chest.

The next day, he walked from the bus to Dinah without pause, cigarette in hand.

"Hi." He said the word at normal volume for once.

She registered his presence and took the cigarette, shoving it into her quilt.

"Stick your tongue… in my mouth." She parted her lips as she had done for the cigarette.

Simon took a step back.

"What? I can't. We're outside. Someone will see."

"No one's here."

He looked around. The cul-de-sac was empty.

"Someone might watch from a window."

"For fuck's sake… Just do it."

He stepped toward her again, bent down, and thrust his tongue into her waiting mouth. It tasted like medicine. He recoiled.

"Sit down… and put your hand under… the bottom of the quilt."

"What do you mean?"

"Reach up… and rub me."

Just then, a brown-faced woman in a white coat opened the door.

"Back!" Dinah yelled with surprising force. The woman disappeared into the house.

"Okay… Rub me."

Intimidated by Dinah's fierceness, Simon sat on the stoop and put a quaking hand under the quilt. At the top of her socks, her legs were bare. She nodded. He continued to reach up. She wasn't wearing underwear. He didn't know what to expect.

"Find the little knob… and rub it… No, not there… There… Not so hard."

Too stunned to feel whatever he was supposed to feel, Simon rubbed until he saw Dinah shiver. He stood up, fearing she was having a seizure.

"Are you okay?"

She didn't answer. He realized she had dismissed him.

For the next several weeks, a pattern was established. He would get off the bus, give Dinah a cigarette, stick his tongue in her mouth just once, then reach his hand under her quilt until she shivered. What they were doing both fascinated and revolted him. He wondered if all girls were like her once you got to know them. Bossy. Rude. Mean. Or if only sick girls were that way.

In his mind, Dinah had become his official practice girlfriend, although he never said so out loud. That didn't mean he loved her. He wasn't sure he even liked her. Maybe he even hated her, even if he liked what she made him do, sometimes.

He had practiced enough. It was time to find a real girlfriend. But after all the fear he had before talking to Dinah, now he feared breaking up with her even more. As if she had trapped him into coming over every day as soon as he got off the bus. As if she had a chain around his neck, yanking him to her, making him do things that he shouldn't do to a stabbed girl.

A day came when he got off the bus and found an ambulance in front of the house next door. It was not the first time. He waited until two EMTs wheeled Dinah out on a stretcher and loaded her into the back of the vehicle. He glimpsed her marshmallow face whizzing by, eyes closed, mouth gasping like a fish. Half-way down the street, the siren began its wail.

Forty-eight hours later, he learned that Dinah died of a heart attack. A complicated mix of relief and guilt haunted him. What if the cigarettes and the rubbing had shortened her fragile life? Horrible thoughts plagued him. His choice to talk to her instead of stabbing himself might have killed her. Maybe that's what it meant to have a girlfriend. What one wants hurts the other.

The next week, he found a box waiting at his doorstep with his name on it and a note. It was from Dinah's mother.

"Dinah wanted you to have this."

In his room with the door shut, Simon opened the box. Parting the tissue paper, he saw that his practice girlfriend had given him one last surprise. Her old sparkle princess shoes.

CHAPTER 15
WHO SHALL BE IMPOVERISHED

It was 2016. Eva's only companion had been her grandmother for twelve years. This worried Edith. The girl was feral enough. At some point, Edith would die, but before then she had to socialize her granddaughter so she wouldn't be alone, doomed to a life by herself, hidden in the hut, fearful of other humans.

As usual, Edith flipped through the pages of "Roots Of The Woods," hoping the author, whoever that was, provided suggestions. The writer of the book used it to commune with Edith. She imagined a grand, unseen network connecting the book, the hut, the replenishing rick of wood, and maybe the entire forest intent on protecting her and the girl, guiding them toward means of survival. Would the spell be broken if other people entered their lives?

The answer came when a slip of paper fell out from between the pages, fluttering to the floor. Edith picked it up. It was the blue-lined kind torn from a school notebook. On it was a message in block printing.

FIND THE NATHAN SISTERS AND FRANK'S GROUP. THEY WILL JOIN YOU IF YOU HEAL THEM.

The Nathan sisters? Edith remembered them. They had been members of the synagogue, known to be animal lovers who had been charged with animal neglect because they exceeded the number of dogs, cats, and wildlife permitted in residences in town. It wasn't because the animals weren't well cared for. They lacked the proper license to be kennel owners. The neighbors complained. There was a court battle.

One day, they loaded all the animals, in cages, into a U-Haul. Before they took off, they stopped at the synagogue to see Rabbi Samuelson. Perhaps they told him where they were headed, but no one else had any idea. They were never seen again. It was assumed they moved out of state. According to the paper in Edith's hand, they settled a few miles away, in the forest.

Frank's group was more of an enigma. Edith didn't know a Frank. Then it came to her. Years ago, when she still worked at the University, there was a professor whose first name was Frank. They fired him because of an ethics violation. He hired a ghostwriter—Larry Anderson was his name. An unforgettable charmer. Frank resigned after a considerable fuss about a ghostwritten paper and stomped off to the forest to live "off the grid" with a few fellow academic discontents. Everyone thought they wouldn't last two days in the woods. Apparently, they endured.

The sisters and the academics chose a primitive existence in the forest rather than the comforts of the modern world. They had nothing else in common. Jewish animal lovers and non-denominational professors might not mix. Although they were younger than Edith, they were too old for her granddaughter. Yet, "Roots of the Woods" suggested them for a reason. They formed a core group that younger people from town might join. If Edith found them, she could see for herself if they would cooperate.

But she wouldn't reveal her name or Eva's. That could be dangerous, if there was still reward money for information leading to their capture after all these years. She would be Great Mother. Eva would be First Woman. Those were the only names they would give the other forest dwellers.

"I can take you to the sisters," Eva said.

She had been subdued since her trip to town. It turned out to be necessary only a single time. The cabinet replenished the groceries she brought back for the rest of the winter. Edith never learned what happened on her granddaughter's journey. She imagined a visit to town might have been a shock after so many years in the forest.

"You know where the sisters are?"

"Yes. I've been spying on them for years. They aren't far."

Edith packed a bag with her healing supplies. Jars of ointments. Pulverized mixtures of forest plants ready for brewing. Feathers, mushrooms, bark, snake skins, and dried flowers for casting spells.

Eva led the way to the sister's woodland residence in a small cave carved out of a hillside. There they were, so indistinguishable from one another that Edith had forgotten their first names. Everyone had called them the Nathan sisters. They didn't recognize Edith, whose graying hair bushed out down her back and who replaced her once stylish wardrobe with used camp clothing. And they wouldn't have known that the muscular sixteen-year-old with the long braid wound around her head was Edith's granddaughter.

Edith coached Eva on what to say, when to remain silent, and when to talk. It was a way of having her get accustomed to engaging with people. The sisters, who had warm smiles, made it easy.

"We are neighbors, and we want to introduce ourselves. This is my grandmother. She is called Great Mother. Even though I'm still young, I'm called First Woman."

The two sisters glanced at each other with skeptical eyes. Edith suspected their unfamiliar names, more like odd pagan titles, didn't inspire immediate trust.

"We live in a hut about half-a-mile southwest of here, near the creek."

The sisters nodded. "We thought we saw smoke from that area. Do you vent a wood stove through the roof?"

"Yes. That's us. We try to keep the wood stove burning smokeless. We don't want intruders. Women living alone are vulnerable."

"We count on one of our animals for protection. We'll show you."

They were led into the cave fitted with town furniture. Two beds with bedspreads. A sofa. A table with chairs. Several cats lying about, some with three legs, some with one eye. Three senior dogs on three dog beds.

"We do our cooking outside."

The outdoor kitchen had a brick wood stove with several compartments of different sizes for baking and a grill insert on top for pots and pans.

"It all looks so comfortable. How did you get the bed and things out here?" Eva hadn't seen proper furniture since she was four.

"We still have the pickup." A sister pointed to a truck parked a few feet from the cave. "If one of us goes to town for supplies, she isn't recognized without the other. We go about once a month for groceries and food for the animals. Over time, we also brought whatever might make the cave homier."

No one mentioned "Roots of The Woods." Edith wondered if she had the only copy in existence.

Chicken wire strung between the trees next to the cave entrance cordoned off a large square area with a shed in the middle. Brown and white hens roamed there, pecking at the ground.

"The chickens came with us when we moved out here. The town doesn't allow poultry. These are good layers. We'll give you some eggs when you're ready to leave."

Eggs. Edith smiled. She hadn't had chicken eggs in years, although she stole eggs from wild birds when she could and fed them to Eva.

There were also two goats tethered to trees. "For the milk." They promised Edith a jug. It would be a treat after the reconstituted dry milk the hut provided.

In another area, cages held injured birds and woodland mammals—porcupines, skunks, groundhogs, bats, possums. Just beyond, a fenced space contained two lame does.

"How do you protect all these from predators?" Eva asked.

"Ah. That's a problem. Bucky is ill. He's our security. Over there," one of the sisters said.

Behind the deer compound was another. Inside, a large black bear was on its side, panting.

"He's tame. But we have no idea what's the matter with him. We're quite worried."

"Would you mind if Great Mother helped? She's a healer," Eva said.

The sisters exchanged skeptical looks again. Then they both shrugged simultaneously.

"Might as well. We can't take Bucky to a vet."

Edith entered the Bear compound and circled the beast several times. It didn't react. She lay a gentle hand on its rump and its neck. She stared at it thoughtfully for several minutes. Then she exited the area. Reaching into her bag, she pulled out various containers until she found the one she wanted and handed it to the girl.

"Great Mother suggests you brew this into a tea. You can add it to a gallon of water. If you can get Bucky to drink two cups every three hours, you should see an improvement by tomorrow."

Eva handed the container to one sister. They passed it back and forth between them, taking off the top and sniffing it, dipping a finger in and tasting it.

"Careful. It's strong," Eva warned.

"We can try, I guess." The sister sounded doubtful.

They walked back to the cave and put a pot of water on the brick oven top to start the brewing, then invited the guests to sit on the cushioned chairs—an unusual experience for both.

"Great Mother wants to know what you miss most about town."

"The synagogue. *Shabbat* services. *Rosh Hashanah. Kol Nidre. Sukkot.* All the holidays with the community. Of course, we have a rabbi, so we do what we can. Only it's just the three of us. They're not authentic services without ten Jews, a *minyan*. And we don't have a *Torah* scroll. We just face east."

Edith pulled at Eva's sleeve and whispered in her ear.

"Great Mother asks what you mean when you say you have a rabbi?"

"Rabbi Samuelson lives in a smaller cave near us. We found him wandering in the forest several years ago. It took a while for his mind to straighten out. He's the one who built the brick stove. And he helped with the chicken wire and the fencing."

Edith was sitting forward in her chair, with her hand on her heart.

"Did you know the Rabbi from town? It must be quote a shock to discover he's been living with us all this time."

Edith shook her head. She didn't want the sisters to guess who she was.

"He studies most of the day. We've been able to get copies of the Jewish texts he needs. He doesn't like it when we disturb him. Perhaps we can introduce you the next time you visit."

Eva was getting tired. She wasn't used to human interaction. It took more energy than hauling water or chopping wood. Edith also drooped. It was time for them to leave.

"We need to go. We have to find Frank and his group. Do you know them?"

"They live about a mile up that trail." The sisters pointed. "We don't have much to do with that group."

"We'll come be in a couple of days and check on Bucky."

Eva and Edith left the sisters with a lidded jug of goat milk and a dozen eggs added to Edith's bag. Edith would spend a sleepless night puzzling over Rabbi Samuelson. The little round man had officiated at Joe's funeral. After she took Eva to live in the forest, he somehow wound up in a cave near the Nathan sisters? With a mind that needed healing? He built a brick oven?

It delighted the sisters when Edith and Eva returned to their cave. Bucky was standing in his yard, swaying, bright-eyed. The security guard was healthy again. Eva said that Great Mother healed both people and animals. Life in the forest had its perils. Illness. Injury. Hunger. If they banded together, they could help each other. While preserving the isolated life they had each chosen, they could form a cooperative to share information, protect each other from outsiders, trade or lend implements, be generous with whatever was acquired but not needed, be friends.

The sisters wanted to think it over. They would have to consult the Rabbi.

"He's very wise. He'll tell us what to do."

They still hadn't introduced him.

It took a year to form the Woodland Cooperative, as they called it after intense discussion. Frank and his group of four grudging academic men needed to benefit from Edith's healing arts several times before they agreed to join. Rabbi Samuelson took months to emerge blinking from his cave. The unlikely group of ten finally interacted.

They met to hammer out a mission statement. The academics argued about the wording far into the night, while the others talked among themselves or snoozed. One of them wrote it out the compromise draft.

"The Woodland Cooperative has as its objective the preservation of life in the forest independent of government authority, modern energy sources, and the norms of society. We pledge to aid each other in maintaining the life-style freely chosen by each member of the Cooperative."

Eva was welcome to visit both the sisters and the academics. She was learning to socialize. Edith still worried about her future among people so much older than herself. It would take more years to convince the Cooperative to admit newer, younger members.

CHAPTER 16
WHO BY PLAGUE

In the early months of 2020, clusters of the coronavirus appeared on campus. The university closed all residences except married student housing. Many of the married students had nowhere else to go, since their parents converted their old childhood bedrooms into craft rooms or libraries. Inside one of the apartments, Simon spent long anxious hours scanning the awful news on TV and internet sites, ignoring the piles of laundry and dirty dishes his wife, Judy, expected him to do. A half-hour before she returned from her job at the hospital, he'd throw a load in the washing machine. He would only do the dishes after the dinner additions.

"When are you going to grow up, Simon?" She scanned the disarray. "The virus isn't an excuse to let everything go to pot."

He'd been attracted to Judy's commanding ways. She was the one who proposed six months before.

"We've been dating a year. It's time to buy a ring. I can chip in."

They were in Walmart deciding on a type of mop—string or sponge—when she made this announcement. It startled Simon into agreeing. He was a graduate student with no income or prospects of earning one until he completed his dissertation, which had not advanced beyond the research stage in several years. Judy was a nurse. "Chipping in" meant that he did not object when she paid for the ring she chose. They squeaked the wedding in during the winter break, before the ban on events of any size. Both families attended. Under the *chuppah*, Simon, damp with perspiration, stamped on the goblet, while Judy smiled sternly in her billowing gown.

She had already moved into Simon's one-bedroom, claiming most of the sole closet, three of the four dresser drawers, and all but an edge of the bathroom shelf for her belongings. An overloaded bookcase for Simon's research materials remained as it had been when he lived alone. Both agreed on the inadequacy of married student housing and planned to move into a larger apartment in town at the semester's end.

By the time the virus spread, it wasn't unexpected when the university closed the residence early, after two staff members became ill. They gave everyone a week to move out. Simon had the nerve-wracking task of searching for another rental just before a state-wide lockdown went into effect. Nothing turned up. The students in the already shuttered dorms grabbed all the off-campus vacancies.

That's when Judy texted her news.

"They results of the COVID test they gave the entire hospital staff last week arrived this morning. I'm positive. Mandatory leave is immediate. They didn't say when I'll get paid. Be home soon."

Simon had the same thought on his wedding day.

This can't be happening.

The unreality of the situation engulfed him. The world was coming apart. He paced around the apartment, picking up random objects. A can-opener. A flashlight. An apple. He wondered why nothing he touched disintegrated. The solidness of everyday objects surprised him.

A few minutes later, he heard the snap of the key turn in the lock. Judy came in and yanked off her sturdy nurse's shoes and white ankle socks. The sight of his wife's unprotected bare feet and her painted pink toenails saddened Simon. A memory of the princess sparkle shoes, left for him by his first girlfriend after her death, popped into his mind. He swallowed, holding back tears. She didn't notice.

"We all kept saying—there aren't enough masks. We're running out. They said re-use them. Ha! It was just a matter of time before we'd be exposed." She glared at him as if it was his fault.

She huffed into the bathroom. Simon heard water gush from a faucet. He waited with his useless shoulders sagging.

When Judy reappeared in her bathrobe, she had composed herself.

"Okay. A bunch of us who tested positive and who didn't work with infected patients are asymptomatic. We might be spreaders who won't get too ill ourselves. That's the best guess from Administration. But you might catch the virus from me. Do you want us to separate for a while to be safe?"

"Separate?" His voice trembled. The memory of the shoes faded, but the feeling lingered. It frightened him more to be on his own than to get ill. But that was illogical thinking, unworthy of a graduate student.

"There are no rentals. The hotels are closed."

"I've got to do this social distancing thing. It's probable that I've been positive for a week. By this time, you might be positive, too. I don't think there is an actual option to live separately, given our financial situation. But I want you to have the choice."

Judy always seemed to be a self-assured problem-solver. He just became an anxious mess, swimming in a rip-current of half-baked ideas. She held out a branch. If he grabbed it, he'd be okay.

"Here's what we'll do. You remember me talking about Frank? In Radiology? He'll trade his camper for the Civic."

"What? Why?" Simon sank onto a kitchen chair. Judy sat opposite him at the table. She ran her fingers through her long blond hair, released from her work-required ponytail.

"I've got it figured out. We don't have a place to live. We'll put our things in storage and stay in the camper in the state park. It's the safest place I can think of to ride this thing out."

She stunned him. His stomach buckled. "We can't. There won't be an internet connection. What about my dissertation?"

He considered caving in to her proposal. But live in a camper in the woods for two weeks? How? Judy reminded him they shouldn't risk exposing any of their relatives or friends. It wouldn't hurt for him to take time off from his graduate work, since they shut the university, anyway. The park remained open, even if the campgrounds were closed. They'd find a place and wait out the quarantine. Either that or homelessness.

Simon left some of his thoughts unsaid. He spent many days listening to the experts. If the hospital cleared Judy to return to work at some point, she was likely to be re-exposed. No one knew if any immunity existed after an infection. Would there be another mandatory isolation? Weeks could turn into months cooped up in the camper with no electricity or distractions. No marriage survived such conditions.

He went along with it. No other solution came to mind. Now that they had decided to flee, he became as calm as Judy. A pleasant interlude in their relationship began. Packing up the apartment together brought them closer. Judy directed. Simon did as she said. In the evening, when they sat on the couch, exhausted, she leaned into him. Maybe it would work out after all, he thought. He pictured the two of them snuggling in the cozy little camper, surrounded by forest, serenaded by song birds.

By the week's end, they were ready. They took possession of the camper, cleaned it, moved everything in they weren't putting in storage, and withdrew cash from the bank. Whatever grocery staples were available were purchased, along with camping supplies from a sporting goods store right before its mandatory closure during the lockdown. Just before taking off, they sent emails informing friends and family of their plan.

The camper was basic. Behind the cab were two seats with a fold-out table and, behind that, a queen size bed. A roof rack bin held the food and a few changes of clothing. A fold-out rear hatch provided a surface for a camp stove.

On the day before student housing closed, they drove to the state park in a cheerful mood. The outing was an escape from the escalating horror of the crisis. No one attended the guardhouse at the entrance. A chain across the camp ground section denied access. They drove on, deeper into the forest, which covered thousands of acres. It was the end of March. The trees budded, promising of a green canopy by April. The cool air foreshadowed the blooming to come. They wound their way through paved roads, then onto gravel ones.

For several days, they parked the camper at different vista parking lots. They both felt well, having no symptoms. The camper was comfortable. The weather was pleasant. This was their chance to explore the forest. Every day, they ventured further into the interior. They were enjoying the adventure.

Then, during one of their longer drives, they came upon a log straddling the road. Simon braked the camper. A crude sign was posted on an upright tree limb branching out of the log.

"Woodland Cooperative. Leader: First Woman," it read.

Below it was another sign with a newer appearance.

"No Trespassing. This is a private community. If you wish to visit or join, you must wait outside for 14 days after any exposure or symptoms of illness. First Woman will find you and interview you if you choose to wait."

They sat there with the motor idling, chugging with impatience. Judy didn't say anything. That seemed unusual.

"What should we do? Turn back?" Simon waited for Judy to tell him. For a long moment, she stayed silent.

"It's late. We have nowhere to go back to. Just park in the little clearing," she said.

"What do you think the Cooperative is? A community just for women? Because if it is, they won't let me in." Heat rose from his neck. He blushed with emotion. The sign annoyed him. Judy just shrugged without arguing, another odd sign.

When it got dark, Simon turned on the lantern. Judy crawled into the bed and zipped herself into her sleeping bag. She fell asleep right away. Simon wondered why she was so tired. Their usual bedtime was much later.

The next morning, he awoke first and made coffee on the camp stove. The sun, a bright globe, hung between the trees. While Judy continued to sleep, he walked back down the road without trespassing by going past the log. There were marvels along the way. Wildflowers, the staccato of unseen woodpeckers, the clean air. He spotted a creek. When it warmed up, he would take a towel and bathe. He relieved himself behind a tree in case anyone was looking, even at a distance.

When he returned, Judy was awake but still in bed.

"My throat's sore. There's a thermometer in my backpack."

His good mood darkened. He knew what a temperature meant. He handed the backpack to her and watched.

"100.2. *Geez.* I'm wiped out. Better get me some potable water. You'll have to help me stay hydrated."

She wasn't coughing. Yet. But neither had to say that a sore throat with a fever was a bad sign. They knew the symptoms of the illness. Simon's stomach jolted, as if he fell from a height. He realized that when they made plans back in married student housing, they assumed that, like many in their age group, they would remain asymptomatic. How could they have been so stupid! They never thought out what they would do if one of them — or both of them — became sick deep in the forest.

This was when Simon was supposed to wear protective gear himself when he was near Judy. But that assumed he was still negative. Fat chance!

"If you still have a fever tomorrow, we should drive back," he said.

She remained silent, turning her head away from him as if she was indifferent or without the energy to care. For the first time since they started dating, he had to rely on himself. He reddened with fear. He dared not give in to panic. Outside of the camper, he walked in agitated circles. His mind wrenched toward the worst possibilities. What if her fever got higher? What if she had trouble breathing? What if she didn't tell him what to do?

The next morning, her fever was 101.4. A dry cough had begun, and she complained about tightness in her chest. Simon drove the camper back though the park. At the guardhouse, he had a phone signal. He called Judy's doctor. There was a voice message.

"The doctor is unable to practice. Please call the hospital if you need medical services. If this is an emergency, call 911."

Stunned, Simon called the hospital.

"The hospital is at capacity and cannot offer services at this time. There are no test kits available in this area. Please leave your name and phone number, and we will contact you when there is medical staff able to serve you. You may call the State Health Department at 317-855-3396 for further advice and updates."

After forty rings to the Health Department, he hung up. Not knowing what else to do, he made a U-turn and drove the long way back to the clearing next to the log. No treatment for the illness existed, anyway. Most people who had rode it out at home. The severest cases were among the elderly with other medical conditions. Judy was young. With some exceptions, women in their late twenties stayed mild.

Her condition didn't change during the next few days. Judy slept fitfully when hot flashes, shuddering chills, and the cough allowed her a few moments peace. Simon gave her sips of water and a cool t-shirt, wet from the creek, for her forehead. She radiated heat. The cough made talking difficult. She batted him away when he offered to hold her.

His thoughts cycled. Did his dread mean he loved Judy the way a husband should love his wife? With all his heart? Or was it what he would feel for anyone in his care with a severe illness? Responsible. Obligated. Uncertain. Lonely. Afraid.

Judy had been his rock. He needed a rock, but need isn't the same as love, is it? He resented his need for her, when he didn't provoke it. But he hated being weak, indecisive, unable to finish his dissertation. Now that his wife might no longer be a rock, he had a constant alarm blaring in his head.

"I don't know what to do," he kept saying, even when Judy was in no condition to give him any guidance. Her symptoms had become severe over the week. Her fever stayed high. She gasped for breath. Simon guessed that she might soon need a ventilator. He drove the camper back to the guardhouse. This time he called 911. A shocking recorded message said there were no emergency services. All the EMTs were out sick. He drove the camper back again.

He had to get help somewhere, somehow, even if he had to cross into the Cooperative territory. Someone there might know what he should do, anyone. Once he climbed onto the other side of the log, he panicked. Maybe he would be turned away. What then? The thought so upset him that he sobbed aloud as he walked, stumbling, on the verge of collapse.

That is when he saw a figure coming toward him on the road. He stopped and waited, bent and heaving, for whoever it was to come nearer and accuse him of trespassing. A young woman, about twenty or twenty-one years old, approached. Her loosely braided hair circled her head. She wore a faded black shirt with a stretched-out neckline, jeans, and muddy boots.

"Hello. I'm called First Woman. You need to keep ten feet back from me. What's your name?"

Her tone wasn't belligerent at all. Simon wiped his face on his sleeve. He stuttered his name.

"What's your situation?"

It was such a relief that she asked instead of ordering him away that he started to cry again. Between sobs, he told her his wife had the virus, describing her symptoms.

"My wife… she has a high fever… it keeps going higher every day… And she's coughing… Sometimes she coughs up blood… she gasps… she's fighting for breath. She needs help breathing… The hospital in town is full-up…" It came out in a garbled rush.

"Hmm. Wait right here until I return." She walked back up the road.

He obeyed her, waiting and pacing, pulling at his hair for the long hour until she returned. She placed two small cloth bags at her feet.

"Stay where you are. I'm leaving these for you. My grandmother, called Great Mother, is a healer. She sent you this. Your wife can't be saved, but maybe it will sooth her. Make a tea from the contents of the brown bag. It will ease her breathing and help her sleep. The green bag is for you. It contains pieces of root. Eat a piece in the morning and a piece at night. They may protect you. I can't guarantee it because you're starting late, but it may."

"What do you mean my wife can't be saved?" He held out his hands, as if pleading.

"Prepare yourself. We will do a prayer circle for her. What's her name?"

"Judy."

"There is a religious leader among us — do you have a preference?"

"We're born Jewish, but anything that helps. Please…"

"Rabbi Samuelson will lead."

She turned, leaving the bags, and walked away. Simon thought of running after her, but her firm stride seemed to forbid it. He retrieved the bags. The woman — who was she? Who would call herself a name like First Woman and why? And Great Mother? Was that Native American? She wasn't a regular doctor. How did he know the bags didn't contain poison?

He was in more control of himself, now. He returned to the camper with the bags stuffed into his pocket. Judy was no better. Once again, he drove to the guardhouse. He still got the same discouraging voice messages from the doctor and the emergency room. No one at the hospital tried to get in touch with him. All he could do was go back to the log.

Once he had parked, he took the bags from his pocket. He sniffed the tea. The smell was earthy and pungent, like soil. The little slices of root in the other bag might have been parsnips, for all he knew. He put a piece in his mouth. It might make him sick, but he had to find out before he gave the concoction to Judy. It had an awful, bitter taste. He spat it out. Then put it back in his mouth. He was suspicious, but what other choice did he have? When an hour passed and the root hadn't killed him, he brewed the tea and gave it to Judy by the spoonful. She relaxed into sleep while still gasping for air.

It took another two soul-wrecking days for Judy's suffering to end. Simon stayed in the camper bed with her, putting spoonfuls of tea between her parched lips, telling her she wasn't alone. He even told her he loved her. It seemed to be true. He wept throughout the process, falling asleep and missing her last moments.

After all the heat had left her body, he fetched a bucket of water from the creek and washed her. A shovel had been placed beside the camper. He ignored it and drove back to the guardhouse. The mortuaries he contacted were all at capacity. Back he went. He spent the rest of the day digging a grave. The hard repetitive work was grim but necessary. He took care of his wife, as a husband should. When he found her too heavy to lift, he dragged her in the sleeping bag from the camper to the grave. He climbed into the hole first and eased her in, to avoid dropping her. Dry-eyed, he shoveled dirt back into the hole.

When he finished, he dropped to his knees beside the fresh mound and spoke to Judy in his mind.

"I don't know what to do without you."

He heard a rustling a few feet behind him. It was First Woman.

"You must remain on your side of the log for two weeks. If you develop symptoms in that period, your wait will be longer. Then you can choose to join us, if you agree to work like you did today. We have people in the Cooperative with many skills, but we are short of laborers. There's lots of physical work to do in the forest. Cutting down trees. Farming. Digging trenches."

"You take men?"

"Yes. We choose people by their skill and willingness to put the needs of the community before themselves. Not by gender or any other demographic. You will have to survive the next weeks before you decide."

No words came to him. He ached all over. It was probably sore muscles. First Woman left.

This time Simon talked to Judy out loud, as if she stood next to him.

"She wants me to join. What do you think I should do?"

He didn't say anything else. His throat hurt too much.

CHAPTER 17
WHO SHALL PROFIT

On March 4th, 2020, Dean Aaron used two chubby forefingers to tap a keyboard on his mahogany desk in his campus office. Outside the window, students drifted between classes. Many didn't wear outer clothing, even in winter. Some wore sandals. It signified what? Indifference? Brashness? He didn't understand young people.

Every morning, his inbox greeted him with more emails than he ever had time to answer, and many texts and voice messages appeared over the next few hours. He prioritized them into files—Hold, Urgent, and the jammed to overflowing Critical file. Without opening anything, he closed the laptop to give his throbbing throat time to relax. Most of the Critical file concerned the Coronavirus. The Administration froze into suspended animation, wondering if COVID would affect the campus, wondering what to do if it did. Much of the correspondence circled around that uncertain subject.

Turning to his voicemails, he noticed one from Larry Anderson. *Larry Anderson.* Of all people. He pictured the younger Nordic-looking man. Like a Viking. Something stirred. Badly, he wanted to touch himself. He forbid himself that. He wasn't gay. He sat straighter in his chair, pressing his hands onto the desk, staring out the window.

The students. How easy it was for them. Wearing sandals in the snow. Tattoos on every inch of skin. Sexually fluid. They understood nothing about the life of a Jewish man in his sixties, raised to wear Gold Toe socks and date women.

"Hello, Professor. It's Larry Anderson, the academic ghostwriter who helped you out a while back."

The familiar voice reminded him of the conversations they used to have about linguistic theory. Aaron hired the ghostwriter to help him with his manuscript, hoping the handsome younger man wouldn't suspect the lustful feelings Aaron didn't choose to reveal. He didn't dare. Being gay wasn't possible. He had his career to consider. The very conservative governor of a very conservative red state in the "bible belt" appointed the university President. Everyone on campus knew how intolerant the President tended to be.

But another type of secret not related to the past nature of their relationship made the voice message from Larry Anderson equally jolting. Aaron didn't want it known that, technically, the ghostwriter wrote "Similarities in Pronouns in Proto-Linguistic Meta-Families," the publication leading to Aaron's promotion. If anyone discovered that he didn't do the work himself, at least not entirely, he would have a disagreeable time with the Ethics Committee.

The voicemail continued.

"Ghostwriting is only one of the hats I wear, Professor. I'm well-connected, having helped other professionals like yourself in government as well as in academia. That's how I've been able to get information about the coronavirus that might be useful for you. Information that hasn't been disclosed to the public yet."

He was being set up by an attractive con artist, just as he had been when he had trouble completing, or even starting, his manuscript in the past. He knew he should delete the message and block the caller. Curiosity, he told himself, made him listen to the end.

"I'm calling you before other administrators I know at other colleges.'

He named three at rival institutions.

"Get back to me ASAP if you're interested."

No. He wasn't interested. This time, he would not be fooled. It had been wrong to allow himself to get mixed up with someone like Larry Anderson years ago. He had been quite capable of writing the damned book himself. He only hired the ghostwriter to assist when he became stuck, and that was just temporary.

On the other hand, it would look bad if other administrators managed to get their hands on advance information before him. No tin-pot college should have a leg-up on a major research university, and no small-time dean should have a leg-up on him. It wouldn't hurt just to listen. He'd hang up if he didn't like what he heard.

"Professor. So glad you called. How're you holding up?"

"I'm fine. What's this about?" He didn't want to sound friendly.

Larry spoke in a hushed tone, as if telling a secret no one should overhear. This would be flattering if Aaron fell for it.

"I have sources, Professor, in the State Health Department. I hear things. Sometimes before the Governor. While they're still developing. Or when they're held up for political reasons. Someone doesn't want the Governor to be unhappy. That sort of thing."

"Okay. What's your information?" Aaron changed the screen on his laptop to World of Solitaire. He clicked on New Deal. It would keep his thoughts from straying.

"I want you to believe my sources are excellent. So I'll tell you two things that will happen tomorrow, March 6th. Neither has been in the news yet. The first confirmed case of the virus in the state is going to be announced. And the Governor will declare a State of Emergency."

Aaron paused before moving the three of hearts on top of the four of clubs. If what Larry said turned out to be true, it would impress the President to hear it from Aaron. He might invite Aaron into his inner circle, instead of allowing him to languish in a secondary administrative building, perhaps as a penalty for remaining suspiciously unmarried.

"I need you to have confidence in me, Professor, like in the old days when we worked on the linguistics manuscript together. When you discover I've told you the truth, call me. In times like these, information is gold. And I can access the gold mine."

The next morning, as soon as he awoke, Aaron opened the digital edition of the newspaper. In a large font across the top of the screen, the headline read "First COVID-19 case confirmed; Governor declares State of Emergency." Larry told the truth. It both amazed and annoyed Aaron that he hadn't believed the ghostwriter in time to alert the President.

Yet, it might have been a coincidence or a lucky guess on Larry's part. He asked him for another prediction, against his better judgement.

"Agreed, Professor. I want you to be satisfied that I'm trustworthy. On March 8th, less than two days from now, the second confirmed case will be announced. It will be a man who travelled to Boston for the BioGen Conference, same as the first case. Let's talk on the afternoon of the 8th if what I am telling you is borne out."

He paused. "By the way, Professor, since we are both interested in the history of linguistics, the expression 'born out' means 'arose from,' but if you add an 'e' to born, you get 'borne out,' meaning 'confirmed.' One silent letter changes the concept."

Aaron's imagination went into overdrive. Why would the ghostwriter mention silent letters that changed meanings in the middle of a pandemic that might kill thousands, even millions of people? He must be hinting about something. Aaron tried his best corral the unreasonable thought that Larry suggested Aaron was in the closet, appearing to be straight when a tiny slip, like a silent letter, revealed he was gay.

Meanwhile, there would be thirty-six hours of waiting until the verification of Larry's second piece of inside information. For two agonizing days, Aaron failed to concentrate on anything else. At this point in his career, influence counted. Larry's intelligence could be a springboard for Aaron, vaulting him to provost despite his questionable marital status.

The President and his advisors had to determine whether and when to close the university. Aaron heard that the President spun his wheels, trying to decide. All kinds of complexities came under consideration, from student fees to the fate of overseas programs. The future of the university might depend on getting it right. Any information about the rate of infection in the state helped. In the absence of testing, foreknowledge would be, as Larry said, gold.

Aaron stayed up late on the night of the 8th, reloading the newspaper website every few minutes until the new edition posted. The same large font announced the second confirmed case. Just as Larry predicted, the victim had attended the conference in Boston.

"Do you believe me now?" Larry didn't hush his triumphant voice when Aaron called him.

"I have to, don't I? You were right both times. What do you want from me to continue to keep me informed?"

Aaron didn't want Larry thinking he wasn't on to him. People like the ghostwriter cost. He had paid through the nose for his help with the book and for continued contact with the handsome ghostwriter.

"I have overhead, Professor. I'm glad you understand this will be business deal."

The ghostwriter named a figure. As Aaron expected, it was more than he could afford. It would require him to take a loan.

"Let me think it over."

"Of course. I'm sure you know—time is of the essence."

Larry put pressure on him. Aaron snuck two fingers onto his wrist. His pulse was rapid. He understood. In a changing situation, information that was priceless one day could be valueless the next. If he waited too long, the President would decide and that would be that.

"I'll call you back in an hour," he said.

His thoughts reeled. Who knew the long-term reliability of Larry or his sources? Did he dare take on such a stomach-dropping loan if the economy hovered over an abyss? What if the pandemic lasted for months, even years, and Larry wanted more and more? What if he failed to pay and Larry dropped him?

But another side crept into his thoughts. Aaron imagined helping the President make a decision whether to close. If the university remained opened too long, students in crowded dorms and over-enrolled classes would spread the virus. If it shut too soon, within the next few days, there would be chaos. He pictured being honored by the President, after the pandemic abated, at a special dinner for his help during the crisis.

"Because of the prescience of Dean Aaron, the university is in good shape today. He is a hero whose name will be remembered when the history of this noble institution is written."

"I just did my duty," he would answer.

He called the ghostwriter back within the hour.

The University closed its doors at the beginning of Spring Break, after Aaron persuaded the President, correctly, that there would be twenty-four confirmed cases by that date. When he predicted a thousand cases by the end of the month and a surge in April, classes were suspended through the end of the semester. Aaron claimed to have an anonymous source. He didn't say it was Larry, the former faculty member who left the university in disgrace after losing a plagiarism case. Aaron became the President's new favorite when he predicted a state-wide lockdown beginning on March 25th.

From that point on, the university faculty and staff worked from home. Larry arranged a daily morning phone call with updates. Other than that, Aaron continued to sort and answer emails in the Critical file.

He had time on his hands. Because the campus and all but essential businesses closed, he couldn't go to the gym, the library, or the opera. Instead, he fantasized about situations in which, for some reason, Larry would be isolated with him. In these imaginings, the young Viking was always the initiator.

"We should comfort each other. Let me hold you." Larry, handsome Larry, would go to Aaron and embrace him. Aaron would allow this without responding. It wouldn't be gay if he just stood still, no matter what Larry did.

But as days passed, his daydreams changed, becoming more reciprocal. Without preamble, Larry grabbed and kissed him. Aaron touched himself, imagining it was Larry. In his mind, the ghostwriter took control. Aaron was forced to respond despite himself. Meanings changed when minor adjustments were made.

Two weeks into the lockdown, Larry made a sly new suggestion during his usual morning phone call.

"My overhead is increasing. I have an idea benefiting both of us without affecting your financial contribution. Interested?"

Aaron held his breath.

"I'm listening."

"You have connections at the university. Some of your colleagues might be receptive to receiving forecasts."

"What do you mean?" Aaron guessed where this was heading.

"You could convince them to trust you with a couple of correct predictions I will supply. I'm expanding to include sources of secret essential supplies, like gloves and masks. You'd be surprised where they're hidden. There'd be many at the university who'd want to invest, I bet."

Aaron had a sudden lump in his stomach.

"But that would be illegal! I don't want to get into trouble."

The ghostwrite spoke in his softest croon.

"Professor. We have our secrets, you and I. It would be terrible if anyone found out."

What was Larry saying? Which secrets? The ghostwriting? The predictions? Or did Larry imply he would out him? Maybe he guessed Aaron was gay from some unwitting gay thing he did or said. He shuddered.

"Are you blackmailing me?"

"I wouldn't put it that way, Professor. I'm just saying I have to cover my overhead. Now, if you prefer to take another loan…"

Aaron had an image of the blond Viking gripping him by the wrists and pushing him down onto the floor. Then rotating him face-downward. He would sob and beat his head on the carpet in useless protest.

During the next agonizing hours, Aaron went back and forth over his choices. Give in to Larry? Or bail and be exposed? Unnerved and restless, he paced from room to room. Their conversation looped in his head. But then it occurred to Aaron that he had as much power over Larry as Larry had over him. If he went to the authorities, Larry would be in trouble. Why had he never thought of this before? Things really could be changed with minor additions. He acknowledged that his fantasies of being controlled by Larry were his own invention. His helplessness was his own invention, whether it concerned his sexuality or his career. Only his fear had prevented him from accepting the truth. But he had nothing to fear anymore. He called the ghostwriter back.

"Well, Larry, I have 'overhead,' as you call it, too. And you have as much to lose as I do if our secrets are revealed."

The ghostwriter jumped right back. "I'm not sure that's true, Professor. I'm not the one with an academic career. But I'm not a selfish man. I'm just trying to make a living. Nothing I've done is against the law."

Was that even correct?

"If you're exposed, you'd be under pressure to reveal your sources. That might make you very unpopular." Aaron won another suit—his favorite, spades—in the solitaire game he played whenever talking to Larry. "I suggest a partnership. If I find investors, I get a cut of their fees."

Aaron figured he would help others if he gave them the information Larry passed onto him from who-knows-where. It was, after all, accurate information. Not the fake treatments or fraudulent self-testing flooding the internet.

Besides, he vowed to give a portion of his profit to charity—fifty percent or maybe five percent. Something.

He would find a reason why meeting with Larry in person was essential business. Although he had more at stake than the ghostwriter, he had the upper hand now. If he gambled with his career, he would have enough power over Larry to be the initiator, if he chose to be. He would decide when the time came.

Aaron was in the riskier age group in the pandemic. He could die. The President could die. The Governor could die. If he was gay and survived, who would care anymore? COVID had changed the world. It freed him to be who he really was. The spoils went to those who saw advantages and took them. Sexual advantages, financial advantages, any advantages. He had nothing to lose.

CHAPTER 18
WHO SHALL BE SANE

The patches on his arms cracked and bled, but the older ones on his legs hardened like shells. Sometimes, he whacked his limbs with a stick to stop the itching. All it did was add purplish welts to the reddened areas.

Samuel lay on a raised mat of the cave. In his agony, he no longer cared what scuttled beneath the boards covering the ground. He became accustomed to the forest and the life forms that crawled, buzzed, slithered, flew, and swam within it. When he took up residence near the Nathan sisters, before they joined with the academics to form the Woodland Cooperative, it was the larger creatures that unnerved him: bears, mountain lions, wild boar. But except for Bucky, their tame bear, these kept their distance. Some microbe or parasite he couldn't even see caused his eczema.

First Woman examined his skin, then given him the directive.

"You must separate yourself from us until you heal. I don't think you're contagious, but just in case. You don't want to give whatever you have to the Nathan sisters. And you might, if they continue to take care of you. There are hunters' shacks outside the compound. Nothing fancy."

He almost sobbed. It felt like a punishment.

"Don't worry. I'll look for a cure and bring it to you." She extended a compassionate hand, then withdrew it before touching him. Instead, she tucked a loose strand of hair into the dark braid snaking around her head.

Samuel is what he called himself now instead of his former name, Rabbi Samuelson. He entered the forest to view the sinkhole that might have killed two members of his congregation, a woman and her four-year-old granddaughter. Although he didn't recall how, he wound up with the Nathan sisters, former members of his congregation in town, after losing his way, and maybe his mind. He didn't remember what twisted thought process led him to give up all that connected him to his former life—his synagogue, his apartment, services, even his dark suit. Now, with his untrimmed beard, long unkempt hair, thinner frame, and ragged clothing, he resembled his ancestors who lived in East European *shtetls*. Until the Holocaust wiped them all out.

When the sisters found him wandering in the forest in a pathetic state—exhausted, shoeless, dehydrated, lost—he was so weak they had to help him stand.

"Rabbi! What are you doing here?" They asked.

"I'm… lost." He gasped out his words.

"We care for injured animals. We can care for a lost rabbi, too."

They led him to a small cave near their larger one. At first, he was too disoriented to make sense of where he was or what had happened. He fell into a deep sleep.

The sisters were there when he awoke, standing in the rough entrance, back lit by the sun.

"We are gathering for a morning meal, if you wish to join us."

He followed them, too stunned to understand anything about his surroundings. Still in a daze, he ate and drank whatever they put before him. How, in the space of a few hours, did he change from a confident man who knew his place in God's universe to the bewildered soul in need of rescue? They saved him. They treated him with kindness. A tight coil within him unwound.

Raised by a stern, remote father and an embittered mother, he entered adulthood without having known a warm embrace. Until he met the sisters, he never questioned the orthodoxies he had been taught. Three times a day, he recited the *V'ahavta* prayer. It commanded him to love God with all his heart, soul, and might. It was aspirational. Nothing a human being could do in reality, he thought.

Nothing he could do. Yet, something the sisters did, caring for so many of God's creatures, including him.

They brought him food, water, and clothing suitable for the forest. Later, they brought him basic Jewish texts they acquired on their infrequent trips to town—the "JPS: *Tanakh*," the Hertz *Chumash*, a *Haggadah*, and others. When he wasn't helping them—figuring out how to build an oven from a leftover pile of bricks, repairing fencing— he concentrated on the pleasures of study. To his surprise, these turned into good years. The combination of outdoor labor, reading in his cave by candlelight, and praying with the sisters brought him into a balance he never experienced before.

Then the Cooperative formed. As its membership increased, a rag-tag group of dwellings filled in the area between the hut of two women leaders—Great Mother and First Woman, the cave of the sisters, and the compound of the academics. The new residences seemed little better than encampments for the urban homeless, but in a secluded wooded setting.

He formed a special bond with the two leaders. The grandmother was born Jewish, but neither she nor her granddaughter were observant. He took it as his duty to educate First Woman about Jewish practice. She listened with respect, but never joined him and the sisters for *Shabbat* meals or services. He found that this did not disturb him, as long as she showed up for her "lessons." Often the tables turned. A teaching from the *Torah* devolved into his personal problems, his loneliness, his low self-esteem, his wish to be better-liked. She became the teacher, repeating something Great Mother taught her, something from the book, "Roots of the Woods."

"If you act like you wish to be, you will become the way you act. If you act like people like you, you will become likable."

He thrived when he took her advice. Although she was at least twenty-five years younger than him, he attached himself to this part priestess, part witch, and part prophet. This young woman, who called herself First Woman and who refused to practice synagogue Judaism, cast a spell on him.

"Samuel. There are tubers in that mound. Can you dig them up?"

Somehow, she compelled him to desire her approval. If she requested that he chop wood or dig up tubers, for the Cooperative or for the sisters, he did so. Before he lived in the forest, he never worked with his hands. It frightened him to think that he was giving First Woman what he should give God. It frightened him to think First Woman wouldn't want what he had to give. Worse, that she would sneer at him for having feelings he couldn't control.

Yet, she treated him with gentleness, not appearing to notice the way he was drawn to her. Was he falling in love? Against his will? Was he ridiculous? The excruciating agony of his feelings worsened until the pain and itching of the eczema overtook it.

It began with a spot on the back of his knee. He paid no attention. As the spot spread, he must have unknowingly signaled his discomfort to First Woman, unless it was knowingly.

"Is something wrong, Samuel?" She was taller than him and bent to cast a worried look into his eyes.

"No… I mean, there's an irritation on my arms and legs."

First Woman showed concern. The wonder of her interest astonished him. Yet, because of the rash, she asked him to leave the compound. She wasn't abandoning him, she said. She promised to find a cure if he stayed in a shack just outside the boundary of the Cooperative. He'd still be nearby, a small comfort, but better than nothing.

Two days after his banishment to the shack, First Woman appeared again. She was carrying a jug filled with a brown liquid.

"This may help you, Samuel. Drink a quarter of it and moisten the patches of eczema with the rest."

He took the jug from her beautiful hands, wishing to touch just one of her fingers.

"Great Mother walked far to find the right mushrooms to brew for you. Besides clearing your skin, it may help you see."

"See what?" If only he knew how to make her want to linger.

"If it works, you can return to the compound," she said as she waved goodbye.

Once alone again, he gripped the jug where her hands held it, imagining her long fingers in his clasp. Following her instructions, he drank the required amount, gingerly peeled off his clothing, and poured the rest over his arms and legs. He remained naked, glad to be freed of the irritating scratchiness of fabric next to his skin.

For hours, he slept. The itching did not disturb him or jar him awake. The sun reached its pinnacle as he came to. For several minutes, he lay on his mat, more comfortable than he had been. Birds of several species tweeted their individualized songs. Frogs croaked back and forth. Insects buzzed and chirped. Leaves rustled. He heard the forest sounds before, letting them blend into the background, without listening to them. It astonished him that they harmonized, as if orchestrated.

When he went outside, the sights in the forest staggered him as well. He spent weeks in the Cooperative, surrounded by trees, without ever taking in their lush splendor. Now, each unique, beautiful leaf on each unique, beautiful tree sprang to his attention, thousands all at the same time. The undergrowth was a rich composite of greenery and wild flowers, separating and blending before his amazed eyes.

He began walking, naked and thirsty for more of God's remarkable creation. Every few feet he stopped to peer at a grass head or a slug inching its way across a bit of moss. Why didn't he bother to view such wonders before? With renewed energy, he made his way through the pathways that opened obligingly ahead of him.

Further and further he went, stopping to drink at creeks, then ascending up a rise, grabbing willing saplings to hoist himself upward. He came to a vaguely familiar spot, where the loose remnants of yellow forensic tape hung from tree trunks. He remembered. Ahead was the sinkhole, the destination he had been seeking when he entered the forest, and the last place he recalled being before the sisters found him.

He drew nearer to the chasm. Without warning, two figures rose out of it and floated above him, at the top of the rise. It was a woman and a girl. The woman was covered with scars.

"You are Edith and Eva, the two who were killed when the sinkhole formed." Samuel spoke in an even tone. It wasn't a surprise to see them. Somehow, he knew they would be there, where they belonged.

"Why are you scarred?"

"My transgression is written on my skin," the woman said.

"What is your transgression?"

"Failure to love the girl."

The girl was silent.

The scars transformed into letters. Samuel recognized c-h-e-s-e-d, Hebrew for love and kindness. The air shimmered. Grooves in the bark of trees, webs made by spiders, and the limestone layers in outcroppings were rearranging themselves to form words. They spelled out the *V'ahavta* — God's commandment to love. The prayer was present everywhere, spread over the entire fabric of the woods.

The rash on his arms and legs brightened and formed the words of his own transgressions. No compassion. Admiration without love. Obedience without gratitude. Rigidity. Envy. He was a failed spiritual leader who had not known how to love God. Slumping onto a log, he waited for the awful shame of it to diminish enough to permit him to walk.

He reached the shack before dark. The jug still contained some of the brew. He poured the last of it over his arms and legs. The rash faded before his limbs dried.

For three days, he thought about what he had experienced. Then First Woman came for her inspection. Samuel was clothed. He rolled up his sleeves and pants bottoms to show her his arms and legs. They were clear.

"Yes. The brew worked. You can come back to the cave. But you will need to wash the inside of the shack and your bedding."

Her loveliness made his chest swell. It was a new sensation.

"There is something I must tell you," he said.

Her concerned eyes stared into his.

"I'm in love with you. And I wish…"

She raised a hand to stop him.

"Don't. Please. It's impossible."

She smiled at him in a rueful, friendly way. Of course it was impossible. But part of seeing the truth was telling the truth, no matter how distressing.

"Ready, Samuel?"

"I'm not coming. I have work to do in town."

"Samuel. The virus is spreading in town. It's dangerous there."

"I know. But my congregants may need me. I can't abandon them at a time of adversity. And I need my congregants. They are my people, my family."

After a moment, she nodded, then sighed.

"Do you need me to show you the way?"

"No," he said. "I can find the way, now."

CHAPTER 19
WHO SHALL BE SERENE

In May 2020, the lockdown was still in effect. Rabbi Isaac had been furloughed after Rabbi Samuelson returned to his position. The pandemic and the subsequent lapse in membership dues necessitated cutting expenses. He gazed out the window at the gray, barren street. The bleak sky shed a dull light.

Loneliness and cabin fever set in. He counted the cracks in the plaster walls and watched ants crawl over the linoleum floor. There was nothing else to do. The pile of books on his nightstand had been whittled down. He watched the dregs on Netflix, the only movies left. No services or *Torah* studies needed preparing. Idleness made him antsy. He paced the living room, ten steps to one wall and ten steps back.

If only he had a girlfriend. But synagogue policy didn't permit clergy to date congregants. And what other opportunities were there to meet Jewish women in the small Indiana town? But now that was moot. Being unemployed meant he could date whoever he wanted.

The membership of the congregation included several attractive single women. He sifted through the possibilities. Martha. Rita. Hannah. He would have to choose. If one rejected him, he would try the other two. They were all equally attractive. He had no preference. He decided to ask them in alphabetical order. The first was Hannah. He sent her a text.

"Hi, Hannah. It's Isaac. You may already know they laid me off. That's bad news and good news. The good news is that I can ask you out. Would you like to have a virtual dinner with me?"

Too nervous to sit around waiting for her reply, he grabbed his keys. Even though drizzle had started and he only wore a T-shirt and shorts, he jogged around the block. How good it was to be outside. A few neighbors on the sidewalks, pushing strollers or walking dogs, wore masks, others didn't. No one carried an umbrella. He forgot to mask, but he kept the required social distance by running in the road. A few times he had to veer to the curb to allow a vehicle to pass.

The sight of other people heartened him. He tried not to stare at the women, at their bare legs pedaling bicycles or striding along the sidewalk. He looked at his phone. Nothing from Hannah, yet.

When he reached the front of his building again, his legs tingled with a pleasant tiredness. He knew he should obey the lockdown regulations by going back inside. But facing confinement in his apartment again after a few minutes of freedom was more distasteful this time than during his previous jogs.

He could violate regulations and go for a drive. No one enforced them, anyway. The only acceptable reasons for leaving one's residence were for essentials, like food and medicine. Now that he was no longer an employed rabbi, he didn't have to set an example. It didn't matter if a whisper campaign about him started.

He noticed his kayak standing against his garage unit wall.

Why not?

He muscled it onto the roof rack of his SUV and drove to the lake, parking at a chained-off boat ramp. Four other cars were in sight. A few other people were scattered somewhere along the lake trail or in the forest that abutted it. After pulling the kayak off the roof, he ducked under the chain, slid it into the water, and squeezed in. The drizzle stopped, and cool spring air raised goosebumps on his arms. He allowed the kayak to drift, paddling when he floated too near to shore. The prickles of worry about his text to Hannah smoothed into random sensual fantasies of anonymous women, their wondrous bodies.

A lazy hour went by. The current drove the kayak through a series of connected lakes. A flock of ducks forked off ahead of him. Gulls skimmed the water, seeking silver-backed fish. Dense pines lined the perimeter. As long as he was on the water, all the stress he experienced fell away. He kept his gaze on the metallic-colored lake.

Whenever he glanced at the trees, the back of his neck prickled, as if he had raised hackles. The last time he visited the state park, years before, he had a strange dream about being stranded on the tree tops. He awoke in the parking lot, in his car, in a panic. He drove back to town, unable to remember entering the woods or falling asleep.

It's just a bunch of trees, he said to himself. A modern man didn't believe in hauntings or the evil eye. Contemporary theology didn't deny science. It supplemented science. God couldn't be explained by science, but forests and nightmares could be. He guided the kayak away from the trees, but not so far away that someone might spot him on the lake.

For another few minutes, he glided along, until something faint caught his ear—a song, someone singing. Or a bird. He checked his phone to see if Spotify or Pandora had switched on. There was no signal. When he drifted a few yards further along, the singing became more distinct. It was a woman's voice. The melody was alluring, but the lyrics were unintelligible. They might not have been in English. Among the cryptic words, he thought he heard his name. His mind must have been taking disparate syllables out of context. Yet, as the song repeated, it became clear that it was his name.

Isaac. Isaac.

And his middle name, too.

Adam. Adam. Isaac. Adam.

He closed in on the source of the singing. It came from the forest, behind the nearest grove of pines. A slight clearing appeared ahead. His curiosity overcame his unease. He stepped out of the kayak and secured it on the shore. There was silence. He stood, waiting, tantalized. Then the singing started again, this time to his left. He pushed into the woods, using both hands to part the saplings,.

He groped his way toward the sound. Whenever he thought he was getting close, the singing seemed to retreat, leading him deeper into the forest. A breeze picked up, blowing leaves in front of his face, obscuring his vision. But the mysterious melody pulled him along. He still heard his name in the garbled lyrics. The singer seemed to call him, drawing him to her.

Turn around, he told himself, trying not to give in. Yet, he kept marching forward, no longer controlled by his will. Of their own accord, his feet stepped over logs and streams, moving him in the direction determined by the song. Bit by bit, he made out the lyrics.

Come to me, Isaac Adam. I wait for you.

A shaft of light ahead led the way. As he approached, the woods opened to a wide space. Through the leaves still swirling around his head, he saw glimpses of a woman, wearing a flowing garment, with long dark hair hanging loose. The song came from her, although her lips didn't move.

He halted several feet away, not knowing what to do.

"Here I am," he said.

Without warning, the breeze strengthened, pushing him forward, until he stumbled inches from the strange woman. She stood so close that her breath tickled his face, but she didn't back away. The breeze intensified into a wind, churning around the two of them. More leaves swept up into the spiraling gust. Its force increased. Objects were caught in the spin—twigs, acorns, pine needles, wild flower petals. Forest debris covered his eyes. The woman slammed against him, as the gust became gale-like, while the singing grew louder. The swirl widened, catching small forest creatures in its circular path—toads, spiders, grass snakes, wrens. Trees groaned, swaying dangerously. Everything in the vortex revolved, crashing against one another, spinning with increased rapidity, until with a final ecstatic burst, Isaac's eyes were uncovered, and looking upward, he saw the face of the sun casting hot, lustful rays down onto him. He fell, hitting his head.

When he awoke, he was in the kayak, paddling against the current. He tried to think. He had pulled into a clearing. That he remembered. After that, everything was blank, like the last time he visited the forest. It had a sedating effect on him. He must have laid down in the clearing and fallen asleep.

An hour later, he hoisted the kayak onto the roof rack and drove back to his apartment. Aside from a headache, his mood brightened.

He had gone to the lake to spend time in nature, kayaking and napping on the shore. He discovered the way to endure unemployment and the lockdown—drive out-of-town once in a while. Go to the countryside or the state park. Experience the beauty of God's creation, not just the four walls of his apartment.

Still, he felt a hollowness in his chest. He had to attempt to find a girlfriend, a companion, and soon. His sudden desire was urgent. It was unhealthy for a man in his early thirties to be alone. It meant he was unfinished, not a complete adult. Hadn't he taken a step in that direction? He didn't remember.

Thoughts jammed into his head that had only been dim concepts. A girlfriend. Another job in another synagogue. Then another idea. Maybe being a rabbi wasn't the only possibility. What about teaching? He had a degree in education. He loved children. Male teachers were always in demand in poor neighborhoods. More ways occurred to him to be a compassionate and ethical guide.

At night, he dreamed. A woman sang to him. He floated down a river on his back, with the sun overhead. When he awoke, he recalled his text to Hannah. How could he have forgotten? Had she responded? He had fallen asleep without looking.

"Hi, Isaac. I would love to have virtual dinner. I'll cook and leave a plate on your doorstep. Friday before services?"

He texted back right away.

"A bottle of wine will wait there for you. We can meet on Zoom."

It was arranged. If she didn't work out, he'd try Martha next.

He might be married in a year. He imagined the wedding, an image of a veiled bride in a flowing white gown, lifted in a chair while a crowd of friends danced around her. She would sing a song he couldn't place, but familiar, with lyrics calling his name.

In his excitement, he ran his fingers through his hair. It was unusually thick, now that hair stylists had closed their shops. Something was snarled in his curls. He untangled it.

How did an acorn find its way onto his head? His cautious fingers groped for other surprises. Pine needles. Twigs. Bits of fur. And most astonishing, a long strand of very dark hair.

CHAPTER 20
WHO SHALL BE HUMILIATED

Larry raised the periscope. He checked the perimeter of his property. Nothing but a couple of startled deer. No sheriff or FBI types nosing around, searching for the entrance to the bunker.

If the social fabric shredded itself during the pandemic, he was ready. He anticipated the end of civilization, whether from disease, war, or climate change, by purchasing a small bunker at the edge of the forest, originally designed in the 1950s as a nuclear shelter for county officials. He got it for a song. The large, damp room needed modernization and renovation. Condensation dripped down the concrete walls. Cracks spidered across the ceiling. But no one driving by would suspect the underground residence existed.

He'd made mountains of cash in the three months since the pandemic began by hacking into State Health Department emails and selling information before its public release until security experts closed the breach. Now, it was early April. Soon, there would be another pile to be made from people receiving the government relief money.

His skill in the art of persuasion convinced others to buy what they did not know they wanted. It depended on the personal touches he mastered—body language, facial expression, tone of voice, stance. Slight shifts in any of these at the right time swayed customers. Blunt instruments like texts, emails, and social media lacked the nuance he needed to succeed.

After he began isolating in the bunker, he spent his days watching both the news on TV and the view through the periscope. The entrance to the state park lay within its range. Vehicles entered, then exited a while later when realization dawned that the park had fewer resources than the town, now that the camp store closed.

Boredom walloped him. He thrived on interacting with others and on the charged up feeling like winning at poker when he convinced them to buy whatever he sold. A release of endorphins. A rush. A dismal let down might follow it during a dry spell, like now, when he had to maintain social distancing to be safe. It made him shake, as if he withdrew from a drug.

Just before his move to the bunker, when his apartment in town became too unsafe because of COVID-exposed tenants touching bannisters and elevator buttons, a letter appeared in his P.O. Box from the local office of the FBI. It requested him to make an appointment for a phone interview. His stomach contracted as if a clenched fist squeezed it. Did his source for the stash of N-95 masks implicate him? Had his hacking activities been discovered? Had one of his customers alerted the authorities?

Not that Larry thought he'd harmed anyone, even if he went around the law. He was an entrepreneur, doing what entrepreneurs did. Whatever people paid him for had actual value, unlike a scammer who traded in bogus things without worth, like false cures for the virus or fake information. Any product or service he sold had quality. If it didn't, he couldn't be convincing. If he sold information, the information was accurate. If he sold medical equipment, it worked as it should.

The bunker kept him safe from both the coronavirus and an FBI probe, leading to an arrest if he was unlucky or careless. But after a mere two weeks, the reinforced concrete walls and low ceilings encased him like an iron lung in the days of the polio epidemic. He wasn't the type to be caged up or alone. But he wouldn't act like one of those fools who risked all by going to a crowded beach.

Then the governor closed the state park. Too many people spent time on the trails without six feet of physical distance. A procession of vehicles exited, after being chased out by the rangers. They placed chains across the park entrance. Larry just had to drive his ATV straight there from the back of his property, avoiding the official gateway, if he wanted to get in.

He knew the forest and its permanent inhabitants. He'd explored its many trails and roads often since acquiring the bunker. Well into the interior, there was some sort of community. It called itself "Woodland Cooperative." A bunch of nuts living off the grid, he speculated. He'd never been interested.

Now, though, if he joined them, he could wait out both the pandemic and whatever legal trouble he might be in. He wouldn't be alone or shut-in. After the danger passed, when travel became unrestricted again, he'd hop a flight to one of the English-speaking countries that didn't have an extradition treaty with the U.S. He had enough money to live well anywhere.

But who knew how long a return to normal would take? He wondered if his skills would rust if he didn't use them for months. The so-called Cooperative was his best bet for waiting out the period of isolation and for keeping his sales tactics from drying up.

His mood lifted. Another challenge lay ahead—persuading the Cooperative members to let him live among them. If they were tree-hugging weirdos, he'd be one, too. He would sell his best product. Himself. His appeal. His attractiveness.

In his ATV, he drove the long dusty gravel route within the forest to the crude "gate" that marked the entrance to the Cooperative—an enormous tree trunk felled across the road. The rangers either hadn't found the obstruction or the Cooperative lay outside of park boundaries.

A sign posted on an upright limb branching from the trunk read "Woodland Cooperative. Leader: First Woman." He had seen it before. Beneath it, a second sign was new to Larry.

"No Trespassing. This is a private community. If you wish to visit or join, you must wait outside for 14 days after any exposure or symptoms of illness. First Woman, our leader, will find you and carry out an interview if you choose to wait."

Larry parked the ATV to the side, then climbed over the log. He had self-isolated for over two weeks and was symptom free. That's what he'd tell anyone he met. He walked into the Cooperative's territory.

About two miles in, the gravel road changed to a winding, rutted, dirt lane. He hiked uphill for an hour or so, using his compass to determine the general direction—southward, into the hillier part of the state that hadn't been leveled by the glacier thousands of years ago.

The forest became denser. A rock landed at his feet, then another. One from the left and one from the right. His breath froze. Looking both ways, he saw nothing but closely packed trees. Another rock whizzed by his ear. He thought of taking the handgun he always carried from his pocket, but there was nothing to shoot at. No movement. Instead, he held his hands palms-out and took a step backwards. Another rock thudded onto the ground on the spot where he had just stood.

An obvious message. Go back the way you came. Once he turned around, the rock-throwing ceased. He made it back to his ATV, all the while having the impression of being watched.

Back in the bunker, he obsessed about his experience. So they don't want me there. Fuck them. Then he had a competing thought. Fuck me if I have to stay in here another minute. The Cooperative people proved to be hard-nosed. He would have to use his complete array of powers to gain their trust. This wasn't the end of his plan. It was the first shot. His confidence grew. A female leader? Women were easy for a handsome man like him.

To begin with, he would have to obey the rule posted on the sign by pitching a tent, and enduring the two week wait until First Woman, whoever that was, showed up. He'd tried short-cutting that demand and almost got himself stoned. It took another twenty-four hours of scheming and insomnia to acknowledge he had no other choice. His bunker was unbearable. It was meant to be a temporary shelter, not a permanent residence. He packed his camping gear, provisions for fourteen days, and took off.

For two weeks, he lay in his tent, hiked short distances, bathed in a nearby stream, and cooked on his camp stove. He read books and wrote in a journal. The lack of internet service or cell phone signal took getting used to. The outdoors oppressed him less than the bunker, but the wait was lonely and depressing. It reminded him of why he disliked chess. The long delay between moves maddened him.

He clenched his teeth. Two weeks in the forest without human company was preferable to who-knew-how-long in either of his other two residences. He would stay the course. It tested his fortitude.

On the morning of the fourteenth day, Larry stood beside the log, in the middle of the road. A speck appeared in the distance. Shading his eyes with his hand, he made out a female advancing toward him. Closer up, he saw a young woman who might have been about twenty, with a dark loose braid wound around her head, wearing an oversized faded t-shirt and jeans. Her feet were bare. Was this the leader? She stopped about three yards away from him, on her side of the log.

"I'm First Woman."

"Hi. I'm Larry. Is First Woman your actual name?" He smiled.

"It's what I'm called. Our leader is my grandmother, but I speak for her."

He had learned to allow his good looks to lay the groundwork with women. If they leaned toward him or widened their eyes, he inferred their interest. First Woman did neither.

"Are you here to inquire about joining us or for some other reason?"

It might have been a trick question. His answer was ambiguous.

"I just thought… If I learned about your group. Maybe you need something?"

"We are self-sufficient. We have what we need. Whatever we don't have, we don't need."

First Woman crossed her arms over her chest. She was being standoffish. Such women took patience. They couldn't be chased. They had to be enticed. He took a half-step back to encourage her to move toward him. Instead, she took a bag out of her back pocket.

What was it? Without thinking, he stepped forward again, trying to see.

"You did as we wanted by isolating on the other side of the log for fourteen days. You don't appear to have symptoms. That's good. But you violated our rules by entering our property despite our 'No Trespassing 'sign."

"Well, I..." He trailed off, unable to deny the truth in what she said.

"There has to be freedom from suspicion on our side if you want a complete interview. Not respecting our sign creates distrust among our members."

"Distrust of what? That I have evil intentions? I don't. Not at all." His hand cut through the air, as if to brush away any doubt.

She tossed him the bag.

"Please remove the contents," she said.

"What's this?" Inside was some sort of lumpy, reddish fruit.

"You can leave right now. But if you wish to continue our conversation and find out more about us, I will require you to eat it while I watch. It will give you severe diarrhea for three days. You will be very weak. I wouldn't advise it if you think you have the virus."

He stared at her, cocking his head.

"You're joking, right?"

"I don't joke. It will show you can be trusted. Please eat it or toss it back and leave."

"But..."

"You have to decide now."

He turned the fruit in his hand and sniffed it. A voice in his head shouted, "Don't."

"How do I know it's not a poison?"

"It is a poison. But it shouldn't kill you."

He looked it over again.

"Is this some kind of witchcraft?"

"There are those who believe I'm a witch. I have to get back. Eat it right away, if you're going to."

He read her attitude as not caring whether he left or stayed. He heard a buzzing in his head. Or was it flying insects, devouring pollen and boring into trees? His hand shoved the fruit into his mouth. He bit off a tart chunk, then another. When he finished, she turned.

With her back to him, she said, "Drink plenty of water. You might wish to strip and stow away any of your camping gear that is not washable."

She disappeared up the road.

As soon as she left, Larry shuddered. What had he done? The woman wasn't his type, yet she cast a spell over him. It was the only explanation. Never would he have eaten a poisonous fruit if he was in his right mind. Dread blackened his thoughts.

An hour passed before the cramping began. It brought him to his knees. Boiling liquid spewed from him. He struggled out of his soiled clothing and shoes, throwing them into the brush. Every few minutes, a new steaming eruption occurred. Crippling pain doubled him over, stealing his breath. For three days and nights, he sobbed for mercy during the hot gushing spasms.

"Forgive me! Forgive me!"

In the middle of the forest, alone, with no hope of medical treatment, with swarms of black flies relishing what repulsed every other woodland being except the turkey vultures circling overhead, with the trees appearing to lean away in disgust and the clouds scattered by the rising stench, who was there to forgive him? His customers? The judge who would hand down his sentence if he were arrested? The Lord above?

In his imagination, he implored First Woman—she who caused his ordeal. Her stern face hovered over him, listening to his pleas with indifference, unless he was having a delirium dream.

By the third day, he lay whimpering on the road in his own filth.

Finally, it ended. Too drained to stand, he reached the creek by slithering and crawling and plunged in. Afterwards, shivering, he stumbled to the tent, zipped himself into the sleeping bag, and dozed off.

When he awoke, something wrapped in a cloth had been left next to him with a note.

"Eat these for strength."

Six brown nuts lay inside. If his energy didn't return, he wouldn't survive. He had to take the chance. After eating the nuts, he fell back to sleep.

At some point, while his eyes were still closed, the voice of First Woman drifted to him.

"You are purged of all contaminants, including any virus in your system. If you wish to join us, you must first drive to the park entrance, where you will get a cell signal. We have taken photographs and messaged copies to you."

His eyes wouldn't open. The voice floated closer. The woman's breath blew into his left ear.

"One of our members has identified you. If you decide to leave and tell anyone about us, we know who'd be interested in seeing the photos. We don't wish to be overwhelmed with applicants wanting temporary protection from the pandemic."

Later, he awoke. He had just enough stamina to find fresh clothing and climb into the ATV. Had First Woman actually said those nightmarish words? At the entrance, he picked up a signal. His newest message contained the sickening photos. Quickly, he clicked delete.

He could have driven to the bunker next, or to his apartment in town, or to the FBI office, or back to the log. Instead, as he sat stunned, with the mortifying photos blocking all other thought, the steering wheel jerked to the right. His exhausted mind was aware of the ATV making a U-turn back into the forest.

CHAPTER 21
WHO BY WATER

It began in January 2020, when hospitals still allowed three visitors for patients in the ICU. Marty was dying of a weak heart complicated by regular pneumonia, not the coronavirus type. Ruth stayed at his bedside, holding his skeletal hand, watching the peaks on the vital signs display get further apart. Nancy, his mother, sat in her wheelchair on the other side of the bed, holding his other hand. Issac, their son, showed up, but Leah, their daughter, would have been the fourth visitor, if four were allowed. Marty slept as the hours crept by.

Then, he opened his eyes, swiveled his head toward her, and spoke in a clear voice, just as he did before he became ill.

"Promise me you'll take care of my mother."

He willed himself into a last fierce alertness. His eyes laser beamed into hers. What could she say? What kind of person denied the last request of a husband of fifty years? Her left hand, the one that held Marty's, perspired. The gold band around the third finger reminded her—you are married. Don't let your husband down.

Nancy waved her free hand, indicating that she could damn well take care of herself.

She heard herself say, "I promise I will take care of your mother, Marty. Yes. Of course."

He resumed the hard business of dying. His rattling breath gurgled to a stop. Neither said a final "I love you." They were the practical sorts, not given to easy romanticism. Yet, he wounded her. His last words concerned his mother, not her. That said it all.

When Marty's father Abraham died, they moved into Nancy's three-story antique-filled house. When a stroke disabled the older woman, and she could no longer manage stairs, they needed to sell the place. None of Marty's brothers wanted to live in a musty old home requiring maintenance and updating. Strangers bought it.

Since Isaac and Leah had grown up and moved away, a smaller place didn't matter to Ruth and Marty. They chose a two-bedroom rental, with the extra bedroom for Nancy, so they could save their money for cruises. Seventeen of them were under their belts. They spent many hours perusing colorful cruise catalogs. Nancy went with them until she needed total care.

"I guess you'll have to cruise on your own," Marty said. He retired from his job as a University advisor to be his mother's full-time health aide. Given the decades-long animosity between the two women, it made more sense than Ruth taking that role.

"Yeah, sure. Cruise by myself. That'll be a lot of fun."

She and Nancy resented each other from the time both showed up at the wedding wearing white, although Nancy claimed the color of her dress was ivory. Each vied to be Marty's favorite. Although she would never say so, Ruth took satisfaction in the silencing of the older woman's sharp tongue, after the stroke robbed her of speech. She tried to hide her jealousy of her husband's increased devotion to Nancy.

What did she expect? Marty would never dump his mother in a nursing home. And he was the only brother old enough to retire. Unless Isaac or Leah came over for a couple of hours, Ruth and Marty couldn't even go out for dinner, something they used to do once a week.

As for privacy, if they managed to be alone for five minutes, the sound of Nancy banging her cane on the floor summoned Marty. Much to Ruth's chagrin, he wound up sleeping on a cot in Nancy's room in case she needed a cup of chamomile tea or an extra blanket during her sleepless nights. Ruth's only comfort was knowing the older woman wouldn't last forever. She would win by outliving her.

The three endured each other for five years. The side of Nancy's face that worked settled into a permanent scowl. Marty's shoulders rounded. The conflicting demands of the two women, neither of whom he made happy, wore him down. Ruth churned with resentment and snapped at her husband over the least thing.

"You bought white rice, Marty. You might as well have bought a bag of sugar. We eat brown rice, the healthy kind. If you weren't so busy pleasing Nancy, you might have remembered."

"I work hard to please my mother because you can't spare a moment to be kind to her. She knows you don't want her here."

Nancy, who heard every word from her room, banged the floor. She didn't need words to make her side of the argument known.

The five years ended when a series of calamities struck in quick succession. Until December 2019, they lived in comfort, if not in peace, in an agreeable neighborhood. Because of the combination of Nancy's social security, Marty's pension, and Ruth's income from her job, they were secure.

In three months, everything changed. Marty died. The clothing store that employed Ruth in the Lingerie Department furloughed her. For twenty-five years, she fitted women who had uneven breasts with bras and helped others choose pricy pink negligees for their wedding nights. Then, the owner of their apartment building succumbed to the coronavirus, and through some legal loophole, the tenants were given immediate eviction notices. The downward thrust of the stock market wiped out that source of income. The money from the sale of Nancy's house had long ago disappeared into the pockets of the brothers. All they had left was Nancy's social security.

In the future, unemployment and other money from the government would be available. But by May, Ruth was desperate. Leah had the virus, and Isaac lived in a tiny studio apartment. Ruth rented a storage unit, had all the belongings and furniture moved into it, piled Nancy into her car, and rented a room at Motel 6 for a week. She and Nancy glared at each other across the narrow space between their queen beds.

"If it weren't for my promise to Marty, you know where you'd be right now? In a nursing home, where everyone has the virus. You'd be coughing your lungs out."

With her good hand, Nancy reached for the glass of water on the nightstand and threw it at Ruth.

"Bitch!" Ruth shrieked.

Once a day, Ruth masked up and went to the Seven Eleven down the road to buy containers of yogurt and jello for Nancy, who needed soft food, and chips and protein bars for herself. At least the motel room had a coffee maker. But the situation was untenable. A friend mentioned a Jewish group in the state forest, called the Woodland Cooperative, that took in strangers. Perhaps they would help. They were about a mile down the logging road nearest the forest entrance.

What else was there to do? No one invited them to use their guest room now that a lockdown was imposed. Once again, Ruth loaded Nancy into her car with a few packages of Depends, wipes, changes of clothing, some food, water, and a collapsable wheel chair. As instructed, Ruth drove into the forest and, after getting lost and wasting two hours, backtracked until she found the logging road. About a mile in, a tree trunk lying across the road stopped her. Two signs were posted on it. One said, "Woodland Cooperative. Leader: First Woman." She had been told to expect that.

The second sign disheartened her. Visitors who wished to join had to quarantine themselves at the log for two weeks. First Woman would come every day to check on them.

Seven or eight vehicles parked wherever they could fit among the trees. A couple with flat tires looked abandoned. As soon as Ruth drew up, a man looking her own age stepped out of a nearby rv. He approached the car. Ruth rolled down her window an inch.

"There's three ahead of you," he said.

"What?"

"Three of us have brought a parent here. The nursing homes are full of virus. We want the Cooperative to take them in. But you're fourth in line."

"You mean they won't take us all?" Ruth looked at Nancy. The eyebrow that worked raised.

"Just saying. You're in fourth place." He returned to the rv.

Ruth noticed that there was a single old-looking person slumped in each of two other cars. Was it possible that they were on their own, with no one to take care of them? It was getting dark. She and Nancy would sleep in their car.

Early the next morning, the same man placed a wheel chair in front of the log, then carried an elderly person out from the rv, seated her in the chair, and covered her with a quilt. He returned to the rv and started it. Ruth honked her car horn. They both rolled down their windows.

"Where are you going?"

"To work at the Fire Department. I'm essential."

"Are you leaving your mother here alone?"

"First Woman will help her. Remember—your mother is fourth." He drove off.

Soon after, two other people drove up. Each put a wheel chair in front of the log and carried one of the elderly people who had spent the night in the forest over to it. They were also covered with quilts, then left there. No one said a word to Ruth.

Ruth following their lead, wheeling Nancy to the log and stood next to her. Her mother-in-law was the only alert elder. She scowled up at Ruth.

"To answer the question you can't ask, no, I don't know what's going on. So don't bite my head off. I'm playing this by ear."

After waiting until the sun was half-way up the sky, Ruth saw someone coming toward them. It must be this First Woman person. The most striking thing about her was the thick dark braid wound around her head. Otherwise, she looked like a typical camper, wearing an oversized T-shirt and jeans. The line-up of elders, all asleep, did not seem to surprise her. She addressed Ruth.

"The Woodland Cooperative is full. We can't admit anyone else. I'm sorry."

It appalled Ruth. She dragged herself and Nancy here for nothing.

"What about those three?"

"It's not possible for us to admit them."

Nancy tugged at Ruth with her good hand. If Ruth read her expression correctly, she wanted Ruth to keep trying. Ruth was near tears.

"Look. We're exhausted. I've lost my job. I'm sixty, too young for social security, and my unemployment hasn't started yet. I'm out of money. We're evicted. We have no place to go. Please."

"I'm sorry." First woman had a compassionate expression, but she didn't relent. Without a glance at the others, she walked back up the road.

For a long moment, Ruth stood there, stunned. How could the Woodland Cooperative allowed five helpless human beings to remain at the log unassisted? What monsters! If Ruth owned a gun, she knew what she would do.

She considered. The others left their parents there. It would serve Nancy right if she left her there, too. And she might have, if it weren't for her promise to Marty. You didn't break a deathbed promise. Not unless you wanted even worse luck than Ruth already had.

With a sigh, she loaded Nancy back into the car. She had no idea what to do or where to go. She drove through the forest with no plan. The road twisted upwards. Nancy kept tugging at her sleeve, but Ruth batted her hand away. She had no patience for her at the moment.

She considered her options. There weren't many. Cram themselves into Isaac's studio. Live in the car in another part of the forest. Stay in a homeless shelter in town. Sell the furniture in storage and rent a cheap roach-infested hovel. All were dangerous or despicable.

Nothing lay ahead but dense pines. They passed an orange cone. Ruth thought she had seen it before. Maybe they were going in circles. The gas gauge registered a hair from the red. There wasn't anything to do but keep going, hoping to stumble upon the forest entrance and head back to town while the car had enough gas. They'd wind up with Isaac, but three people in one room would be a stop-gap solution until something better turned up.

Nancy kept up the annoying pokes and nudges. Ruth kept pushing her back toward the passenger door.

"Quit it. How can I think if you keep prodding me like that?"

The road reached its highest elevation, and the trees thinned. They were on top of a ravine, overlooking a river.

Nancy began thumping the roof with her cane.

"What? Do you have to toilet? Is that it?"

Ruth just thumped harder.

"No. I don't know what to do. Stop thumping the roof. You'll damage it."

Nancy started poking again. Ruth reached her limit. Taking one hand off the steering wheel, she pushed Nancy with force, smashing her into the passenger door. Furious exhalations whistled through Ruth's teeth. A few seconds later, Nancy struggled back into an upright position and, without warning, hit Ruth in the face with her cane, cutting her forehead. Blood flowed into Ruth's eyes.

"Damn you!"

Ruth's foot stomped down on the accelerator. She turned and punched Nancy hard on the bad side of her head. The older woman slumped in her seat. Ruth tried to wipe the blood from her eyes. She couldn't see the road. Snapping sounds were inside her ears, unless it was saplings breaking. Her head hit the car roof. Nancy was sideways. What had she done?

As the car careened off the cliff and fell toward the river, Ruth apologized.

"Oh, my God. I didn't mean it. I don't know what came over me. I'm so sorry."

CHAPTER 22
WHO SHALL DIE

In the distance, they heard three bursts. *Pop! Pop! Pop!* It was hunters getting closer.

The weekly meeting of the Woodland Cooperative was in progress. Fifteen uneasy members listened. They sat at two picnic tables and on stumps and logs scattered about the clearing. The younger members, all in their early twenties, guarded the access road leading into the compound. First Woman stood. Her dark braid hung down her back. An oversized T-shirt draped over her bulge. Great Mother, now blind and silent, sat next to her.

Everyone had the same thought. Food shortages in town brought more hunters into the forest. At some point, the dwindling population of deer would vanish. And there would be more intrusion into Cooperative property.

First Woman resumed her speech.

"Five people are waiting at the entrance of the access road. They understand they have to quarantine there for two weeks in case they are infected. But we don't know if they're maintaining social distance from each other."

Among the fifteen present were the two newest members, a single man, Larry, and a young widower, Simon. The Bergs, with their toddler son, Calen, sat together at one table. The Nathan sisters were across from them. A sub-group at the other table was dominated by Frank, the former professor.

"I have a report from the members guarding the road. The new arrivals are two groups. A woman of about sixty with her ninety-year-old mother. And three elderly people, also in their nineties, who belong in nursing homes. Their families might show up once or twice a day to take care of them. They dumped them there, thinking being in the forest is better than chancing infection in an old-age facility."

A communal gasp arose.

"Do they think we're a COVID-19-free nursing home?" Larry asked.

First Woman put protective hands on her stomach.

"Because Samuel went back to town, we might be able to accommodate one extra healthy, able person at our present level of resources. But if none of the five are contagious, and we permit them all in, it means we would have to ration food. And we have no way of caring for anyone who needs assistance."

"What if more show up after that?" Jenny Berg looked down at her son as she spoke. She worried about having enough for him to eat.

Simon raised his hand. He took charge of the cultivated areas of the forest. "It won't be possible to expand the gardens unless we do some clear-cutting."

Murmurs arose at this suggestion. It was against Cooperative principles to remove trees. They were stewards of the woods. If more farm land was the answer, it would mean leaving the forest.

"The goats don't produce enough milk for us now. It's fortunate that the hens are laying. As long as Bucky keeps predators away."

Jenny brought the discussion back to the arrivals. "If we admit the mother and daughter, we'll be one over. But at least the daughter would take care of her mother."

Her husband Leo spoke up. "Taking care of an elderly person is a full-time job. Neither would make a contribution to the Cooperative. They would be drains on our resources."

"Like Calen?" Someone asked. No one followed with," like Great Mother?"

Frank stood up before the discussion got ugly.

"I remember my parents talking about bomb shelters in the 1950s. The owners often armed to keep out the hordes wanting in, if bombing started. This may be our situation now. We have a hidden, infection-free place to live in together. But now the hordes are finding us. We have to decide what to do."

First Woman turned to him. "It's worse than that, Frank. If we don't take in the old ones and their families stop showing up, they'll die on our doorstep."

"That's not our responsibility," Larry said. "Besides, once there's a vaccine, the virus won't be a problem. The hordes will disappear."

"It might be months away. Even years." Simon said.

Several people spoke at once. Morality collided with survival. Let others in, and they threatened the existence of the Cooperative. Keep others out and bear the responsibility for what happens to them.

"Great Mother will meditate on what to do. Let's adjourn for now."

They rose. Everyone knew that First Woman's grandmother had visions. They trusted whatever she came up with. Her prophetic abilities always kept the Cooperative intact. She had the foresight to suggest felling a tree across the access road and putting up the "No Trespassing" sign. When news of the virus reached the colony, she decreed the two-week wait for newcomers wishing to join. Abandoned vehicles and tents on the far side of the log provided shelter for those who didn't have accommodations of their own.

After the meeting, Edith and Eva returned to the hut that had been their home since Eva's grandmother brought her there as a small child. The older woman had changed greatly since arriving as the victim of her deceased husband. She had morphed into a healer, a visionary, and the leader of the Cooperative, although her granddaughter still spoke for her. She would have been unrecognizable to her friends and acquaintances back in the town.

The first thing Eva did was to give her grandmother a meal— berries, bread made from wild wheat, smoked fish—knowing she needed nourishment before a trance robbed her of awareness, perhaps for many hours. She lit candles to take her through the night, then sat with her on their mats in a lotus position and waited.

Nothing would begin before Edith expressed her doubts. They talked. None of the people at the log were in good shape. Four of the five were disabled. If their families abandoned them, pressure would grow on the Cooperative. The more compassionate members would either try to care for them, and the many others who followed, or face moral devastation. Even if healthier people showed up, they carried the risk of infection. The forest couldn't sustain a larger group.

Eva directed her focus on what mattered most—her own swelling womb. Edith put a hand on her granddaughter's bulge. Both breathed deeply, imagining each inhalation pulling air from the upper atmosphere down into their bodies and circling inside them before being exhaled back to the heights. As dusk transformed to darkness, and nothing was visible beyond the three candle flames, Edith floated a vivid picture into Eva's mind of the room that was hers before she came to the forest. She saw herself as a small child picking up each of her belongings—a doll, a ball, a bag decorated with unicorns. Then the girl she had been spun around and reached for something on a higher shelf—a Noah's ark. Tiny figures of Noah and his family shared the ark with two bears, two elephants, and two tigers. Two birds and two monkeys sat on the red wooden roof. The solemn little girl handed Eva the ark, then vanished. For several hours, she sat with the toy in her hands, waiting for Edith to convey its meaning.

All night, she drifted between sleep and wakefulness. Still clutching the ark, she heard Edith's voice over her right shoulder.

You must choose. The past or the future.

By the time the last candle sputtered into a rising tail of smoke, she understood her grandmother's plan. When she looked down, her cupped palms no longer held the ark. At that precise moment, she felt the quickening, the flutter of the new life within her. Now her hands cupped her bulge. She made her terrible choice.

At the next meeting, First Woman spoke to the group. Her gentle tone had a harsher ring than usual.

"The only way for the Cooperative to be safe is to go across the big lake to the deeper woods and find a new, hidden spot. You can rebuild someplace distant from the shore, where you won't be seen. There are no trails there. You'll be very hard to find."

"What about the old people at the log?" Jenny's voice quivered.

"I'll tell their families we can't admit them. I'll make sure they'll be okay."

She gave Jenny a hard look. The younger woman blinked, leaning back in her seat, swallowing her next question. First Woman waited. No one spoke. They wouldn't challenge her when she conveyed the authority conferred on her by Great Mother.

"Leo. You're a carpenter. You must guide everyone in constructing a raft that can take the entire group, including the goats and hens and Bucky, to the other side. You must hurry. Frank is right. The hordes are coming, and the virus with them," she said. "You must sail at night, when the outsiders can't see you."

Once Leo began organizing the raft-building, Eva walked up the access road. The straightforward part of the plan was in place. Her grandmother's voice stayed with her, whispering in her ear. *Choose. Choose.* In her peripheral vision, she saw the tail of smoke that came from the candle, still there, drifting around her head like the familiar voice. Great Mother sent it to guide her.

As she approached the log, five figures lined up across the road. Four were in wheel chairs. Had they waited all day for her to come? She nodded at the youngest, the only one standing.

"I'm First Woman."

The squat, gray haired woman seemed to be the caretaker of the older woman beside her. "I'm so exhausted. My only obligation is to my mother-in-law. But I can't let the others starve or sit in their own mess. I'm the only one here who helps them, most of the time. I'm doing the work their families should be doing." She was a senior-citizen herself. Tears ballooned on her lower lids.

"Take your mother home. The Cooperative is no longer accepting new members. I'm sorry."

The daughter's expression changed to outrage. "I'm sixty. Too young for social security. I lost my job. I lost my home. We have nowhere else to go. Take us. Please."

"I'm sorry. I can't..."

Nodding toward the other three, the daughter said, "What about them? Are you admitting them?"

"It's not possible. Can I help you load your mother and her wheel chair into your car?" First Woman pushed the mother to the vehicle before the daughter objected.

As the two drove away, First Woman walked back to the remaining three. They were sleeping in their chairs, one with her head thrown back, mouth agape, and the other two drooped forward, with their heads almost touching their knees.

The past or the future.

She sighed. What were their families thinking? Is dying in the forest from the weather or starvation or a predator more merciful than dying of the virus? Were they so confident the Cooperative would take care of their parents? She had to use Simon's camper—the one he abandoned when he joined, still parked near the log. The keys were hidden in the wheel well.

The three elders would fit on the bed installed in the back of the camper. But they had to be lifted. Eva considered the possibility of miscarrying if she lifted them by herself.

"I'm choosing the future, Bubbe. But I need your help while I take care of the past just this once."

She waited, willing her words to flow to Great Mother's ears. It must have happened. A thick branch crashed down, landing at her feet. It brought a length of strong vine down with it.

"Thank you, Bubbe," she said.

After wrapping one of the frail elders in a blanket from the camper, First Woman wheeled her over to the rear hatch. Next, she wound the vine around the blanket, and, from a position inside the camper, pulled the elder onto the bed. She did the same with the other two. It was safer to pull a weight than lift, she hoped. The three did not stir when she bumped them in. Perhaps they were already comatose, near death, or even dead.

Eva drove the camper to the official forest entrance. It had just reopened. She parked and stood near the still empty guardhouse. It wasn't a long wait. A car pulled up. The driver rolled down his window after tying on a mask.

"Do you have a phone?" Eva stood several feet away.

"Yes," he said. "Is there a problem?"

"Yes. I need you to call 9-1-1. There are three elderly people in the camper over there in terrible shape. Please request an ambulance."

While the driver talked to the dispatcher, she slipped away. It was a long walk back to her hut. She needed sleep. For the second time, she felt the fluttering. The future she carried within her seemed unharmed. As she advanced up the road, she noticed the tail of smoke from the last breath of the candle lit the night before. It moved ahead of her, leading the way, beckoning, urging her on, billowing into the rough shape of her grandmother. From that point on, Eva knew she had to do whatever was necessary to put the past behind her.

For the next two days, she rested in the hut on the mat next to her grandmother. She lay on her back with her hands on her bulge, thinking. The five-year experiment in communal living was in jeopardy. If the virus didn't dissipate, more outsiders would bombard them. It would be safest to move to the other side of the lake. That would buy time. Sooner or later, the group would be found. There would be a split. Frank and his group would want to arm. In time, some larger group with more lethal weapons would overcome them. The rest would wind up enlarging their numbers until the virus caught up with them or their communal lifestyle was compromised. She envisioned this unspooling as if it was a movie projected onto the ceiling of the hut.

When she rejoined the group, the raft was ready.

"We must make three trips. Most of us can fit on the first crossing. Then the Nathan sisters with the goats, hens, and Bucky. Last, our provisions." Leo had his hands on his hips, surveying the construction.

First Woman stared straight at him. "Leave tonight. I'll finish up here and follow you with Great Mother in the dinghy."

"Follow us?" He didn't expect an answer. The Cooperative members knew First Woman had secrets.

"Leo, you must lead the group until I catch up with you. There will be confusion. It's difficult to start over."

"Any problems at the log?'

"I turned the new arrivals away. But if I went back, there would be a new batch by now."

She returned to her hut to pack. She wished she still had the bag with unicorn decorations. If it hadn't been taken from her during her only visit to the town when she was sixteen, it would be over a quarter-century old. It even appeared in her vision from the past. A different bag, created in the woods from hides, could be filled with items for the future. Candles. Matches. Clothing. A few biscuits. "Roots of the Woods." She would have to carry her grandmother on her back.

That night, after the last crossing by the group, she slipped the bag and her grandmother into the dinghy. First, she took out the matches. She needed them to light the torch she had brought from the hut. Then she set each dwelling on fire. They reminded her of the occupants, how lost they had been when they joined, what she had given them, how the forest helped them find themselves. The only one she couldn't bear to torch was her own hut, where she had been raised long before the Woodland Cooperative existed.

The conflagration would be visible from the log. It would discourage newcomers. Yet, there wouldn't be much damage to the forest. It was May. Too much moisture remained in the undergrowth to provide tinder for a raging blaze.

The fire provided enough light to row the dinghy across the lake. She pulled into shore about a half-mile downstream from the raft. This was the part of her plan that could go wrong. The future depended on her doing it the right way. Edith stayed in the boat. Eva would do the rest by herself. The fluttering grew stronger. She was being kicked in the ribs, as if the future told her to hurry.

When she neared the encampment, she lit the candle. Everyone was on the ground, asleep on mats. A few stirred, saw it was her, and went back to sleep. Where were the Bergs? She found them, stretched out with Calen between them, at the edge of the gathering. First Woman blew out the candle, bent over, and picked up the toddler.

Jenny lifted her head.

"It's okay. I have him," First Woman said.

Jenny murmured and fell back to sleep. Calen never woke. He slept on First Woman's shoulder. He would grow up to be her child's companion, a safe-guard in case everyone else was wiped out. She glided back to the dinghy and lay the boy on a folded blanket in Edith's lap. If she rowed hard, she would put a good distance between the dinghy and the raft before dawn. Then she would find a place for them to hide in the forest. She pictured a spot in a huge hollowed out tree trunk, in the densest part of the woods, unspoiled by any previous human intrusion, protected by a thick tree canopy and nature's guardians of the wild—snakes, ticks, poison ivy. These Edith could help her tame.

She and Edith were the past. She would care for the future until the future took care of itself. She was responsible for stealing a child and leaving elders for someone else to save. One day, there would be punishment for what she had done. She betrayed the trust of the Bergs and the group. The forest would determine her fate. It wouldn't take much. A nip she didn't even feel from a bat, a spider, or a mosquito. An inability to find the medicinal roots to counteract the venom. Or a careless moment when rock climbing during a foraging expedition. Or a quick movement startling a hunter who would mistake her for a doe.

The time for Eva to die would be when her unborn child and Calen were old enough to be on their own. Before then, Eva would bring her grandmother to the Nathan sisters, swearing them to secrecy. She would give "Roots of the Woods" to her child. Edith no longer needed the book, now that she was blind. It didn't matter. She had it memorized.

What Eva had to do now was get far enough from the group so that when Calen awoke, his parents wouldn't hear his cries.

CHAPTER 23
WHO SHALL BE INSANE

Leah jogged several circuits around the block where Larry lived, even though the lockdown was in effect. She had to drive to his neighborhood. If the police stopped her, she would say she had to go to the supermarket, an essential business. She wouldn't say she traveled miles out of her way, parking her car and hoping to glimpse the man she loved, if he left his apartment just as she happened to run by.

A brief look at her handsome Nordic beloved would be enough, she told herself. Yet, she dreamed of more. Larry would come down his front steps, then look up. Their eyes would meet. His head would lean to the side. He knew her, but how? Then his eyebrows would raise in delight. Of course. She was Leah, the woman who had bought one of the N-95 masks from him. He had only seen her for the minute it took to make the illegal sale, but he hadn't forgotten the dark-haired thirty-eight-year-old woman, who might have passed for twenty-eight at a distance.

She had been through enough to feel like a forty-eight or even fifty-eight-year-old. The murder of her husband Josh, the death of Dinah, followed by the death of her parents and grandmother, the soul-shattering depression that followed, the loneliness, the disappointments of online dating, being furloughed from her job in the early days of the pandemic, and now the lockdown — all marked by the long, white scars of wrist-slits hidden under her sleeves.

Until Larry.

Their transaction took place in front of his apartment building, before the lockdown in April 2020.

"If I want more, can I buy them from you?" His finger whisked hers when he handed her the plain bag containing the mask. Her entire body tingled. Something passed to her from him, like an erotic contagion. Neither of them wore protective gloves.

"I may go to the Panhandle for spring break. If I do, I'll call you when I get back, if I have any supply left."

He was going to the Panhandle. Later, back home, she thought she remembered him winking. He had invited her to meet him in the resort town, hadn't he? How amazing that a man like him should show interest in a woman like her. She had never thought of herself as attractive or as anything special. Not even her parents or her husband Josh had ever said she was special.

She googled the route to Panama City. She decided not to take the mask. Nothing should get in the way of Larry recognizing her if they ran into each other. She made a reservation at a centrally located beach-front hotel that would serve as a base for her search. Larry, the adventurous man of her dreams, caused her to chase after him and plan a romantic capture.

What she found when she arrived were crowds of college-aged people wedging themselves into the restaurants and bars and matting themselves together on the beach. If Larry was among them, she failed to locate him. No one realized the extent to which spring break would spread the virus.

Back home, she waited for him to contact her. Nothing. She called his number, letting it ring twenty, thirty, forty times, leaving voice messages and texts several times a day, sometimes at ten-minute intervals. When she didn't hear from him, she wondered if he had been arrested or hospitalized. Maybe he lost his phone in the Panhandle. Was he avoiding her, wanting her to play hide-and-seek with him?

The last possibility made her rake her face until blood ran. Make-up concealed the scratches. Meanwhile, the governor closed down the state. Everyone was ordered to shelter in place, except essential workers. Leah found one excuse after another to go to Larry's neighborhood.

After a week, she worked up her nerve to park in front of his apartment. She tried to will herself to get out and ring his doorbell. Her stomach twisted. She exhaled in sobbing bursts. Ten frozen minutes later, she gave up and drove away.

Back in her house, she paced, yanking her hair. She would never see her beloved if he didn't open his door when she was there or if fear stopped her from getting to his doorstep at the right moment.

A sudden, jolting thought dizzied her. She held onto a chair to keep from falling, then sat.

She imagined Larry staring out the window, seeing her jog by. He wished she would stop and knock on his door. If he didn't have a fever, he would run out to her. Ever since they met, he'd been waiting for her, sleeping through all her texts and calls, hoping she would come to him. By now, he might be on the floor, too weak to reach his phone, gasping for breath.

She had to find out. She had to save him. By nightfall, she had gone back to his neighborhood again. The directory near the locked entrance to Larry's apartment building said he lived in apartment number 103. That would be on the first floor. She circled the building. The windows were too high for her to see inside. Around the back, she found a broken metal chair. It looked like it could hold her weight. Beneath each window, she propped the chair, climbed up, and looked inside. Most were covered with blinds or drapes. A few had no window treatment, but she didn't see any ill-looking, still-handsome blond man immobilized on the floor or on a sofa.

Not sure what to do next, she sat on the chair in the dark. Something scurried by, a cat or a rat, she couldn't see which. She heard a sound, a meow or a squeal. Unless it was Larry, calling to her.

Leah. Help me. I'm here.

She shot up and ran around the building, shouting, "Where are you? I'm locked outside."

Just as she reached the front, one of the tenants came out. Leah slipped in. She ran through the halls, yelling Larry's name. Residents cracked their doors, telling her to pipe down, to leave, or they would call 911. When she found 103, she pounded on the door with her fists, sobbing and choking.

It never opened. Two masked security guards showed up and escorted her back to her car. Larry still called to her, pleading.

Back at her house, she spent several days drifting between fits of weeping and numb listening. At night, she roamed the house, watching the time on her phone flip from minute to minute, and still no call from Larry. Her dry lips cracked, though she drank water all the time. She only ate a few Saltines.

Even though she was miles away, she still made out the sound of Larry's calls for help, unless it was the swoosh of the water heater or the whir of the air conditioner. To distract herself, she turned on the tv. At a press conference, the President said something about the days ahead being hard. His eyes bore right through the screen into hers. He talked just to her, telling her that without Larry, her days would be too hard to bear.

At least she knew now, after locating Larry's door within his apartment house which windows were likely to be his. When enough time had elapsed, she drove back. The metal chair leaned against the building, still where she left it. She placed it against the window that was probably Larry's, climbed up and looked in. The interior was dark. He must have been too ill to get to the light switch. At least she determined he wasn't on the floor of the room she could see. A home office, she guessed. All the other windows were dark, too, as if the apartment had no tenant.

When she tiptoed around to the back of the building, she noticed the dumpster filled to overflowing. She dragged the chair to it. Perhaps one of the garbage bags contained a clue to Larry's condition. She rooted around, untying bags, tossing the contents onto the ground. A few times, she took bites of leftover food, imagining she kissed her beloved by putting her lips on the same spot his lips had touched.

There was nothing to be learned from the food scraps, used tissues, plastic wrap, and other debris in the dumpster. After using a rag from the trash to wipe her hands, she left.

Days followed of almost continuous texting and leaving voice messages sent to the phone number a friend of a friend had given her when she first contacted Larry. Leah's mood changed. She suspected he wasn't answering on purpose.

It dawned on her—a woman opened the door and held it open long enough for Leah to go in. Of course! She was leaving Larry's apartment after instructing Larry not to open his door if Leah knocked. She meant to send Leah a message. Leah couldn't have Larry. He belonged to another.

Leah's breath hissed between her clenched teeth. She threw herself onto her bed, twisting the sheets, falling into a fitful sleep. Someone laughed at her. But it was only the alarm on her phone. She fell back to sleep. When she awoke, she felt light-headed and feverish. A hard, dry cough started. She knew what it meant.

Without bothering to comb her hair or change clothing, she drove back to Larry's neighborhood, to the supermarket nearest his building. No doubt all the tenants of the apartment house shopped there, including Larry's girlfriend. Leah took a cart, as if she was an ordinary shopper. She had remembered to wear the N-95 mask. There were only a few customers allowed in the store at a time. That was good.

As if she searched for something in particular, she cruised up and down the aisles, stopping in the empty ones. It didn't matter to her which section of the store she was in, as long as no one was around. Lowering her mask, she took jars and cans off the shelves one at a time, licked the top of each, then returned them to their places on the shelf.

Experts advised people to shop quickly. Leah pictured Larry's girlfriend rushing through the supermarket, tossing items into her cart, not bothering to peer closely at each one. Later, if she wanted a pickle with her lunch, she might twist open the top, then eat a spear with hands that touched Leah's dried saliva. If she wanted a few potato chips, she would open the bag Leah contaminated.

COVID-19 overwhelmed the hospitals. There weren't enough ventilators. There was no treatment. The thought comforted Leah that the three of them — Larry, his girlfriend, and herself — might all drown at the same time, if not together, as the edema filled their lungs with thick milky liquid.

She wrote a note, pinning it to her shirt, to be found with her body. "I bear no grudges."

CHAPTER 24
WHO SHALL LIVE

Snaking around mottle-barked sycamores and towering cottonwoods, splashing through creeks, swinging on tendril vines, scampering up slopes, jumping across chasms, sprinting, darting, leaping, and running for the sheer joy of it, Azura raced ahead of Calen.

Laughter robbed him of the breath needed to catch up to her. It always happened this way. Without warning, she would take off. In the moment it would take him to realize she had gone, he lost any advantage. But he delighted in watching her bound through the forest with the grace of a bobcat.

They weren't brother and sister. Mama, who was called First Woman, borrowed Calen when he was little and not given him back. That might explain why Azura had more brains than him, even though she was younger. She knew how to steal things from the hikers and campers who visited the forest, useful things like food, clothing, and matches. She also took things she liked—a doll with eyelids that opened and closed and an earring with a sparkling green stone. These treasures were hidden in their dwelling.

Mama had been sick for a year before she died. "Roots of the Woods" hadn't healed her. It either lost its power, or it meant for her death to happen. A year before that, she found the Nathan sisters, resettled in their cave with their animals and Bucky. They agreed to allow Great Mother, now in her mid-eighties and blind, to live with them until Eva's health improved. Instead, her health declined.

She shrank to the size of a young doe, barely able to move her twig-like arms. Between gasping breaths, she told Calen he might have relatives in town who had been looking for him for all of his fourteen years. But Calen didn't have an interest in anything that might separate him from Azura. And no one could have been a better mother to him than Mama. He didn't need actual parents or relatives.

When Mama neared the end, Azura asked her about her father.

"His name is Isaac." Mama took several minutes to get these words through her cracked lips.

"Where is he?"

"In… the… town."

While Azura digested this, Mama perked up, adding, "You'll have to be very careful if you try to find him. If the police catch you, they won't let you come back to the forest."

Azura's eyebrows knitted in puzzlement, like they did when she overheard conversations between hikers who discussed things with no meaning—cell phones, laundromats, voting.

After Mama died, the Nathan sisters offered to take care of the young teens. Azura refused their offer. They could take care of themselves. Besides, Azura had "Roots of the Woods." It might still be useful.

Her curiosity grew about her other parent, her father. She wouldn't miss Mama so much if she found him.

"I wonder if we look alike." Her hair, which she hacked with a knife whenever it annoyed her, was the same dark brown as Mama's long braid, but wavier. Mama had been tall and muscular. She was petite and agile.

Calen never vomited unless Mama made him if he ate the wrong mushroom. But when Azura spoke of going to town to find Isaac, his stomach twisted. What if they looked alike? What if that made her want to stay in town with him?

What if she said, "You don't belong with us, Calen?"

His dull brown eyes and hair didn't resemble hers or Mama's. Everything about him was dull.

"You can't go to town. The police will get you." He tried to think of every awful thing that would prevent her from going. "The hikers and campers talk about needing money to buy food. You don't have money. You'd be hungry."

Azura said nothing. Whatever she thought or planned to do, she kept secret from him. He reminded her every day of the dangers.

"It's not safe. People steal your things."

Another month passed. Azura seemed like her old self, not the self who wanted a father. She and Calen chased around the forest as usual. They hauled water, fished, hunted, collected roots, and stayed hidden from visitors, as they had done when Mama lived. Calen's stomach smoothed.

Then, one morning, Azura shook him from sleep. The bats still flew about. The birds just started their wake-up chirping in the pale morning light.

"Come on," she said.

"What? Where?" He re-curled himself on the sleeping mat in their hut.

"Get up! We're going to town." She kicked him, but not hard like she would if she was mad.

Before he sat up, she ran out the door. He didn't have time for his morning pee or cup of water. If he didn't hurry, he wouldn't see which way she went. He followed the rule—keep up or lose her.

They ran to the forest entrance, slowing to sneak around the guard house, even though the attendant wouldn't be at his post that early. Beyond the entrance lay a day's walk to the town. The road was straight, allowing Calen to keep Azura in sight even when she sprinted ahead. His slower, steadier, plodding, one foot in front of the other, gave him time to catch up when she stopped to puzzle over road signs. She read a little and sounded out the letters.

"S-t-a-t-e. State. R-o-a-d. Road. 4-6. Forty-six."

At the outskirts of town, she slowed to his speed. They met one astonishment after another. Houses. Buildings as tall as trees. Shops with glass fronts, like huge car windshields. Too many people to hide from, although no one looked at them in an odd way.

The road led to the center of the town, where a large, important-looking building stood, surrounded by cars both parked and moving on streets webbing out from all sides. People moved in and out of the building, up and down its massive steps, or sat on benches scattered on the grass in front. Many dressed in fancier clothes than visitors to the forest wore.

They crouched behind a trash can that lay against a smaller building across from the important-looking one and watched, amazed. So much activity, noise, colors, smells, and unfathomable sights. Calen hunched down, trying to make himself as small as possible. He would have squashed himself into the trash can, if he could fit. Azura craned her neck, interested in the new surroundings.

"If I go in the building, someone might tell me where Isaac is," she said.

Calen shuddered. "What if the police are in the building?"

But she had already crossed the street, dodging vehicles, heading up the stairs and through the massive doors. He found her standing in the middle of a huge round space, head thrown back, staring at a domed ceiling as high above them as the tallest tree in the forest.

Down one hallway spoking from the room, a mustached man washed the floor. He wore the same type of clothing they had seen on campers. Old, faded clothing.

"I'll ask him," she said.

They walked toward the man and waited for him to notice them.

"What are you looking for," he asked.

"Isaac."

"Isaac Who?"

"I don't know."

"There's no Isaac in any of the county offices here."

"I need to find him."

The man leaned on his mop. "Isaac. It's a name from the bible. The Old Testament. Abraham's son, who came near to being sacrificed. You kids know your bible?"

Azura and Calen gave each other a mystified glance.

"Maybe," she said.

"I'd go to the Jew church and ask there. I think they had a pastor named Isaac." The man pointed the direction. "It's about three miles out from here on Third Street. A red brick building."

After leaving the important building, Azura and Calen looked at all the street signs until they found the one that Azura read as "T-h-i-r-d. Third." With so many trash cans along the way, finding food wasn't a problem. Azura recognized cigarettes among the trash from seeing campers smoke. They were bent and used, but not all the way. It was a lucky thing that she brought matches. She lit two cigarettes and gave one to Calen. He doubled over with a coughing fit, while she walked ahead, blowing smoke back at him and laughing.

He recognized police and police cars. They sometimes showed up at campsites and put someone in the rear seat after binding their hands behind their back. He scanned the area, skipping his eyes over anything that made little sense, to see if any police were around.

Just then, Azura grabbed his sleeve. Four kids near their own age up stood in a group ahead. Three boys and a girl, looking their way.

"Hey, Girl. Wanna fuck?"

"How much you want to let me fuck your girlfriend?'

"I'll give you some weed if you let me fuck her."

Azura rushed Calen past the four who had collapsed against each other with laughter. She pulled him along, looking over her shoulder, in case they followed. The mocking words of the group rattled in his head. Azura pinched her lips, the way she did when she was mad. Calen hoped she wasn't mad at him.

They walked in silence for a while. Azura didn't look at him. Then she spoke in her usual, not mad voice, as if the group hadn't annoyed her.

"Remember that doll I loved so much? The one with the moving eyelids? It went missing one day. I thought it was alive and left. Just shows. Nothing you like is for keeps."

His stomach twisted. He had been the one who smashed the doll and hid the pieces. It scared him to think of what she would do if she ever found out.

They reached the red brick building when the sun was low in the sky. A woman with tight curls locked the door from the outside.

"I'm looking for Isaac," Azura said.

"You must mean Rabbi Isaac. He's a school teacher now. I can give you his address."

"Can you just tell us how to get there?"

"Do you kids want a ride?"

Did she mean she would take them in her car? Calen wasn't sure, but Azura hopped in the front seat. With a bad feeling, he slid in the back.

The woman asked questions. What were their names? Which school did they go to? Were they Jewish? He sat still, not knowing how to answer, but Azura did her best.

"I'm Azura. My brother is Calen. We're from out of town. We don't go to school here. Isaac is a relative of our mother."

The woman stopped the car in front of the house she said belonged to Isaac.

"I think I should call Isaac and tell him I've brought you." She began punching her phone with her finger.

Azura shot Calen an alarmed look. Her lips moved to form a word. "Now!" With that, she shot out of the car. Calen jumped out after her.

"Hey! Where ya going? You're heading to the wrong house." The woman yelled out the driver's side window, shaking her tight curls.

By now it was dusk. A few houses away, a man walking a dog and young children riding bicycles all looked in their direction. A few minutes later, a police car drove up to the woman's car. Everyone pointed at them. Azura shoved Calen behind a large bush near the doorway of a house that looked just like Isaac's.

"Come. Hurry." Azura shot up and ran between the houses. Calen followed her. They zigzagged through yards, climbing fences, using skills they had mastered climbing trees in the forest. They didn't see any police officer behind them. With caution, they edged around the houses, circling back to Isaac's. Both the curly-headed woman's car and the police car had driven away.

"Let's wait in the back until it's dark. I just want to look at Isaac. But I don't want him to see me," she whispered.

Once in the back yard, they lay down behind the foundation plantings, breathing in the familiar scent of the earth. The town had been exhausting. It was nothing like the forest. They were tired and hungry. Using their fingers, they raked up some hardened soil, so much dryer than the forest loam, putting bits into their mouths. Mama had taught them this way to fill their stomachs when there was nothing else to eat.

Calen fell asleep. He dreamed that Mama was the woman who gave them a ride. He sat in the back seat, watching Mama's curls bounce. She looked over her shoulder at him, saying, "You took that doll."

Azura shook him. It was too dark to see her.

"I'm going inside. You coming?"

Darkness smothered everything. But Azura only needed a thin sliver of moon to see. She slipped in an unlocked door. Calen thought it was a terrible idea, but he followed right behind her. Inside, the house was like many huts shoved together, some on top of the others, connected by a staircase. No one was in any of the lower huts, although sounds of ticking, hums, and gurgles made Calen wonder if any animals were there. They crept up the stairs.

The door to the first hut they came to was open. A man and a woman slept in there, sprawled on a raised mat. Azura stared at the man. If he was Isaac, he would be her father. Calen didn't move. He held his breath. What would the man or woman do if they woke up?

After a few minutes, Azura pulled Calen out of the first upper hut and into another. A sweet smell Calen couldn't identify filled the space. Azura pointed to a kind of box. Inside a tiny being, a baby slept with its thumb in its mouth.

Azura picked it up, handing Calen some pads and a bottle. He wanted to scream, "No!"

But Azura had already run down the stairs and out the back door. Calen ran a few steps behind her. The baby stayed quiet. As they passed under street lights, Calen saw its scrunched-up face with squeezed shut eyes. Its body was wrapped in a blanket.

They began the long walk back through the town, leading to the forest. The baby stretched its mouth into a grimace and made squealing noises, but walking calmed it. Azura stopped to unwrap it. He was a boy.

"He'll need more of the milk babies drink from bottles," she said. They had seen babies at the campsites and park shelters.

Back in the center of town, Azura asked people passing by for money to feed her baby brother. Soon, she had several dollars. No police came around to stop them or take the baby, but people asked each other if someone should call social services.

"You kids shouldn't be walking around at night with a baby. Where are your parents?"

"They'll be here any minute," Azura said, hoisting the baby higher onto her shoulder.

The group of kids who harassed them earlier still lounged there, half visible under colorful lights from signs on buildings and from the lit ends of whatever they smoked.

"Fast work. She's gone and had a baby already."

"I'll make you another one. Any time, you girl."

Azura ducked into the doorway of a building. Calen was soon at her side.

"We have to find a store that sells baby milk. Can you run?"

He thought he could. It was a couple of miles to the edge of town. When they stopped to catch their breath, they noticed an enormous building, bigger than the one in the center of town. Azura read the letters on the side.

"W-a-l-m-a-r-t. Walmart."

Cars were in long rows in the front and around the sides. People came out of the doors with carts of food. Many small children and babies, some riding in the carts, were with the adults. Azura, Calen, and the baby blended right in.

"I'll go in and get stuff for the baby. You wait here among the cars, in the front."

At first, the crush of people, the bulging carts, the slamming of car doors, the chaos of vehicles changing places distracted him. He thought he saw the group of kids who yelled at them in town, but maybe it was another group. Just in case, he crouched down between two cars. It seemed he waited a long time. What would he do if Azura slipped out the back with the baby? He cowered. Finally, he saw her, carrying the baby and rolling a cart, just like everyone else. She told him to take the bags.

They crossed the field of cars.

"I'll call the baby Abe," she said.

Watching Azura clasping the baby tight to her chest under the last of the gigantic building's light before entering the darkness of the road to the forest, Calen had an odd sensation. Inside he buzzed like a big agitated hornet.

For the first time, he knew what it was to hate.

CHAPTER 25
REPENTANCE: CALEN

When they arraigned Calen, a man called a "public defender" described him as a "feral child who does not know right from wrong." Until his arrest, he lived all his life in the forest with his adopted sister, Azura and, for a few days, the baby he murdered. Without parents or any adult supervision, without education, without medical care or proper nutrition, with limited language, he "bears as much responsibility for his crime as a fox in a henhouse," the defender said.

The judge stared at Calen, who was among the most disheveled juveniles to have graced her courtroom. They charged him with second degree murder.

His head lowered. It bothered his eyes when anyone looked at him or when he had to look at anyone. He gazed at the black Nikes he had been given and forced to wear in the jail cell. He knew what shoes were because he had taken pairs from camp sites while backpackers slept. When the snow came, he stuffed his feet into them for warmth. But he did not like the way they squeezed his toes together.

After they chased and captured him, they took him to town in a police car. He had been to town once before—with Azura when they stole the baby. The grey buildings, the streetlights blinking red and green, the cars whizzing down roads, the smell of exhaust, the sirens and hissing buses, were familiar. Everything else was new. He had never been in a courtroom. They made him sit at a special table. The "public defender" sat next to him. The "prosecutor" sat at another table across the aisle. They took turns standing and speaking to the judge. He didn't understand anything they said.

The judge told him he had to have "a psychiatric evaluation to determine if you are competent be tried as an adult. If not, you will be tried as a juvenile. Do you have any questions?"

They took him back to the jail cell, a room with one wall of bars. Although the cell had four metal shelves with mats, he was the only occupant. He picked a lower one, pulling the blanket over his head, so he wouldn't see the procession of staff wanting a peek at him. The Baby Killer. The Feral Boy. The Wild Child. The Silent Teen.

They may have thought he couldn't speak. They were wrong. He chose not to speak. And he did know right from wrong. Mama, who raised him and Azura, taught them. It was wrong to tell anyone where their hut was located. It was wrong to speak to hikers and campers. It was right to bury Mama when she died.

He tried very hard not to kill the baby. His hands had folded into fists. Every day, he pried his fingers apart. But the time came when they tightened like snakes coiled around mice. His fingernails dug into his palms. He couldn't stop his fists when they took control.

After, he slammed his knuckles into trees until they bled, to punish them. Azura screamed and hit him with a stick about twenty times. He let her do it. She wanted the baby back alive.

"I'll get you another one."

"I don't want another one. I want *that* one," she said.

She took the baby to the gatehouse and showed the attendant, hoping he would know what to do. That was how the police got involved. When they caught Calen and asked if he hurt the baby, he nodded his head "yes."

But he didn't do it. His hands hurt the baby. He just watched.

The next day, a man with a ring of hair the color of the road came into the cell. He sat on the shelf opposite Calen.

"My name is Dr. Thomas. I'm the psychiatrist who'll be doing your evaluation, today." He had a pad of yellow paper and a red pen.

"Can you tell me your name?" When Calen didn't answer, Dr. Thomas wrote something on the pad. Calen had never seen anyone write before. The squeaking sound of the pen hurt his ears.

The psychiatrist kept looking at Calen and waiting. Every few minutes, he made another mark on his pad. Calen tried to say his name, but his tongue refused.

"Okay. I'll tell you what I found out about you. Your sister told me your name is Calen. You're fourteen years old. She's twelve. You two have been on your own for a year, since Azura's mother, who is your adopted mother, died. Is that right?"

Calen nodded. His mouth tasted like dry leaves. The pen squeaked again.

"She told me you both came here to find her father. When you reached his house, you entered and stole the baby, Azura's half-brother. You took the baby back to the forest and murdered him. Is that right?"

Harsh rays pierced the cell's small, high window. Dust motes floated in the air. Calen didn't think what the psychiatrist said was right, but if Azura said it was, maybe that's what happened.

He shook his head "yes." The pen squeaked.

"Can you tell me why you murdered the baby?"

"Dunno." The word popped out. Calen wanted to say the psychiatrist should ask his hands, not him.

"Did you plan to kill the baby ahead of time?"

"Dunno."

After Dr. Thomas finished, they brought in food, the same kind left in the campsite trash. A cheese sandwich. A square box containing milk. An apple. Chips in a small bag. He could have eaten twice as much. In the forest, he could always eat bits of bark or earth when food was scarce. Nothing in the cell could fill his stomach except stuffing from the mats or fragments of green paint he scraped from the walls with his front teeth.

People came and went, in and out of the cell. A man who shaved off Calen's matted hair. A woman who stabbed his arm and stole some of his blood. Someone who took him to the shower room and who gave him clean clothes.

Across from his cell was an identical cell, with four grown men locked inside. They kept calling to him.

"Hey, kid! Baby killer. How come y'killed a baby?"

Word spread to the other cells. Shouts of "Baby killer!" swept up and down the block. Calen hid under his blanket. He missed Azura. She was probably back in the forest, crying about the baby. She cried more for him than she had when Mama died.

He still didn't understand what was so special about the baby. It was just… a thing.

Back in court, the public defender, the prosecutor, and Dr. Thomas were all present.

The judge said, "I remand you to an adolescent psychiatric facility until you gain competency. Then you will be tried as an adult. Do you understand?"

The place they took him to, called Valley Hospital, was a "locked door facility," meaning no one could leave the building without permission. They told Calen this when they admitted him. The rest confused him.

"This is not a prison. It's a place to get treatment, to learn to behave appropriately. Privileges depend on behavior. There are four levels of privilege. Since you are just admitted, you will start at level one."

An Orientation Specialist, called Pam, sat behind a desk across from him, in a small room. Her job was to explain the rules. No fighting. No name calling. No throwing food. Take all prescribed medications. Attend all assigned classes and groups. Lights out at 9 p.m. She gave him a paper to sign, agreeing to the rules. Since he couldn't read or write, she told him where to make an "X."

They assigned Calen bed number 8 in the boy's dormitory. It was just a place for sleeping. During the day, they herded both girls and boys into a large dayroom, into a series of smaller group rooms, or into the offices of therapists and medical staff.

At first, they kept Calen in one of the smaller rooms with the other New Admissions—three stunned boys. Pam read over the reasons they were there. Drug addiction. Truancy. Running away from home. Battery. Theft.

"Calen, would you tell the others why you are here?" Pam's voice was soft, but her eyes were hard.

"I'm supposed to have killed a baby," he said.

Three sets of eyes jolted toward him.

"Are you the Baby Killer? For real?" The boy who asked seemed astonished, as if he had met a celebrity. "You've been on tv, man."

Seventy-two hours later, when the New Admissions joined the others in the Day Room, everyone knew what Calen had done, except for the ones too medicated to care. They sat at tables with their heads on their arms, dozing. No one came near Calen. He kept his eyes on his Nikes.

The door to the Day Room opened. To his amazement, Azura entered, accompanied by Pam. When she saw him, she marched to the opposite corner of the room, turning her back on him, allowing Pam to introduce her to a couple of girls.

A hollowness began in Calen's stomach that wasn't hunger for food. It made his eyes moisten and drip. Azura and Mama helped him fill the awful hollowness that sometimes came upon him, even in the forest. Mama held him tight. Azura talked to him and let him follow her. But Mama died, and Azura stayed with the girls. He realized she was still mad at him.

The next day, a therapist named Rick asked Calen if he wanted to do a "Conflict Resolution" with Azura before they discharged her from Valley Hospital. Discharged meant she would be leaving.

Leaving? The hollowness grew so large that Calen feared he would burst apart, scattering into pieces across the Day Room.

Rick explained that Conflict Resolution was a way for Azura and him to talk about what happened to the baby. It would help both of them heal from their crimes.

Calen agreed, if it meant Azura would speak to him.

Rick told him more. Her DNA test revealed that the baby's father was her father, too. The probability was ninety-nine percent. She would go to Juvenile Detention for kidnapping her brother. Meanwhile, her father agreed to establish a relationship with her. When she finished her sentence, they would seal her records. She would have a fresh start with the support of a parent.

Conflict Resolution took place in one of the small rooms. Rick, Calen, and Azura sat together with the two teens across from each other. A large chart hung on the wall, filled with simple illustrations of faces, each having a different expression, with the word describing the expression beneath.

"Here are the rules," Rick said. "Each of you gets to tell the other about how and why you committed your crime. One is the listener, and the other is the speaker. The listener repeats what he or she heard the other say."

Azura began. "Before Mama died, she told me who my father's name. I just wanted to look at him. You came with me. When we found his house, we snuck in his bedroom. I saw him there. My father. Asleep. Then, I saw the baby in the next room. I took the baby and ran out, back to the forest."

Rick said, "Don't say 'the baby.' Say his name."

"I called him Abe."

Rick asked Calen to repeat what Azura said, using the baby's name. He stumbled through it.

"Tell Calen why you stole Abe from your father."

She bit her lip. "Like… I saw my father… and I wanted him to come back to the forest with me. But he was asleep… So it was like the baby, I mean Abe, was a part of him."

Rick made her point to the face on the Feeling Chart she made when she saw her father. The word beneath was "sad." Then he asked her to point to the face she made when Calen killed Abe. She pointed to "furious."

Rick asked Calen why Azura had been furious.

"She wanted the baby, I mean Abe, to be alive."

"Why do you think she wanted the baby alive?"

"She liked it."

Now Calen had to point to a face he made at that time. After a long pause, he picked both "sad" and "mad."

Rick pressed harder. "Tell Azura why you killed the baby?"

"I didn't. My hands did."

With that, Azura erupted from her chair. Her face was the "furious" one on the chart.

"Your hands did it? Your hands? Your hands are you, Calen." She yelled at him.

"I should cut my hands off."

"Then you'd be the one without hands who murdered Abe. You'd still be the Baby Killer."

It was the last thing she said to him.

Calen fell into a big black hole. He spent his days with his head on his arms, like the medicated kids. Sessions, as they called them, with Rick were the only thing he had to look forward to after they discharged Azura. The big man with the mustache didn't call him Baby Killer or tell him he was a bad person. The feeling Calen had when Rick invited him into the group room, just the two of them, was the smiley face, the "glad" one. But sometimes, he wanted to leave the session when Rick asked him to point to the expression he had about Mama's death or Azura's anger. Rick made him stay.

One day, Rick surprised him.

"I didn't tell you everything Azura told me about you. I understand her mother, the one you both called Mama, took you when you were two-years-old. Do you remember that, Calen?"

The question startled him. Yes, he knew, but he also didn't know. Mama told him, but he didn't remember. An image came to him. The dinghy. Mama rowing. Her finger to her lips making a "Shh" sound. He told Rick.

"Why would she be shushing you?" Rick looked straight at him, leaning forward.

"Because I was being loud?"

"Loud how?"

"Maybe… crying?"

"And why would you be crying?"

"Missing my real mother?"

The hollow sensation expanded again. His eyes dripped. He would have broken to pieces if Rick didn't hold him together.

There was more. How Azura was all he had after Mama died. How he feared she would like Abe better than him. How that made him hate the baby. How the baby may have felt the same way Calen did when he was stolen. How he killed Abe, but blamed his hands.

Rick asked one more question, the toughest one of all.

"What do you imagine the baby felt while you murdered him?"

Although he tried to find it for months, no face on the Feeling Chart fit the answer to Rick's question. It was left to Calen's despairing imagination to invoke.

CHAPTER 26
PRAYER: CALEN

In 2030, the fifth year of Calen's incarceration in the Sexual Offenders Unit of the prison in Terre Haute, he received his one and only letter.

His cell mates eyed the envelope with interest.

"Who'd be writing you?"

Before opening it, he turned it over several times with his wary fingers. It was a plain white piece of mail, with just the address and a stamp on one side and a triangle flap, already opened by the administration, on the other. It didn't have a return address.

During incarceration, he learned to read. It fascinated him to see how letters combined to spell a word. Like his name, Calen. It took all five letters in the right order for it to be him. Scramble them, and he wouldn't be he.

To others, he was the notorious Baby Killer. Two best-selling books had been written about him, dozens of articles, and scholarly works by academics interested in the psychology of feral children. A documentary film had been shown on tv, produced by the Justice for Incarcerated Juveniles Organization.

In the Sexual Offenders Unit, he stayed by himself. They placed him there for his own protection from the general population. The murder of a three-week-old infant made him a "Freak." The others were split into two groups—sexual abusers of children and serial rapists of adults. He winced whenever he thought about what he had done. Others were sure to think he was the worst of the sinners in the Unit. But the image reflected in the dull bathroom mirror was of an ordinary looking young man, with medium brown hair, medium brown eyes, medium height, and medium weight. What roiled inside of him, the cyclone of self-torture and regret, didn't show on the outside.

He didn't open the letter until the others went to the recreation area to watch the news on tv. He stayed in his cell. Inside the envelope was a printout on white paper. He sounded out the words under his breath.

My name is Rabbi Sam. I am your uncle. For a brief time, I was a member of a forest commune. Jenny Berg, your biological mother, was my niece. I convinced her and your father to join to escape the virus. After I returned to town, you were stolen from your parents by the woman who raised you. Your mother died of COVID-19. Your father disappeared after her death.

His uncle was a rabbi?

There was more. Meanwhile, tension mounted in the recreation area. He stuffed the letter into his pocket, intending to deal with it later. He had to stay alert in case of unrest. There was always the possibility of danger, even a riot. From the cell, he saw inmates rising out of their seats, yelling at the tv.

"The Fuck! They're going to let us die in here. Just like the last time."

"They treat us like fucking cattle. Packed in. No masks. No soap."

The news item was about the spread of the mutated coronavirus, COVID-30. The vaccine developed a decade before was ineffective against this new strain. Guards turned off the tv and herded the inmates back to their cells before things could get ugly. A rising odor of perspiration drifted through the Unit, the stink of fear and outrage.

Low murmuring rumbled through the cells, the swirl of rumors. They were sex offenders, worthless to the public. Testing and distancing would be a waste of money on them. If they all died, so much the better. They would be sardined together with no protection in order to become infected as fast as possible. It was a death sentence for all of them.

When they served dinner in the cells, everyone concentrated on eating. The men shoveled whole portions of mashed potatoes into their mouths, entire dinner rolls, and large forkfuls of ham, while gulping down their Kool-Aid. They pondered while they ate.

When they finished, the angry discussion continued. What if they planted a spreader among them? Someone placed in the Unit by the administration. A human cluster bomb, capable of spraying the area with virus when detonated. Suspicions mounted. The inmates looked each other over with distrustful eyes. Then they looked over at Calen, sitting slouched on his bed, trying not to be noticed. This in itself made him noticeable. Someone said the spreader had to be someone like the Freak, the Baby Killer, the one who thought his shit smelled sweet. Calen's cell mates ordered him to lie in his bunk facing the wall. They didn't want his COVID breath spewing on them. They pushed him against the pocked cinder blocks.

It was a bad situation. Even Calen knew that. He reached into his pocket and tore off a piece of the letter with his teeth. He intended to swallow it so the others wouldn't read it.

"Hey! Look! He's eating the mail he got today. Someone get it!"

Two of his cell mates held him while a third grabbed the piece of paper before he bit off more.

"What's it say?"

They passed the half-chewed piece of paper around. No one touched the germy part that had been in Calen's mouth.

"His uncle's a rabbi. The Freak's a Christ killer!"

"A baby killer *and* a Christ killer?"

"Stay back from him. He'll make you sick."

Two guards opened the cell door, motioning Calen out.

"Give him his letter," one said.

They pushed the paper back to Calen through the bars. He was ordered to walk a few feet in front of the guards to a solitary cell. No one had to explain why.

After they slammed the door shut and bolted it, Calen fished a piece of the letter from the inside of his cheek. The wet glob could still be read when he spread it out and lay it next to the dry part.

You have broken the 6th commandment: Thou shalt not kill. That infant you murdered was the half-brother of your sister-by-adoption. In a way, that makes him your brother, too, and complicates your crime. Even though no one raised you in the tradition of our people, I urge you to find your own way to pray to God for forgiveness. As long as you are sincere, God will be merciful.

Just as he finished reading, the din in the Unit grew louder. Sounds of banging on the cell bars and shouting interrupted the agonizing shame ignited by the awful letter. The guards yelled. He couldn't make out their words. Whatever they said increased the cacophony. A steady roar swelled throughout the Unit.

Then, one voice rose above the others.

"Kill the Freak!"

After a momentary pause, others joined in. It became a chant, repeated, along with the banging.

Alone in solitary, Calen had spikes of panic. He flattened his back against the cold cell wall, then spun around, facing the wall instead, as if he could push himself through. A carbonated sensation arouse in his legs, traveling upward, like bubbles bursting under his skin. He spun around again, as an almost visible plume of tiny bubbles escape through his nose and mouth. With each exhalation, the plume enlarged, escaping toward the Unit through cracks in the walls and under the cell door.

The baby he murdered was named Abe. His uncle claimed they were like brothers. When he thought that the baby was almost his brother, something else bubbled up from inside him—racking sobs. Each one shoved the plume with more force, spreading it along the floor of the entire area. The chanting in the Unit paused. Calen's weeping was the only sound. Then the alarmed voices of the inmates rose again.

"What the fuck is it?"

"Look! It coming from solitary."

"The Freak's spreading the virus. He's killing us!"

Calen paid no attention, thinking about his uncle's words in the letter. They told him to find his own way to pray for forgiveness. He hadn't been to church much, but he had seen church on tv. He knew to get down on his knees and clasp his hands in front of him. This he did on the cell floor, beside the foot of the bed. He had to find the right words, his own words, "sincere" words. Not words that lied. He didn't know how.

Deep sobs still spilled from his throat. They morphed, becoming higher pitched, until they sounded like a baby's piercing squall. It was his baby brother, somewhere in the cell. Calen noticed a box he had not seen before, squeezed between the head of the bed and the wall. It looked like the box that contained Abe the first time he saw him. He now knew the box was called a crib. He stood and peeked over the edge. There was Abe, flailing his arms and legs with each loud wail.

He picked the infant up with one hand under his head and the other under his body, as his sister had done, nestling him on his shoulder. There was no room to move. He stood in place, rocking, speaking with softness.

"There, there. It's okay."

Abe quieted. His fuzzy head wobbled against Calen's cheek. He eased himself back down on his knees, taking care not to loosen his hold on Abe.

Screams came from the Unit, from inmates and guards yelling at each other. There were other noises Calen couldn't identify. Thuds. Crashes. Shatters. Then the constant beeping of the fire alarms drowning out all other noise.

A few minutes later, the first trail of smoke sailed through the air vent, then under the cell door, overlapping with the virus plume going in the other direction. Shouts of "fire" from the Unit reached the solitary cell.

Calen rocked Abe while still on his knees, moving back and forth. Tears rolled down his cheeks. Abe wheezed. As thicker smoke shrouded the cell, he gasped out a prayer.

"God, please. *Cough.* Save this baby. *Cough.* Scramble all the letters from my name so they'll be no me anymore. *Cough.* For what I have done, burn me to ash."

CHAPTER 27
RIGHTOUSNESS: CALEN

The Prison Reduction Act passed in 2035 in response to public fears of disease spread by crowded institutions. They released all inmates who had been non-violent during incarceration for ten consecutive years with implants that monitored their location, heart rate, and any illegal substances in their system. Travel outside a proscribed area, a heart rate indicative of an altercation, and drug abuse alerted the monitors. Any convict not responding to a monitor contact might be subject to re-incarceration.

Calen was one of those released. The prison system gave him a coat, a city bus ticket for transportation from the prison to a shelter, and a coupon from McDonalds for three meals. A masked guard accompanied him to the outer door. Once he exited the prison, he was on his own—except for the implant. His monitor would instruct him through the part that reached his ear. The voice might be a person or a robot or the two combined. Calen wouldn't be able to tell.

During the two-week orientation after they installed the implant, Calen had the option of giving the voice a name.

"Uncle Sam," he said.

The approval came with a commendation for choosing a patriotic name. The authorities didn't know that Calen had an actual Uncle Sam, a relative who sent him a letter in 2030.

Uncle Sam's first instruction, after Calen's release, was to buy lunch at the McDonalds across the road, since the bus only stopped at the prison once an hour. Calen had never been in a fast-food restaurant. He had to be guided through the transaction by the monitor. He had never been on a bus, either, and had to be guided through that process, too—how much to pay, where to put the money, and where to sit, alone if possible. The monitor noted that his heart raced. The authorities viewed this as normal for a convict who'd spent the last five years in solitary and who had little experience in a town before that.

During his time in his lone cell in prison, Calen always carried the baby he murdered on his shoulder. The infant, Abe, never grew older than three weeks, the age he had been when he had been killed. Calen took him with him beyond the prison doors. Whenever there was danger, he prayed to God to protect the Abe. During a prison fire years before, Calen suffered lung damage, but the baby wasn't hurt, thanks—he believed—to the mercy of God. Calen needed inhalers and medical checks. Abe had healthy lungs. His crying was still lusty.

Abe fussed on the bus. The hissing sound of the doors opening and closing upset him, even though Calen held him close. At the stop near the shelter, Uncle Sam told him to get off. That quieted Abe.

The shelter was in a former indoor sports area, converted into housing for the homeless after the digitalization of all competitive events. Large gatherings had been outlawed. Uncle Sam told Calen how to use his implant to gain entrance. Just inside of the door, the residence required him to step into an enclosure that checked for contraband and screened for the virus. Once cleared by security, they issued him a keycard. His room number was 4057A on the men's side. One of a bank of single person elevators carried him up to the fourth floor.

Room 4057A had a half-sized door, low to the ground. A ladder beside it reached another half-door on top of his—4057B. His room opened onto the bed in a bee-hive style room, four feet in height, containing a twin-sized cot, a sink, toilet, and a closed container for belongings. On the wall next to the bed was a metal door for trash. A tiny window at the head of the bed and a monitor at the foot above the door completed the furnishings. A button on the wall activated a cover for everything and turned the entire room into a seated shower, after which all moisture was wicked away, eliminating the need for towels. The only thing he couldn't do was stand.

After crawling in, he put Abe on the bed and lay next to him. He touched the ceiling with his outstretched hand. This was his new residence, a cube under another cube, smaller than his solitary cell had been, but modernized. He would no longer have the worry that Abe would become overheated, chilled, bitten by a rat, swarmed by roaches, or infested by the filth of the prison. Abe smiled, unless it was just gas. Maybe he liked his new home. Calen's heart rate lowered to normal.

They gave him forty-eight hours to adjust to his room. Meals were provided when the trash shoot converted to a delivery system. He slept on and off, as he had done in solitary, dreaming about his childhood, raised in the forest with his sister. He endured painful memories of his crime. Every day, he prayed for forgiveness and thanked God for the second chance he had been given with Abe. He promised to protect and care for the baby this time.

For years, he had asked, "What else should I do?"

He awakened from one of his naps to hear Uncle Sam tell him, in a lower voice than usual.

Love thy neighbor as thyself.

The preachers who visited the prison often said this. After Uncle Sam said the same words, Calen spent some hours thinking. In prison, where cruelty abounded, it was hard to love anyone. Ever since he murdered the first Abe, he hated himself. His sister hated him, too. He hadn't had contact with her in more than a decade. During his five years in solitary, the only one he learned to love was the second Abe.

He wondered who his neighbors were in the shelter and whether he could love them. When he heard the door to 4056A open, he peeked out. A large man grunted as he emerged, feet first, extracting himself bit by bit from his half-door. He was very stout, heavily tattooed, and breathing audibly. When he could stand, he wiped his red, perspiring face on his sleeve.

Calen stuck his head out and said, "Hi."

"Fuck off!" The man headed toward the elevators.

This was a neighbor it would be hard to love.

Uncle Sam asked, "Are you having an altercation?"

His heart rate must be up. He closed his door.

"No, just talking to a neighbor."

"Use your inhaler. Then take three deep breaths."

He did what the monitor told him to do.

When the forty-eight hours elapsed, Uncle Sam told him to go outside to the park across the street. Carrying Abe, he descended in the elevator and left the shelter. A busy street lay between the residence and the park. He was guided to the corner and instructed on the meaning of red and green traffic lights.

The park had a wide expanse of grass dotted with trees and benches connected by a walkway. The sight of trees brought Calen joy. Although they were spaced out across the park instead of in a dense growth, he hadn't seen trees since his childhood in the forest. In solitary, all he viewed out the high window was a square of sky. The little window in his room in the shelter looked out at another part of the building.

He didn't know what to do in the park. After strolling for a while on the walkway, he sat on a bench. He switched the baby from his shoulder to his chest, turning him so he could see the greenery.

"Bird. Cloud. Bush." Calen pointed to things Abe should learn to recognize.

There was a rumbling on the walkway. Calen saw a person wheeling a cart piled with items coming toward him. He shifted Abe back to his shoulder to free a hand, in case he had to defend himself. When the person came closer, he saw it was an unmasked woman with hair stringing out from under a close-fitting hat, wearing layers of old clothing.

"That's my bench." A strong odor oozed from her.

"Can I sit here with my baby?"

The woman stared at him before answering.

"Don't steal my stuff."

The woman sat on the far end of the bench.

"Are ya from the psych hospital?"

"No. I just moved into the shelter."

"Then you gotta be just outa the prison. You got a monitor, don't ya?"

The woman was hard to understand. Her mouth caved in. She had no teeth.

"What's ya name?" She rummaged through items in the cart nearest to her seated position.

"Calen."

"I'm Gert. I'm an alcyholic. Gotta have a nip." She fished a bottle of MD20/20 from the cart and offered it to him."

"Can't. The monitor."

She nodded, raising the bottle to her lips and swigging. Calen noticed a piece of fabric poking out from the heap in the cart.

"Can I see that?" He pointed.

"Don't touch my stuff. I'll get it out."

The clattering of objects shifting as she pulled the fabric out awakened Abe. He fussed. When the fabric was freed, it turned out to be a large blue shawl.

"I'll trade or sell it to ya. What will ya give me for it?" She stood, draping it around her shoulders, turning to model it.

"A McDonald's coupon?"

She paused, looking from him to the shawl.

"Okay, seeing yer just out of prison and don't have nothin'."

They made the exchange. Calen looped the shawl across his chest, tying it at the back of his neck. He laid Abe face up in the center of the sling. The infant stopped crying. His lips puckered in a sucking motion. Calen drew a bottle out of his coat pocket and popped the nipple into Abe's questing mouth.

"It looks good on ya. Should keep ya warm," she said.

Gert had become Calen's bench neighbor, someone he had to love. He wasn't sure he even liked her. But he should try.

"Can I sit on the bench with you tomorrow?"

Gert flapped her hand at him, as if shooing him away.

"Just don't ya touch me. I ain't into sex no more." She tipped the bottle into her mouth again, swallowing hard.

"Time to return to the shelter." It was Uncle Sam.

Back in his room, Calen thought again about loving his neighbor as he loved himself. But he didn't love himself. The only one he loved was Abe. Maybe he should try to love his neighbor as he loved his brother. Would he be able to love Gert as he loved Abe? The only women he ever loved were his mother and his sister. Prison wasn't a place to meet other women. Gert traded the shawl for the McDonalds coupon. That was a start. Now that his hands were free, he would be able to work. He owed that to his bench neighbor.

The next day, Uncle Sam guided him to the employment office. They required him to work to pay the government rent for the shelter and for meals. The only job available for an ex-convict with no education and limited reading skills was garbage sweeper. It would be outdoor work. He accepted, agreeing to start the next morning. It involved following a sanitation truck with a large sack and retrieving trash the automated lift missed. When the sack was full, he emptied it into the truck. Sometimes, he had to use a broom if small particles escaped. Abe accompanied him in the sling. The baby was too young to leave with anyone else. The driver of the truck never said a word about him.

But the first time they worked together, the driver lifted his mask and spat on the ground before hopping into the cab.

"There ain't no jobs. People are going hungry. The economy is busted. And the government gives work to scum like you? Plus shelter housing and meals?"

Calen didn't know what to say. The driver was his job neighbor. It might be beyond him to love a man who spat at him.

After work, he would meet Gert in the park at her bench. One day, as they sat together, someone he recognized approached. It was 4056A. Calen took off the sling and laid Abe on the bench, swaddled in the shawl. The huge man stopped in front of them.

"That's my girlfriend. If you don't want trouble, leave now." His voice was gruff.

"Ex-girlfriend. We broke up, remember?" Gert said.

4056A didn't respond to her. His beefy fingers bent into fists. Calen rose. The top of his head came up to 4056A's shoulders. In prison, he became used to larger men threatening him. They didn't scare him, as long as knives, razor blades, or acid weren't involved.

"The baby's sleeping. I'm not waking him up just because you say to leave."

"Baby?"

4056A looked with a confused expression from Calen to Gert. His hesitation gave Calen an advantage. If Calen lowered his head, he could run at 4056A and ram his chest with force, knocking him over. Then he could stomp his head.

But before he acted, a high-pitched voice spoke.

"You'll go back to prison. Besides, it's wrong."

It was Abe, speaking his first words. Calen whirled around toward the baby, amazed by this milestone. Then his neighbor pushed him to the ground and kicked him several times in the ribs. Calen curled into a ball with his arms protecting his head.

Gert yelled. "Stop! Enough!"

Uncle Sam said, "Is there an altercation?"

The police arrived and arrested 4056A. An officer wrote out a report based on Gert's version of what happened. EMTs came to patch up Calen. They taped his chest and treated his cuts and bruises. He refused their suggestion that he accompany them to the ER for an X-ray.

Back in his room, Calen lay on his bed in pain. That didn't matter. The same thing happened in prison and, before that, in the psych hospital. Inmates fought. You got beat, or you won. Either way, there was pain. What mattered was that Abe spoke his first words. And he stopped Calen from hurting the neighbor he should love. He was still a free man because of the baby.

There was a rapping on his door. When Calen peeked out, he was tapped on his brow. Looking up, he saw the head of 4057B peering down at him, holding a yard stick.

"Hi. I'm 4057B. Thought I'd introduce myself. What's your name?"

"Calen."

"Prison, rehab, or psych ward?"

"Prison. Although I've been in the psych ward, too. When I was younger."

"I'm from rehab. I'm in recovery. I spend most of my time off work at meetings."

4057B had pleasant brown eyes, thinning hair, and a wrinkled face.

"You want to come up for a visit?"

"If I can bring my baby."

"You can bring an entire tribe. I've got lots of space." 4057B's head receded into his room.

After tying the sling around his neck and placing Abe in it, Calen climbed the ladder next to his door. He crawled in. His neighbor was a tiny man, less than five feet tall. He was standing next to the bed with his head almost touching the ceiling.

"It's ridiculous. The upper cubes have five foot heights, and who do they stick in them? Little guys like me. Big guys get the four-footers below. Make any sense to you?"

"I guess not."

"It's how government works. Always screwing up."

He sat down at the end of the bed near the window. Abe had his eyes open. Calen could tell he was listening to every word.

"Do you read Ayn Rand?"

"What's that."

"She wrote *Atlas Shrugged*. It's the only book you ever need to read. Tells you everything."

"My reading ain't too good. Comic books are easier for me. I don't mind the superheroes ones."

"What's your philosophy?"

Calen shook his head. Abe was quiet.

"I'm a libertarian. It's about what you believe. I don't believe in the government, any government. What's your belief?"

Calen thought. He wasn't used to hard questions.

"I guess I believe *love your neighbor as you love yourself.*"

"I'd say, love yourself and forget about neighbors. Very likely, they have no love for you."

Later, he discussed 4057B with Abe. The baby had mastered language. He could lie in his swaddling or on Calen's shoulder and give his opinion in his squeaky baby voice.

"You should always do the right thing."

"Sometimes I don't know what that is."

"I'll help you."

A warm sensation grew in Calen's chest. He had all a man wanted. A room. Meals. A job. A girlfriend. A new friendship with 4057B. A park across the street. And, because God answered his prayers, a second chance to love his baby brother. He was happy.

CHAPTER 28
PRAYER: ISAAC

Isaac felt like an actor playing the part of himself, "Isaac," ever since his Grandfather Abraham died after telling him his terrible secret. For the first ten years of his marriage to Hannah, he cast himself in the role of "husband." Inside, doubts plagued him. Was he playacting or did he really love his wife? How can anyone tell whether what they are experiencing is true love? Was there someone else out there who was his soul mate?

He checked often. If Hannah made the special meatloaf he liked, topped with Swiss cheese rather than ketchup, did he feel gratitude or love? When he held her hand, was it affection or just enjoyment of the warmth? Would sex be as good with any attractive woman, or was it good because it was with Hannah? He would put this question to the test if he wasn't a firm believer in fidelity.

The miscarriages made the matter worse. Every time Hannah had a positive home pregnancy test, every early ultrasound showing a beating heart, made his own heart race with joy and hope. He drew his wife close at such moments, having the brief certainty that she was the one for him. He was a fourth-grade schoolteacher who liked children, and he was sure he would love the woman who would provide him with a family, wouldn't he?

If only her hormonal rages, her crying spells, the medical tests and procedures that became more expensive as they advanced didn't complicate their relationship. And the months of depression every time she lost a pregnancy.

"I just don't think I can do this anymore. I may not be up to it again," she would say.

It was *her* body. He had to respect whatever decision she made. If she stopped, he had to accept it, never mind his own selfish, sexist, infantile, male needs.

"I will be here to support you no matter what." He said the correct thing.

The questioning would return right away. If she stops trying, will I love her or hate her? Can it be true love if I even have to ask?

He needed a test that provided a definitive answer and put an end to the uncertainty that preoccupied him for hours, even waking him in the middle of sleep. Every Friday night, the couple would go to services at the synagogue. At every service, both of them prayed that God would give them a child. Now, Isaac prayed instead for assuredness, for something that determined once and for all whether he loved Hannah.

They had developed a routine of only discussing fertility issues on Saturdays.

"We've been at this for nine years, Isaac. I'm thirty-five." She sat opposite him at the kitchen table on a Saturday, twirling a strand of her dark hair. "That means two risk factors for having a child with developmental problems. My age and the fertility treatments. Supposing I can ever carry a baby to term. Dr. Anders claims I might get to viability with his latest procedure. That's a third risk, if it means having a preemie."

Could he love a woman who couldn't have a perfect child?

"I'll say what I always say, Hannah. It's you who have the burden. It's your choice."

"Okay. I still need to hear what you want and whether we are together on this."

At a younger age, they both wanted a baby, any kind of baby. In their thirties, mid-career, with demanding work loads and long hours, a special-needs child might be too much of a challenge. Too much for Isaac. Too much for Isaac to love the child.

"Of course it would be a disappointment to wind up childless. Having a child might disappoint in another way, if he or she is autistic or blind or whatever. I'm not sure. From what I've seen at school, the parents of the kids in Special Ed love their kids and the parents of mainstreamed kids love them. There's no difference."

Unless there *was* a difference. Just because parents greet their children with similar-looking hugs and smiles, no matter what their ability, did they feel the same?

Several Saturdays later, they decided to try one more time. They would pray first. Issac had a request.

"This will sound crazy, but instead of going to services, I want us to go to the state park, find a beautiful spot, and pray there."

He turned his embarrassed face away from her.

"It does sound crazy. I enjoy going to the park, but not to pray. I need to be in a congregation, near a *Torah*, to be close to God."

"Yes, but… there are parts of the park, if you go beyond the picnic areas and the lodge, that are, as strange as it is to say, magical. It's hard to explain. I've only experienced it twice."

"You never told me."

"I don't remember any details. I haven't told you because I only recall the sense of… mysticism. I have a memory of being in the forest. Not of why or of what happened."

Hannah took his face in her hands and looked into his eyes. He hoped he didn't reveal his discomfort.

"Isaac."

The one word, his name, said in a tone just above a whisper, conveyed so much. Her protectiveness, her nurturance, her forbearance, her compassion. All the qualities one wished for in a partner. Hannah was a perfect wife. She would be a perfect mother. If doing voodoo in a park resulted in a healthy pregnancy, she would do it — for him.

The next day, they drove to the park. She packed a lunch. Signs directed visitors to campgrounds, picnic areas, trails, and vistas. They followed the arrows to the vistas, turning the first two down for not seeming right to Isaac. The third one, farther away, up a gravel road, ended in a scenic spot above a waterfall. First, they stopped in the vista parking lot and gazed out at miles of tree canopy. Then, they drove down to the bottom of the waterfall and parked. No one else was around. They found a place to spread a blanket. Both sat and ate their sandwiches. The waterfall splashed down into a pleasant circular pool. Birds chirped, insects buzzed, a gentle breeze feathered coolness across the area. They agreed it was a lovely place.

But was it the magical spot Isaac had either experienced or dreamed up? This is what Hannah asked.

"Well, it might be. I'm not a hundred percent sure. It's very nice. Maybe God is here right now, and I don't know it, as Jacob says in the *Torah*."

"So, do you want to try praying, anyway?"

She raised inquisitive eyebrows, giving him the choice.

"I guess we have nothing to lose," he said.

They agreed that they would do the *Amida*, the Jewish Standing Prayer. Hannah went to the car and returned with their prayer shawls.

"Let's do the first lines together, and do the rest in silence," he said.

Hannah nodded. Together, they stood and chanted.

Blessed One, open my lips, that my mouth may declare your praise.

Once the silent part began, Isaac prayed from his heart, asking God to grant Hannah a normal, full-term pregnancy. But even while praying, annoying questions drifted into his head—the same ones. How did he know if he really loved his wife? Would he be certain if she didn't lose a pregnancy? He feared God would frown on him for allowing these thoughts to intrude on the *Amida*.

He opened his eyes. The water cascaded down the high rock face, bubbling into the pool. As he looked, the shadows and highlights on the vertical surface merged into a dim image. The prayer faded from his lips as the image became the face of a familiar woman with a dark braid of hair topping her head. He had a vague recollection of seeing her before, but didn't remember where or when.

The image disappeared after a few seconds. Isaac turned to Hannah, pointing at the waterfall.

"Did you see that? Did you see?"

He had a dizzy spell. Hannah ran to him and caught him before he fell over.

"Are you ill? Here. Sit down on the blanket." She eased him down.

He perspired, chilling at the same time. Hannah wrapped both shawls around him.

"I think you have a fever." She put her cool hand on his forehead. "It's a good thing you had your COVID booster this year. It can't be that."

On the drive home, he made a slow recovery.

"I don't understand what happened."

"It's a bad idea to pray in the forest. Next time, let's go to the state park for picnics and do our praying in the synagogue. Besides your spell, I'm full of mosquito bites."

In lighter moments, she joked about mosquitos loving her. The word "loving" had triggered Isaac's obsessive thoughts, before going to the forest. But the thoughts hadn't returned. Instead, the image of the woman in the waterfall kept floating back into his mind.

A month later, Hannah was pregnant, and by natural means, without a fertility treatment. Praying in the park worked after all, unless it was a coincidence. Isaac's obsessive thoughts returned.

Did he love Hannah or love the fact that she would have his child? Would he be able to love a woman whose body would change if the pregnancy went full term? There was no guarantee of that happening and plenty of reason to doubt it would. Meanwhile, he had been noticing other changes common to even the most attractive women in their mid-thirties—crinkles around her eyes, graying at her temples, extra weight. Each of these "flaws" gave him more reason to pause.

Isaac wasn't a callous man. His ethical and psychological training in the Yeshiva helped him be well-liked in his former job as assistant rabbi. Now, he violated the most basic of Jewish principles when he doubted his love for his own pregnant wife. She was created in the image of God, and that alone was reason to love her. He didn't want to have doubts. They seemed to come from outside, to enter his mind like an invading virus he couldn't ward off with rational thinking. He tried hard to combat the alien thoughts by denigrating himself, calling himself superficial and unworthy of his marriage. If he didn't love her, he didn't love himself either. He despised himself. It was a vicious cycle. He hated himself for not being sure of his love for Hannah, which made him hate himself and incapable of loving Hannah.

If only he stopped ruminating about it.

Meanwhile, Hannah's pregnancy advanced to viability, the minimum time a fetus might survive outside the womb, twenty-four weeks. Every week beyond that Hannah did not go into labor was cause for celebration. Every week beyond twenty-four lessened that chances for disabilities.

"Your idea of praying in the park is working," Hannah said, with cautious jubilation.

She paraded around the apartment in underwear, thrusting her growing bulge in his face.

"Want to feel the baby kick? Put your fingers right there." She grabbed his reluctant hand.

He fought to disguise his disgust. It seemed he very much wanted a baby with Hannah without having to endure Hannah's pregnancy. It's temporary, he told himself. After the birth, she will get her figure back, and I'll find her attractive again.

Sometimes Hannah suspected.

"You think I'm repulsive, don't you?"

He protested.

"How can you say that! I love your body. It's beautiful. What makes you think I would feel any other way after ten years of waiting for this?"

"I don't know, Isaac. You always say the right thing. But you never look at me if you can help it. I've seen you turn your head away when I come into the room."

"You're imagining things. It's your hormones." His voice was insistent.

"You don't touch me anymore."

"Yes, I do!"

Did his lies mean he loved her or did he just wanted to spare her feelings? He shuddered to think what would happen is she knew the truth.

Isaac tried something new. Every time he had a "bad" thought, he would counter it with a prayer — the *Sh'ma*, the most important Jewish prayer. At that very moment, another obsession sprang into his head.

"Praying won't tell me if I really love my wife. *Sh'ma Yisrael, Adonai Eloheynu, Adonai Echad. Listen, O Israel, God is our Lord. God is One.*"

For a few seconds, he had relief. But soon the "bad" thoughts came back, and he had to pray again. For hours, this pattern continued. He had trapped himself by tying the prayer to the thoughts. Both cycled in his head. And all the while this torture plagued him, he had to pretend enthusiasm for Hannah and her pregnancy.

They stumbled along in this way, Isaac concealing and Hannah suspecting, as their relationship eroded until Hannah's water broke on her due date. She turned to him with pleading eyes.

"Isaac, I'm so scared. You've got to be with me on this."

At once, an inexplicable miracle occurred. His heart filled with equal parts excitement and regret. Tears sprouted, running down his cheeks.

"I'm with you," he sobbed. "All the way. I'm so, so sorry. I don't know what happened. From now on, I'll be making it up to you."

His brain was in upheaval. He meant what he said. On the drive to the hospital, he repeated his apology.

"It's going to be okay, Isaac. In a few hours, we'll have our baby boy. Stop apologizing and concentrate on driving. We have the rest of our lives to figure out what happened to you. Or not. It isn't important right now."

She was right. He had been under some sort of spell, ever since he prayed in the state park. There was something about that forest, ever since his grandfather died. He agreed with Hannah. It no longer mattered. They were going to have a baby.

Several hours later, Isaac held his perfect, healthy son in his arms for the first time. With absolute certainty, he loved the tiny creature with his whole heart. And Hannah was the love of his life.

Later, he would be convinced that though the forest almost destroyed him, the *Sh'ma* saved him.

How could it have been anything else?

CHAPTER 29
REPENTANCE: ISAAC

After the murder of their newborn, after the capture of the two children who kidnapped and killed him, after the funeral and the seven days of Shiva, after the quieting of the media, after the casseroles and brownies, after the recommendations of support groups and therapists, after the prescriptions for Xanax and Lexapro, Issac and Hannah were left with their sorrow and each other.

Isaac didn't see how to help himself, much less his wife. He drifted from numbness to intense spells of sobbing to alcoholic melancholy. Hannah did the same. She didn't get out of bed. He didn't go to bed, spending the night pacing and mumbling to himself. Neither had the courage to enter the baby's room and remove the empty crib, the changing table, and the dresser full of onesies.

Isaac tried hard not to get into recriminations. Hannah wasn't to blame, yet he wanted to scream at her.

"Why did you let this happen?"

She, too, cast him bitter looks, although she didn't say what she stewed about. Isaac guessed. It seemed best to leave their newborn in his own room from day one instead of the more customary arrangement of keeping the baby in the parent's bedroom for the first month or two, where he would be monitored. It was safer to keep him separate, in case one of his parents became infected. An additional benefit was having a good sleeping habit established by the time maternity leave was over, and they both needed uninterrupted sleep to work.

Isaac didn't remember who came up with this idea first, but Hannah did all the research, read all the articles, and consulted more experienced mothers. He went along with her ideas, deferring to her nesting arrangements. If the baby slept in their bedroom instead of his own, the kidnappers would have awakened one of them. He would be alive today.

And who left the back door unlocked? Isaac racked his brain. He didn't use the backyard. It must have been Hannah's fault. She planted things, flowers, tomatoes. She was in and out of the yard with a trowel or rake.

At times he pulled himself together, remembering the vow he made before the baby's birth to be a better husband. He steeled himself.

"Hannah, do you want to talk about it?"

"No." She pulled the quilt up to her neck.

"Can I do anything?"

"No."

"Well, I tried," he said to himself, both relieved and guilty for being relieved.

The house fell into disarray. Neither of them cleaned, did laundry, or bathed. They ate straight out of cereal boxes or ice cream tubs. Who cared? They were on leave from work and without energy for visitors. If the doorbell rang, they didn't answer. No one saw the state they were in.

The Homicide Officer in charge was Detective Conners. He kept in contact. It was no surprise when Isaac received a call, but the request to speak to him alone was unusual.

"Alone? You mean without Hannah?"

Isaac sat in his home office with the door closed. He always switched to speaker phone to include his wife if the detective phoned.

"I wanted to speak to you first. It's a sensitive subject," Detective Conners said.

"Okay." Isaac gripped the arm of his chair. Calls from the Homicide Department were never good news.

"We ran DNA tests on both of the suspects, Azura and Calen, and on your son. There is no match between the two kids. They are not siblings."

"Well, okay." That didn't matter to Isaac.

"We traced the boy to the parents of a child kidnapped twelve years ago. It's over a ninety-nine percent match. Another officer will attempt to contact his family."

Isaac didn't respond.

"The girl, however, is a sixty percent match with your son. They are likely half-siblings."

A fog descended. Isaac heard the detective's senseless words. "What?"

"Yes. Azura and your son are half-siblings."

"How can that be?" Isaac stood without awareness of leaving his seat. He shoved his hand into his corkscrews of uncombed hair.

"Well, sir, the only plausible scenario is that you are her parent. That's why I wanted to speak to you alone, in case you don't want your wife to know. The girl maintains the reason she kidnapped the baby is that you are her father. We know she had a mother. We located her remains in the forest. I'd advise you to submit your DNA to rule yourself in or out."

"No, no, no, no. This is a misunderstanding. I'll take the damn test. I'll tell my wife after the results are in. You'll see. Our son was our only child. The girl lied. Her test must be a false positive."

Forty-eight hours later, the result came in—a 99.9 percent match. He was the girl's father. But how? He saw her on tv, never in person. She looked very young, a dark-eyed fawn of a girl, a girl he loathed for kidnapping his baby boy and contributing to his death.

He had to tell Hannah. The bedroom smelled stale from unwashed clothing, perspiration, and body odor. The curtains were drawn. Isaac no longer slept there. He dozed in chairs, on the sofa, or in the guest bedroom. Hannah bunched herself up under the queen quilt. Her chestnut hair, the only visible part of her, lay in a dull fan on the pillow.

"Detective Conners called. There has been a paternity test. It seems I'm the girl's father."

A blur of pillows and the quilt quaked the room. Hannah shot up and out of bed.

"It seems? What do you mean 'seems'?" She shrieked.

"The test is ninety-nine percent positive. I'm her father, and the baby is… was her half-brother." He gave it to her straight.

"Oh, my God. You have a daughter, and you didn't tell me. Oh, my God!" She doubled-over, clutching her shirt in her fists, then straightened.

"I didn't know."

"That girl is twelve. You conceived her thirteen years ago. It would have been 2020. That's the year we started dating, Isaac."

"It is?" That hadn't occurred to him.

"So, did you fuck someone before or after we started dating?"

"2020. That's the year we isolated and wore masks, at least when I dated you in the spring. I don't remember having sex with anyone. How could I have?"

"There's only one way, Isaac. You put your damned prick into the girl's mother's damned cunt. That's how."

Hannah never used vulgarities. That shocked him as much as anything else he learned that day. Her fury gave her more energy than she had in weeks. For two hours, she ranted and grilled him. How could he not know? Why wasn't he honest with her? Was he thinking of the other woman while she was pregnant with their son? Did he cheat on her?

Exhausted beyond the point of caring, he blurted out what he knew.

"It happened in the forest. I thought I fell asleep there and dreamed it. There was this woman with her hair whipping around in the wind. And when we prayed at the waterfall, I saw her image on the rock face. I realize this sounds insane."

"It doesn't sound insane, Isaac. It sounds like a lie."

She threw herself on the bed, yanking the quilt on top of her. He was banished.

He returned to his office and called Detective Conners.

"If I'm her father, what does it mean?"

"You should see a lawyer. You're not the father in a legal sense because there's no birth certificate. But you're her biological father. What you do or don't do about it is up to you."

He tried to explain this to Hannah.

"Detective Conners says the girl isn't my legal daughter."

This was ripe cause for more fury.

"That's not the point. You have a daughter you claim you knew nothing about and who I for certain knew nothing about who killed our baby! My baby. Now I'm left with nothing, no child, no baby, nothing. But you! You have a daughter. You aren't childless. You have something."

There was no denying what she said. Yet, he'd loved their baby with all his being. He'd never loved anyone so much. The loss devastated him. Having another child didn't mitigate the loss. It just added a confusing layer of anguish and guilt, since his child caused their baby's death and Hannah's rage.

Without being able to talk to his wife, Isaac pondered his situation alone for several days. Until the DNA test, he hated the girl. Azura. He still did. But his feelings weren't the central issue. As Detective Conners said, "What you do or don't do about it is up to you." Isaac had a right to abandoned her. Or what? Write her a letter? Send her books? Visit her? Nothing seemed more distasteful. The detective put the responsibility on him. Even if he did nothing, he still made a choice. Everything shifted from what his daughter did to what he would do.

After working up his nerve, he talked to Hannah again. He went back to the bedroom. To his surprise, she was up and dressed in clean clothes. Her hair was wet from showering. She pulled creased sheets off the bed.

"What do you want," she said.

"You're up."

"Yes. I have an appointment." She didn't look at him.

"With who?"

She didn't respond. It must be with a lawyer. He'd deal with that later.

"I don't know what to do about the girl, my daughter."

She glanced at him with cold eyes.

"Well, don't think I'm going to give you permission to do anything about her, if you mean have some sort of father-daughter relationship with her. But I will give you a choice—her or me."

He remembered the day he asked Hannah to a virtual dinner, on the same day he kayaked near the forest. He heard singing and pulled into a clearing. That's where he encountered the long-haired woman while in some kind of delirious state. Evidently, he wasn't dreaming. The woman was real. As soon as he returned home, he called Hannah. He chose her, not some dream woman he forgot. That woman faded, like people in dreams do.

While he was still under the spell of the forest, he phoned Hannah about a date without forethought. It turned out to be the right decision. They married. Didn't that in itself make it right?

Who was he kidding? Right decision, wrong decision. His baby was dead, and he lost his wife. A dark chasm opened. Never, not even on the day of his son's disappearance, did he feel such awful pain. Even if he had done nothing wrong, it was all his fault. It was he who hadn't protected the baby. It was he who hadn't checked the back door. Blaming Hannah avoided responsibility.

Because of his negligence, the baby had been murdered, choked. A helpless newborn, too fragile to do anything but submit to brutal hands. The baby's suffering was beyond his ability to imagine, yet he imagined it. A slow death. A quick death. A grotesque death. He pictured it all.

He didn't deserve to live. Thoughts of suicide circled in his head. If only he had a gun. But a gunshot would be too quick and easy, anyway. He needed a painful, torturous means to make things right. A plunged knife in his guts, perhaps. He'd do it while Hannah was with the lawyer, sparing her the ugliness of a divorce. She'd be better off without him. He'd failed as both a husband and a father.

A shower curtain beneath him would prevent blood from staining the carpet. He wouldn't add to her burden by leaving a mess for her to clear up. Or he could do it in the backyard, letting the soil absorb his bodily fluids.

He hurried into the kitchen and opened the knife drawer. It contained a cleaver, paring knives, steak knives, and a wicked-looking thin knife with a seven-inch blade. He stared at it, knowing it was a now-or-never moment, that the time had come. Before fear stopped him, he must act. Right away. The seconds it would take to reach the yard would be too long. He grabbed the thin knife and without bothering to remove his kakis, drove the blade hard into his soft fatty abdomen.

Sirens approached when he awakened. He must have passed out. Hannah was on her knees, bending over him, her mouth opened in an oval shape. She made a sound he couldn't make out. Or maybe the woman in the forest said something he struggled to understand. As everything dimmed, he heard her voice.

Take care of our daughter, Isaac.

CHAPTER 30
RIGHTEOUSNESS: ISAAC

Isaac was asked to take part in a Victim Offender Mediation process with Azura, the girl responsible for the death of his newborn son. A therapist named Rick, who phoned him from the adolescent psychiatric facility that held the girl, made the suggestion.

"It will be your opportunity to tell Azura how her crime has affected you. She's twelve years old and may be released from Juvenile Detention when she's fifteen or sixteen. She needs to know the consequences of her behavior so she won't offend again." Rick had a deep voice and a New York accent.

"The consequence of her behavior is that my son is dead." He stared at his inbox. More than two hundred unread emails had piled into it. He hovered the cursor over the "Delete All" box.

"What I can tell you is that many victims find the process is a helpful part of healing."

"I'm not the victim. The victim was three weeks old. I'm the father of the victim and the father of the offender, according to some lab DNA test. But to hear about it on tv, you'd think the girl is the victim. So excuse me if I have my doubts." He clicked the cursor. All the unread emails vanished.

"Please think it over. I'm only offering this because it wasn't Azura who murdered your son. They charged her companion Calen with that offense. Azura is remorseful and prepared to tell you so."

Under pressure from Rick, Isaac agreed to think it over just to end the call. The Juvenile Justice System had a way of putting the ball in his court. He had to choose whether to get the damn DNA test. He had to decide whether to have any kind of relationship with the girl. Now he needed to decide about this Victim Offender thing. The unfairness irked him. Why did the system force him, who had been put through so much, to make all the decisions?

He faced another sleepless night. The stitches in his abdomen itched. The bed in the motel where he booked a room while looking for an apartment was comfortable enough. Ambien put him to sleep when he took it at midnight. By one, he was wide awake again. If he drank enough, he might doze off for another hour around four. He had plenty of time for considerations and reconsiderations of his situation.

They stuck him with a daughter he didn't want. She didn't ask to be born. That was his doing. At the Yeshiva, he was taught that God's presence is in everyone. And that everyone should be as loving to others as God is. Didn't this apply to his daughter? God's presence had been in his son. And, at one time, in him. In the past, he had similar thoughts about Hannah when he failed to love her. This confusion of theological ideas convinced him to accept Rick's offer, with reluctance, even though treating the girl in a loving way didn't seem possible.

He called Rick to begin the process. They had a long conversation.

"Azura was raised off the grid in the forest, where she learned to distrust everyone except her mother and Calen. She is a very naïve child. I'm worried about how she will survive in Juvenile Detention. It's a very rough atmosphere, there," Rick said.

He didn't have a response. She belonged in Juvenile Detention for what she had done. But what did "rough atmosphere" mean? He didn't want her to be beaten up or exposed to kids who would turn her into a gangster. He wanted her to suffer as much as he suffered, but mentally, not physically. Crying. Regretting. Feeling the full weight of guilt. Having black spells of depression.

In the lobby of the Valley Adolescent Psychiatric Hospital, they gave him paperwork to fill out and a mask. Then they escorted him through a maze of hallways that avoided all areas where the young patients congregated.

"For confidentiality."

They left him in a small, windowless room, with several chairs and a chart with facial expressions tacked to the wall.

"Sit anywhere," they said.

A paper cup filled with tepid water was handed to him. They closed the door and left him alone. When he put his hand to his chest, he felt his heart pumping hard, as if he uprooted a tree. He told himself to leave while he had the chance, that he didn't want to do this, that it was a mistake. Yet he sat.

After about fifteen minutes, the door opened and a large man with a bulging mask, hiding a thick mustache, entered. He introduced himself as Rick. The girl, Azura, followed him, wearing a cloth mask. Her dark hair was gathered into two ponytails, one above each ear. She was much smaller than Isaac expected, no taller than the ten-year-olds he taught in the fourth grade. He had pictured her being bigger, fiercer, defiant. Instead, a frightened child confronted him, whose thin arms dangled from an over-sized shirt emboldened with the logo "Valley Hospital." Her head remained bowed while she took a seat opposite him, as Rick told her to do. The therapist sat as well.

"So. Here we are. Let's start with names. I'm Rick. And you?" He gestured toward Isaac.

He refused to say "Dad" or "your father."

"Isaac."

Now Rick pointed at the girl.

"Azura." Her voice was just above a whisper.

"Azura, you have been through a mediation before, with Calen. You know how it goes. Each of you gets a turn to speak, while the other one listens. Then the listener repeats the gist of what the speaker said. Agreed?"

Isaac wanted to protest. He was the aggrieved party. The girl should be made to listen to him. It sounded like Rick gave them equal status. But if he argued, it would lengthen the ordeal. He nodded his head.

"My understanding is that you both called the baby 'Abe,'" Rick said.

Azura's downward gaze jolted up to Isaac's for a brief instant. Dark brown eyes.

"After my grandfather, Abraham," Isaac said.

The child couldn't have known. It had to be a coincidence that they both called the newborn by the same name.

"Right. When you talk about him, don't call him 'the baby. 'He was a human being with a name. Azura, why don't you go first. What do you want to say to Isaac about Abe?"

She continued to look downward. Isaac saw her eyelids twitching and slight movements of her mask.

"Look at Isaac when you're ready to speak."

After a couple of sniffs, she looked up, right at him. A gush of tears sprang from her eyes, squeezed shut, then opened again with effort.

"I'm sorry…"

"Tell Isaac what you are sorry for."

More tears soaked her mask.

"For taking Abe…" Before she could say the last word, she was sobbing.

Rick gestured to him. His big hands hung from arms resting on his legs as he leaned toward the participants.

"Can you repeat what Azura said?"

The sight of the distraught girl brought a bursting sensation to Isaac's chest.

"She said… she said…" He doubled over with sobs.

"Keep going. What did Azura say?"

"That she's sorry she took Abe." He cried harder than he ever had. Words spilled from him between sobs. "You ruined my life. You took my son, Abe. It tortured me to think of him going hungry, of being cold, in a wet diaper, with strangers, in pain. Then when I learned he was dead? Even worse torture, imagining his last moments, gasping for air, not knowing what was happening to him."

Rick put a hand on his knee, signaling for him to stop.

"Azura, what did Isaac say."

"That it tortured him to think what Abe went through." She continued to cry. Like a smaller child, she balled her fists in her eyes.

"Do you have more, Isaac?"

"My wife, Hannah—she left me when she found out about you. I'm living in a motel with nothing. I don't have my son, my wife, or my home."

They both sobbed. Then Azura stood.

"Kill me! Kill me! Please. Kill me right now!" She grabbed her shirt, trying to rip it, twisting and wringing it, pleading and shrieking. "Kill me! Kill me!"

Rick reached over and pulled her to him. He nodded at Isaac.

"There are tissues on table if you need them." He drew a device from his pocket while still holding the agitated girl. "Could someone please come and show Azura's father the way out?"

Back in the motel, Isaac lay face-up on the bed. His heavy arms lay like broken wings at his sides. He had seen what he thought he wanted to see—suffering equal to his own. Suffering that exceeded his own. The despair of a suicidal twelve-year-old child who happened to be his daughter. He should have been satisfied.

On impulse, he phoned Hannah, knowing it was unwise.

"I just want to talk. Can we talk?"

"I doubt it." She sounded weary.

"I saw the girl today at Valley Hospital. Can I talk about it?"

"Isaac. Really?" She hung up.

Not knowing what to do with himself, he left the motel and walked through the seedy commercial area, passing liquor stores, convenience stores, a Dollar Store, Dennys, Hardees. The ugliness suited him. If he saw a flower, he might weep again. No chance of that in this neighborhood.

He came to a roller skating rink. It surprised him that any still existed. He hadn't skated since high school, maybe middle school. A posted sign described the sessions—the early ones for children, the current session for teens and adults. He went in, paid the admission fee, and traded his shoes for skates. The interior was dim. Strobe lights swirled harsh colors over the walls and ceiling. Classic rock drowned out all other sounds.

He clomped to the rink edge, then took a tentative step onto the floor, gripping the railing. It didn't matter if he fell. If he wound up in the emergency room with broken legs, it would settle things. Someone else would decide what to do with his sorry life. Not caring, he pushed off and, to his astonishment, found that he remembered what to do.

After gliding around for several minutes, his tight shoulders loosened. For the first time since his son's disappearance, the awful melancholy lifted. He drifted along, swaying to the percussive beat of the music, with nothing required of him other than lifting one foot, then the other. He swirled around for another ten minutes. Then all males were ordered off for a female-only session.

He took a seat off the wooden floor and watched as teenaged girls skated, holding hands, laughing, and waving to the boys on the side-lines. They were normal kids, in jeans or short skating skirts, having a good time.

Seated next to him was the only other adult man in the rink. A strong cologne smell wafted from him. He began talking to Issac.

"Look at that one, the blond with the red top. See her? I could fuck her until the sun comes up. Know what I mean?"

Isaac got up and clomped away. The guy was a creep, a pedophile. The blond girl was young. With a shock, he realized she was close to Azura's age. It nauseated him. He traded in the skates for his shoes. He was too disgusted to stay.

Back in the motel, he thought about the Victim Offender mediation. He should still loathe Azura. For months, he had stoked his smoldering hatred of her to keep it blazing. Anything less betrayed Abe. He owed it to his son to hate his kidnapper.

If only Azura was more of a monster, instead of a lost, frightened child. Since their meeting, he had a harder time hating her. In Juvenile Detention, she would miss the normal experiences of a teenage girl, like skating parties. He shuddered, imagining guys like the creep in the rink, able to do whatever they wanted with her. Such a vulnerable kid.

Rick's words came back to him.

"She is a very naïve child. I'm worried about how she will survive in Juvenile Detention. It's a very rough atmosphere, there."

He was her father. His feelings didn't matter. If he never stopped hating her, it was because he was only human. But that day, he had connected to God's presence within her when they wept together during the mediation.

Now he knew why he had survived his stabbing attempt. The knife had not pierced his intestines. The wound was superficial. God had been merciful, giving him a second chance. Like He gave his grandfather.

He came around to the idea of consulting a lawyer about asking the court to give Azura to him instead of sending her to detention. A consultation wouldn't obligate him. He could decide later whether to put the lawyer on retainer, to go through the process of adding his name to her birth certificate, to request guardianship.

Each step would be an opportunity to stop or move ahead. After failing to protect his son, it was on him to protect his other child—or not. In time, he would come to know the right thing to do.

CHAPTER 31
REPENTANCE: LEAH

The five-day Jewish Grief and Renewal Retreat began at 10 a.m. in the Oak Room of the lodge in the state park. Chairs had been set up in a circle. A coffee urn, cans of diet soda, a bowl of spotted bananas, and a neat arrangement of Entenmann's Frosted Donuts had been placed on a side table. Boxes of tissues waited in strategic locations around the room.

Nine participants filed in with shy glances at each other. All had been immunized. Masks weren't required anymore. They seated themselves with hesitation, since no one directed them to any particular chair. After a few minutes, a tall, wiry thirty-something man entered with a confident stride and sat in the last vacant seat.

"Hello, Friends. My name is Simon. I'm your facilitator, and this is the Jewish Grief and Renewal Retreat. Is everyone here signed up for this? Yes? Good. So, ground rules. Confidentiality. What's said here doesn't leave this room. Agreed? Respect. We don't interrupt or criticize. Agreed? It's okay to pass and take breaks. Yes?"

Everyone looked more at ease. Someone—this man, Simon—was in charge and would tell them what to do.

"Let's go around the circle. Just say your name, something about yourself, and who you lost. I'll start. My name is Simon. I lost my wife, Judy, who died in April 2020, of COVID-19. Then I lived in the Woodland Cooperative in the forest until it broke up. Now I'm back in town."

Simon looked toward an older man seated on his right.

"My name is Aaron, and I'm a dean at the university. I lost a friend I never even had. This friend never knew how I felt. So not even a friend, to tell the truth. Just someone I loved from afar."

He looked downward with an embarrassed smile.

"Thank you, Aaron. Who's next?" Simon asked.

"Me. I'm Leah. I'm very nervous. This is my first time doing anything like this. My life has been filled with tragedy. Years ago, a schizophrenic man murdered my husband, Josh, and severely injured my daughter, Dinah. She died of a heart attack when she turned sixteen. After that, my mother, Nancy, and grandmother, Ruth, drove off a cliff in the forest and drowned. No one knows why. There's more, I'm afraid. You might have heard of my niece, Azura. She kidnapped my brother Isaac's baby." She touched her dark hair and inhaled. "Then, like you, Aaron, I fell for a man who didn't know I existed. For some reason, that loss hit me harder than the others."

"Thank you, Leah. Next?"

"I'm Hannah, Leah's ex-sister-in-law. I used to be married to her brother, Isaac. But we came separately. We haven't seen each other in years. I'm an old hand at these retreats. I've attended three others since my baby Abe was killed. You may have seen it on the news. He was kidnapped by Leah's niece, Azura, the one she mentioned. Azura turned out to be my ex-husband's secret daughter. Her adopted brother murdered my baby. It's complicated. We need a chart to explain all the connections."

Hannah grabbed a tissue and dabbed at her eyes.

"Thank you, Hannah."

The five remaining participants took turns with stoicism or anxiety or tears. There was a recovering alcoholic, two widows, a man whose teen-aged son had committed suicide, and an older woman mourning the loss of her dog—her only companion for fifteen years.

"I realize it's silly to make such a fuss over a pet." She was the only one who openly sobbed.

Later, after the first day's session, Leah found Hannah sitting on an Adirondack on a deck, drinking wine.

"Join me?"

Leah smiled, eager for company. They sat next to each other all day, sometimes glancing at each other, at first with suspicion, but in a friendlier manner as the hours passed.

"What do you think of Simon?" Hannah asked. They had a silent understanding not to speak about anything personal.

"I just figured out how I know him. Simon's family lived next door to mine. That's a small town for you. We're all linked, especially those of us who are Jewish. He's okay. Not too *frum*. I mean, I'd like a spiritual experience, but not a Conservative one."

"He's cute, isn't he?" She took a casual sip of her wine.

"I guess." Leah sat in the adjoining Adirondack. "Why?"

"All the retreats I've been to turned into fuck fests, with everyone getting jealous of anyone the leader favored. In two of them, the leader switched his favorite every day. Both turned into warfare. The last one ended half-way through."

"Why do you keep signing up?"

Hannah laughed. "Eternal hope. And I figured a Jewish one would be cleaner. Not that I mind hooking up with someone. I just don't want the ugliness. I've had too much ugliness in my life as it is."

Leah wondered whose life had been uglier—hers or Hannah's.

"What about Aaron, the dean? He's older, but still nice looking."

"Forget it. He's gay."

Leah looked at Hannah with amazed eyes. Her own life had been so sheltered. She knew nothing of fuck fests and figuring out sexual preferences.

"How do you know?"

Hannah shrugged. "He said 'friend 'instead of 'woman. 'Gay men in his generation say 'friend 'to cover up."

The second day of the retreat was devoted to the grief part of the program. Those who wanted to would say *Kaddish*, the prayer for the dead, at the end of the session. Everyone told the others about who or what they lost. It surprised Leah when Hannah, who she thought of as cynical, wept hard while recounting the loss of her newborn, then appeared recovered during the lunch break, then wept again during the afternoon session.

The alcoholic, the two widows, the father of the suicide, and the woman who lost her dog were all emotional. Even Simon was tearful when interjecting bits and pieces about the death of his wife. Aaron and Leah were the only two who remained dry-eyed, even when their turns came to tell their tragic tales.

Leah thought Aaron had an excuse. He couldn't lose what he never had. But what kind of human being was she? The years of caring for her disabled daughter, the surgeries, the hospitalizations, one emergency after another, the horror of her last heart attack, the ambulance, the death certificate, the funeral—and not a single tear? In fact, she didn't remember ever crying. What she recalled was exhaustion, hours on the phone with insurance companies, never daring to sleep in case her daughter had a seizure or pain.

Now, she felt inferior, as if she were a retreat failure, an outsider, the one the leader wouldn't favor. Not that she wanted a fuck fest with Simon. That was not why she signed up. But she wanted to be worthy of the group. That day, she hadn't been sad enough for them. The ground rules were "no criticizing," but she criticized herself.

In the dining room, she noticed Aaron eating alone. She decided to join him. Hannah would have been a preferable companion, but Leah feared the other woman's scorn.

"Can't you manage any sorrow for your daughter?" She imagined Hannah thinking, even if she did not say those words out loud.

When she approached, Aaron half-rose and motioned for her to join him. He gave her a rueful smile. She wondered if he thought he had a right not to cry. Men don't cry in public, no matter how sad they are. Even gay men. She was a woman, a mother. She was supposed to cry.

"What do you think of the food," Aaron said.

It seemed they were going to discuss trivial subjects. Not their sorry performances in the sessions.

"Typical park lodge food," she said. Hamburgers. Salads. Steak.

"What did you think of the afternoon?"

"I'm not sure. I didn't do very well."

His eyebrows raised. "What do you mean?"

"I must have appeared cold-hearted. My daughter dead. My husband murdered. And I don't seem to have the proper emotions about it. I had to train myself to be calm when my daughter had surgeries. I forgot how to have feelings."

Aaron shook his head. "It may sound odd, but I envy you. You have a story to tell. I don't even have that. All I have is a wish that didn't come true. I fell in love with my business partner, Larry, and never told him."

So. Hannah was right. Aaron is gay. Larry. Larry?

"That's funny. The man I fell for is named Larry. I was just one of his customers, nothing more."

"During the last break, I talked to Simon about my Larry. He told me a Larry was a member of the forest commune he belonged to. That Larry was a handful. Kind of immoral, it seems."

"Hmm." It was curious that a group of ten people knew three immoral Larrys.

The Renewal portion of the retreat began on the third day.

Simon explained. "For the next two days, we will deal with our regrets and have a chance to repent. The Hebrew word for repent is *Teshuvah*. The literal meaning is 'return. 'We will help each other return to the state we were in before we did whatever we regret doing."

Simon paused, looking around the circle at each of the participants before continuing. Leah looked away before he could meet her gaze. She wished she had the courage to leave. But she didn't want Simon to be disappointed in her again. Was she falling for him, as Hannah said she might?

"For example, I regret not being able to save my wife from the virus. That's easy for you to understand. But I also regret that when I was six, I couldn't save Leah's daughter from being stabbed. We were neighbors. It doesn't matter if my regret is reasonable or unreasonable. What matters is that my inability to save them feels like a blot on my soul. Don't try to be logical. Many of our regrets won't be logical. Try not to censor yourself today or tomorrow."

The first person to volunteer was the woman who lost her dog. There was a procedure costing thousands of dollars that might have extended the animal's life for a few months. She had enough savings. In the end, she didn't choose the surgery, and the dog died. She'd betrayed her best friend for money.

"If the surgery had cost a hundred dollars, I would have done it. If it cost a thousand, I would have done it. Even five thousand, seven thousand. But ten thousand? There was some line I couldn't cross. My dog was worth seven thousand to me, but not ten thousand. I can't explain it. I'm chewed up inside about it."

Leah had almost bankrupted herself paying her daughter's medical bills. It shamed her to recall her relief when her daughter died. No more horrendous co-pays. It was horrible to remember. Badly, she wanted to get up and get a donut. Badly, she wanted the entire tray of donuts. All that stopped her was not wishing to be rude in the middle of anyone's turn.

Simon instructed. "When you give feedback, it's not about whether a dog is worth some amount of money. It's about what this brings up in your own life."

Leah couldn't imagine confessing her thoughts to the group about the financial worth of her daughter, although she had done much worse than being glad not to receive bills from the hospital.

Hannah had a turn.

"When my baby was kidnapped, the F.B.I. agent kept pestering me about ransom amounts and rewards. Never pay a ransom, he said. The demands will just keep escalating if you do. Leave everything to us. But it's okay to offer a reward as long as it's for information leading to a conviction. A conviction? I didn't care about a conviction. I just wanted my baby back."

Someone passed her the tissues.

The others took their turns, regretting deeds of mistreatment, abandonment, infidelity, neglect, and exploitation. Hannah wondered if she had been too hard on her ex-husband for wanting a relationship with his daughter. Aaron admitted to black-marketing and other unethical acts to please his friend. Leah was the only one who passed and who then castigated herself for it.

"I'm a coward," she kept telling herself.

In the evening, she hid in her room rather than eat with the others. Instead, she used the vending machine to buy candy bars and Oreos.

The next morning, she awoke before dawn. The fourth day of the Retreat wouldn't start for four hours. She took her coffee out to the patio. The sunrise cast a silvery glow on the trees surrounding the lodge. The sky was clear and the air pine-scented.

Sarah, the name of the woman with the dog, sat on a bench.

"I hoped to see another early bird. Care to take a hike on such a lovely morning?"

"I suppose. I'll just finish my coffee," Leah said.

"Years ago, I worked in an office at the University with a woman named Edith. She and her granddaughter disappeared. They may have hiked up the hill when a sinkhole formed. I've been wanting to visit the site."

Leah had heard about the sinkhole. Edith was the mother of Deborah, the first wife of her deceased husband Josh. She was curious about the site, too. Josh's older daughter, Eva, might have died there.

A half-hour later, they had climbed to the top of the hill and looked down into the hole. A posted sign read "Danger. Unstable earth."

"The thing is, if the hole widened and took me, I'm not sure I'd mind," Sarah said.

"Hasn't the retreat helped?"

Sarah looked outward across the vista, an expanse of trees extending for miles.

"Oh, I haven't found anything that helps. I've always been single. I've always owned dogs. They last ten or fifteen years, until they die. I'm happy enough while they're young. But I've always been depressed, more or less."

They both stared down into the hole. It was about twenty feet wide and twelve feet across. They couldn't tell how deep. A slab of the former hill top on the far side of the hole dangled into the abyss, still attached.

Sarah turned to her.

"How about we jump in together? Right now."

"What?"

"I don't have the nerve to do it alone. We can hold hands and count to three. It will be over in a few seconds."

Leah froze.

"You're the one at the Retreat who seems like me. Fed up. Ready to end it. Let's do it."

What if Sarah pushed her or seized her hand and yanked her into the hole? She tried to clear her head. Fight—push Sarah in first, or flight—run before Sarah grabbed her. Any movement might cause Sarah to react. She might be older, but she had the energy to bound up the hill. That meant she had strength, maybe more than Leah did. Leah didn't dare budge.

"We better go back, now. We don't want to miss the beginning of the session." Leah tried to sound normal. She waited for Sarah to pounce.

"I'll stay awhile. You go." Sarah faced the hole. She seemed to shrivel. Leah saw this as her chance for escape.

"Will you be okay?"

"As much as ever," Sarah said.

"Alright. If you're sure." Before Sarah answered, Leah turned and started down the trail. Was it the right to leave Sarah? Should she tell Simon?

Back in the Oak Room, she took her usual seat between Aaron and Hannah, biting her tongue while waiting to see if Sarah would arrive. She could shout out to everyone that the older woman needed help. She could whisper to those next to her, passing the dilemma on to them. Meanwhile, Simon took his seat next to Aaron and looked at his phone. He didn't appear to notice that all the participants had arrived except one.

"Shall we begin?" Simon said.

She needed to say something before someone volunteered to work on repenting. Once they started, it would be against the rules to interrupt.

"Who hasn't had a turn yet?"

The participants looked from Leah to Aaron to the man whose son had committed suicide. Those three had done no Retreat work the day before.

"I'll go this afternoon," said the man whose son killed himself.

The group waited in silence for Aaron or Leah to volunteer. The thumping of Leah's heart was so loud, she was sure it was audible to the others.

"I'll defer to you, if you want to go first." Aaron's voice sounded to her as if it was at the wrong end of a megaphone.

Leah stammered. "It's just that… Sarah isn't here. I can't go until she gets back."

"Has anyone seen Sarah?" Simon's brow furrowed, as if he had just noticed one participant was missing.

They shook their heads.

"We were together at the top of the hill. She didn't come back with me."

Simon smiled. "Here she is."

Sarah walked to her usual seat, the only empty chair left, next to the two widows.

"So sorry, everyone. I see I'm late."

The group expected Leah to continue, as if she had chosen to take a turn. That wasn't what she intended. The relief of seeing that Sarah hadn't jumped into the sinkhole changed into the terror of telling what she most regretted. It was fight or flight again.

"Do you want the group to help you begin?" Simon's voice was gentle.

"I… I…" Leah cast pleading looks around the room, hoping for rescue. If she blurted out her regret, it would be over in seconds.

"We're right here with you, holding your hands," Simon said.

"I had the virus, a mild case, and I guess I went crazy, only a crazy person would do such a thing, an awful thing, I was angry, jealous angry, and I… I… spread the virus on purpose."

She spoke fast, spilling her words on to the group in a jumble. Everyone stared at her, no longer smiling. In a minute, they would give feedback. Hateful feedback. Feedback she couldn't bear. Intolerable feedback.

Before it started, Leah jumped up and ran from the room. Would the participants chase her down the lodge hallway? She didn't look back. Let the hotel keep her belongings. Except her purse. Her wallet.

Car keys. She would come back for them later, at night, while everyone at the Retreat slept in their hotel rooms, when no one would confront her.

She dashed to the trailhead leading to the sinkhole. Breathing in gasps, she climbed as fast as she could. There were splashing noises from the swimming pool or a waterfall or—she shuddered at the thought—Simon or one of the others calling her name. She didn't dare turn around. She reached the sign. "Danger. Unstable earth." Was it meant for her? Was she dangerous and unstable?

She needed to catch her breath. Looking around for a log to sit on, she saw a bench. But it wasn't empty. Aaron and Sarah sat there. How did they get up there before her? They grinned, as if they planned to outsmart her. As she stared at them, they transformed into her deceased parents, Ruth and Marty..

"Momma? Papa?"

"Do you want us to help you begin?" Ruth asked.

Leah approached them.

"I've been so bad. I'm so ashamed."

"Come," Marty said. "Sit on our laps,"

Leah sat on the pillowy thighs of both parents, leaning against them.

"I don't know what to do," she said.

"You must make *Aliyah*," Ruth said. Her hair was gray, no longer the salt-and-pepper that it was when Leah last visited.

"What do you mean?"

"You must go to the promised land."

Marty pointed a tremulous finger toward the sinkhole. "Look! It's just over there."

As Leah stared at the collapsed slab on the far side of the chasm, it shimmered and changed. The stone facade became the walls of Jerusalem, the Old City, flanked by the City of David. Part of the wall swung open to reveal the Souk, the Kotel, and the Dome of the Rock.

"The promised land. Right there," Marty said.

"We'll walk you to the edge and hold your hands. Then you must go on your own," Ruth said.

They rose, with Leah in the middle and a parent on each side, holding hands. As they walked to the edge, the bird chirps sounded like shofar blasts.

"We'll count to three, then let go," Marty said. "One, Two, Three…"

Ruth and Marty let go. Leah rose, as if on a breeze, and wafted toward Jerusalem. The rest was a blank.

A short session took place on the fifth day of the Retreat. The participants would leave after lunching together. They entered the Oak Room and took their usual seats, except for Hannah and the man whose son had committed suicide. He took his chair and placed it adjacent to hers, squeezing in next to Leah's. Hannah had her hand on his knee. He kept a possessive hand on Hannah's shoulder.

"Let's go around the circle so that everyone can say what this retreat meant to them," Simon said.

Smiles bordering on joy replaced the embarrassed sniffling of the previous four days.

"I'll go first." It was Sarah. She wore a long, flowing, colorful skirt and a youthful red top. "I signed up because I was very depressed. Some of my thoughts were frankly suicidal. But the past few days were a turnaround for me. The forest, the beauty, and just the fact that you all listened. It was a revelation."

"Thank you, Sarah. Who's next?"

Everyone told of their good experience, of the lifting of the burden of guilt, of redemption, of finding God, of a new lightness in their being. They all thanked Simon, their facilitator and their thoughtful guide on their journey from grief to joy.

Leah went last.

"I didn't take full advantage of the group sessions. Maybe you don't think I gained anything. But something happened—I can't explain what or how. All I can say is that I'm changed, different."

"There's no need to explain," Simon said. "Just stay with it and see where it takes you."

"Yes." she said.

At lunch, Leah sat next to Hannah. They hadn't spoken much after the first day.

"You have a new boyfriend," Leah said.

"He's a retreat boyfriend. It won't last. Just like all this good feeling. We'll go home. There they'll be—same old yellow floral curtains, same old rust-stained sink, same old sticky space bar on the computer. Back to the same old life."

"Not me."

"Oh?"

"I'm in Jerusalem."

CHAPTER 32
PRAYER: AZURA

Azura celebrated her twenty-second birthday in the Women's Rehab Unit of Block 742, Pod 56. Her room number was 3729B. From her tiny port window, she viewed the bleak housing block opposite, identical to hers. Dozens more were in this one section. With half the country devastated by viruses, unemployment, chronic psychiatric disorders, imprisonments, and the drug epidemic, the government subsidized thousands of bee-hive rooms to keep homelessness from sky-rocketing.

She might have opted for the relative freedom of life in the streets, but roving gangs made that too dangerous for an unprotected young woman. In return for safe quarters with meals, they required her to wear an ankle monitor able to detect drugs or alcohol in her system. If she didn't stay clean, they would kick her out.

Even after a year in a locked Rehab facility, she still craved Steel Wool. During her last overdose, she died three times, the EMT said. Steel Wool had been the only thing that calmed her, more so than Snow Ball or any of the cocktails. Now that drugs were forbidden her, she had to figure out other ways to keep from spiraling down.

In Rehab, she had taken classes in relapse prevention. They gave her techniques to use if a stressful situation arose. Call her sponsor, a woman named Meg. Go to a meeting. Focus on breath. Recite the Serenity Prayer.

God, grant me the serenity to accept the things I cannot change; the courage to change the things I can; and the wisdom to know the difference.

That sensible prayer was all the religion she needed. With its help, she accepted her room, for instance. Four feet high by five feet wide by six feet deep. Not much larger than a coffin, just a sleeping cell. In the evening, occupants crawled through a half-sized door onto a bed. In the morning, they crawled out and went to work. It wasn't designed for hanging out. For that, there were parks, gyms, libraries, and malls.

Azura repeated her Twelve-Step program as a precaution, now that she lived a less structured life outside of a locked facility. In all her years of doing the program, she never completed Steps Eight and Nine. "Make a list of all persons we had harmed, and become willing to make amends to them all" and "Make direct amends to such people wherever possible, unless doing so would injure them or others."

She kidnapped her infant half-brother, Abe, resulting in his death. Ten years before, in 2020, she apologized to her father, Isaac, but not to her step-mother, Hannah. The prospect terrified her. No doubt Hannah hated her. She might not be willing to allow Azura to make amends. Why should she? Besides, Hannah and Isaac divorced. She had no idea where Hannah was.

How would it be possible to make amends for the death of a newborn? An apology didn't seem like enough. Her mind curdled when she tried to think of an appropriate atonement. Meg said she would figure it out when she was ready. What she didn't want to do was anything that might injure Hannah by re-awakening her grief.

In the bible, atonement meant "an eye for an eye." Hannah might demand that Azura kill herself. Or that she stop taking measures to prevent herself from contracting Covid-30. What then?

She would have to consult her father, Isaac, even though he had been barred from visitation while she remained in Rehab because of his use of drugs. He was the rabbi of the Jewish Ecstatic Congregation in the Woods. After taking up residence in the same hut her mother had lived in as a girl, he began conducting Saturday morning services at the base of a waterfall in the forest, where he claimed to have visions. Mystical Jews followed him, but the more numerous non-Jews were welcomed. Hebrew prayers were supplemented with chanting, psilocybin mushrooms, and sometimes LSD.

The Serenity Prayer taught Azura that there was no changing her father. She could only change herself. Abstaining from drugs was the most important change she made. Another was avoiding her father when he pressured her to accept his odd mood-altering theology. On the other hand, he might know where Hannah was and how to approach her.

On the next Sunday, when she didn't have to work, when he wouldn't be leading his version of *Shabbat* services, she took the bus to the entrance of the state park. She would have a long walk to the hut. The forest was always more home to her than the town, even though she hadn't been there in the past decade. Most of the time, she'd been locked up in a psych ward, jail, or Rehab, or had been in stung out in some motel room. Now that she was sober, she relished being in nature. Every one of her senses awoke, stretched, and greeted the surroundings with pleasure. Here is where she'd been happiest, although she no longer had the skills to live in the forest.

When she arrived at the hut, her father was there, looking like the biblical patriarch he was named after, with his full beard, long hair, and robe. He embraced her, which she didn't much like. Not only did he refuse to wear a mask, he was also a kind of stranger, since she didn't meet him until she was twelve. For a short time, she had lived with him. She left when he began changing, giving up his job as a teacher, spending more time at the waterfall, taking drugs to induce visions, becoming more of a madman, in her view.

Some had called her mother a witch because she used roots and plants as cures. If her mother had been a mad woman, she never seemed so to Azura. She never used forest products to get high. Azura's life with her mother may have been primitive, but it had order and dependability. It was only after her mother's death that Azura stole the baby and careened into drug abuse.

Getting right to the point, she told her father the reason for the visit.

"I neglected to do this for too long, but I'm ready to apologize to Hannah. Do you have any idea where she is?"

Isaac picked up a book from the table. He gazed at it as if Hannah's whereabouts were written there. Azura noticed the text was in

Hebrew. Was it a Hebrew version of "Roots of the Woods?" She had the original in her bag. She always took the book with her wherever she went.

"Hannah?" Isaac said the name as if it familiar, but he couldn't quite place it at first. "Yes. Abe's mother. Where she lives."

He stood. "We can find out at the waterfall."

"Dad, this is not something to pray for. God doesn't have an address book. Either you have it or you don't."

He gave her a knowing smile. "*Elohim* knows everything, Darling. Everything. You never can tell what He'll choose to reveal."

She would have to humor him. "Okay. Lead the way."

He grabbed a stout branch leaning against the wall.

"A staff! You look like Moses," she said.

"I'll take that as a compliment, even though your tone is sarcastic."

They reached the waterfall. Isaac took a position facing east. He extracted a bag from his pocket, opened it, and popped something into his mouth. Azura made a displeased sound. He offered the bag to her.

"This will help."

"I can't. I'm wearing a monitor. Besides, you don't carry my drug of choice."

"Which is?"

"Steel Wool. I don't like hallucinogens. They make me feel too weird."

"They're supposed to. Insight comes with weird sensations. And you can tell whoever monitors the monitors that my drugs are part of a religious ceremony. That makes them legal."

"The monitors will appreciate knowing that." Could her father be that naïve?

Isaac closed his eyes, extended the staff toward the waterfall, and began chanting, swaying back and forth.

"*Baruch Atah Adonai. Blessed are You, Holy One.*"

Azura stood next to him, waiting. He would be praying for at least twenty minutes. When she lived with him, she attended his services. She remembered the process. The "visions" didn't happen until the ingested mushrooms or tabs took effect. Most of the time, she just observed. He wouldn't offer drugs to a minor. At times, twenty or thirty people would be high, all hallucinating at once. She'd back away, never sure what would happen.

"Every time, I get a little closer to God. But it's not without danger. If I get too close, I'll be consumed. I'm seeking the right distance, you see." This is what he told her when she lived with him.

After every *Shabbat* service, she asked him. "Did you find the right distance?"

"Maybe. If I go a nanometer closer, and I'm consumed, then I'll know."

This frightened her. You can't tell if you are too close, he seemed to say. It would be like apologizing to Hannah. There was just enough, and there was too much. Too much was dangerous. But she didn't know how much too much was. A personal conversation instead of a letter? The wrong words? "An eye for an eye"?

Her father became more animated.

"Look! Behind the waterfall! Do you see?"

She saw nothing but the familiar cascade of water spilling down the rock face. Isaac carried on, pointing and shouting, sometimes groaning, sometimes breaking into "Hallelujahs." When he finished, he staggered back to the hut, leaning on his staff, and then fell asleep. None of this was unexpected. Azura waited. He would be awake in a couple of hours.

When he roused, it surprised him to see his daughter, as if she had just appeared. Then he remembered.

"You want Hannah's address."

"That's right."

He dug through a pile of papers stacked on the table and another beside it on the floor.

"Where is it? I saw it recently," he muttered. "I forgot I kept it 'til just now."

After several minutes of searching, he handed her a yellow piece of paper with an address but no name.

"Are you sure this is hers?"

"I'm pretty sure. That's her handwriting. If you show it to her, she will know I gave it to you. It will prove who you are."

She stared at the paper. "She's in a good neighborhood. Not a government housing one, like my building."

Isaac didn't ask where.

"By the way. Some people who attend my services are pitching tents out here. I'm starting a cooperative, like your mother did, deeper in the forest. The name will be Ecstatic Woodland Cooperative. You might consider joining."

Azura still stared at the address.

"What should I say to Hannah?"

Isaac raised a hand, palm outward.

"Wait. That reminds me. These visions — they can go as fast as they come. You've jogged my memory. I heard Abe. He had a message for you about Hannah."

She put an incredulous hand on her hip.

"Dad. You had a verbal message from a newborn who has been dead for ten years? Really?"

"Yes. Of course. He is with *Elohim*. Everything is possible for those with *Elohim*. As I keep telling you, distance matters. I came close today, but not too close. Close enough receive Abe's message."

She considered. Her father was delusional, unless he wasn't. If a message was the bridge to Hannah, she should at least listen.

"Okay. Give me the message?"

"*Teshuvah.*"

"What?"

Isaac's smiled. It wasn't mysterious to him for a three-week old to say that word.

"*Teshuvah.* Hebrew for 'repent, 'or to be more literal, 'return'."

She shook her head. "That's it?"

"That's it."

"What does it mean?"

"That's for you to figure out. It may be a warning. Or a prediction."

She recited the Serenity Prayer under her breath. Even if she couldn't control his belief in drug-induced visions, she could control her own belief. Such as the impossibility of anyone hearing a message from a dead baby.

And yet…

"I've got to go. The last bus will be here soon," she said, putting the paper in her pocket.

He took a step toward her.

"Remember. The Ecstatic Cooperative. I'd very much like you to join."

The wisdom to know the difference.

"I'll think it over. After I make amends to Hannah."

He stepped aside so she could leave.

"Good luck with that," he said.

She understood what he meant. She was more likely to hear a dead infant speak in a waterfall than to think Hannah would allow her to apologize.

CHAPTER 33
REPENTANCE: AZURA

Three months later, COVID-30 peaked, and much of the country endured another lockdown, as it had off and on for years while the virus mutated and vaccine makers hurried to catch up. Lockdown periods were hardest on the millions living in bee-hive government housing. With ceilings between four and five feet high, residents had to spend long periods prone on their beds or sitting. Experts suggested exercises to prevent formation of embolisms, the primary cause of emergency room visits after the virus.

Azura had entered the second trimester of her pregnancy and had to take special precautions. The virus passed from the mother to the fetus. She was in Group One, reserved for pregnant women, senior citizens, and people with chronic illnesses. Group One couldn't leave their rooms. All essentials had to be delivered to them. They weren't allowed any human contact.

At least morning sickness, which should have been called "all-day sickness," had abated. Now she was ravenous. Her government-issued meals doubled in calories because of her condition, but they weren't enough. She spent her allowance, the pittance left over from her unemployment benefit after payment for room and board, on snacks.

The father of her baby was an older guy named Larry. They had only hooked up once. It meant nothing. She didn't plan to tell him about the pregnancy or that she refused to consider an abortion. Although she had been sober, she remembered little about the encounter. He dealt in pharmaceuticals and used to supply her with

Steel Wool, before she went to Rehab. They still kept in touch, although, in a technical sense, she relapsed by being in contact with a dealer.

Narcotics Anonymous meetings remained available on zoom, and she still did the Twelve-Step program. For over three months, since visiting her father in his forest residence, she'd been working up the nerve to do Steps 8 and 9—making amends to her ex-step-mother Hannah for kidnapping her baby. Now that Azura was pregnant, her shame and regret for what she had done deepened.

She taped the print of the ultra-sound of her fetus to the wall. Although it was hard to make out, the beating heart of her child lay somewhere beneath the more defined shape of its head. For hours, she cradled her small bulge in her hands. The tiny fetus, no bigger than her thumb, was the only thing that had ever been hers. Little Adam, she called him.

She intended to contact Hannah before Little Adam's birth. After, when she was drowning in responsibility, she'd lack the courage. Hannah's physical address was also taped to the wall, along with her email address, which Azura paid to acquire. She wrote a short draft, telling herself she'd decide whether to send it later.

Dear Hannah,

I'm the daughter of Isaac, the one who took your baby, which resulted in his murder by my adopted brother. For years, I've wanted to make amends. Now that I'm pregnant, I realize more than ever how much pain I caused you. Will you allow me to apologize and to come up with a way to atone?

Very very sincerely,

Azura.

Her finger hovered over the "Send." Many possibilities tangled in her head. Maybe Hannah wouldn't reply. That was likely. Maybe she would send a hate-filled reply. Azura wouldn't blame her. Maybe she would be nice. Fat chance. Maybe she'd get Azura in trouble. Somehow. Maybe her reply would be so horrible, it would drive Azura to relapse, damaging her baby and getting her kicked out of her room. She tried to imagine a reply that would be any worse than the words she already had in her own head.

Over and over, she went through these possibilities. When exhaustion took over, she clicked on "Send." It was over. She had a few seconds of relief. Then the anxious waiting started. She bit her nails. She bought more snacks and ate most of them in a sitting.

It surprised her to receive a reply from Hannah only ten minutes later.

I received your email. My husband, Simon, and I would like to set up a Zoom meeting with you. We have a way for you to atone, if you mean it.
Hannah.

Azura closed the box of cookies. She thought a slow email process would follow, if Hannah replied at all. After each email, there would be a time to reflect and consider a response. But a Zoom meeting. She would see Hannah's pain or fury in real time. And this Simon, her husband—it would be two against one. But if that was Hannah's condition, she owed it to her to comply.

They set up a meeting for the next day. Azura stayed awake all night thinking of how to apologize, the right words to say, many words or few words. She couldn't decide. She would have to just rely on her wits when the time came. Her appetite tanked. She didn't finish her breakfast.

The room had a built-in monitor on the wall that could swing out for use while in bed, either sitting or tilted while lying down. It was a large screen, better for Zoom than her phone. When she logged in, there, without introduction, were the disembodied heads of a man and a woman, only inches away. The woman had dark curls, graying at the temples, and fine wrinkles around her severe dark eyes. The man was narrow-faced and balding, with cruel, thin lips. In the smaller image of herself, her government-required buzz haircut made her face look enlarged, balanced on a fragile neck.

In silence, they looked each other over.

"Let's get started. I'm Hannah. This is Simon, my second husband. He knows everything about your father." The woman sounded confident, blunt.

"I'm Azura. Thank you for letting me do this."

During another pause, Azura held her breath. *Say it. Say it.* She commanded herself.

"I… uh… realize it's years too late. I want to make amends for what I did to the baby, Abe, your baby. To you…"

She swallowed, feeling tears well up, unsure what to more to say.

"You're pregnant." Hannah barked out the fact.

"Yes. Four months."

"And you want to atone."

"Yes." Hannah took charge, leading the conversation. Azura felt obliged to answer.

"We have a way," Simon said.

Just then, Azura remembered. "*Teshuvah*," she said.

Hannah blinked, then looked at Simon, before gazing at Azura again.

"I'll tell you what you can return," Hannah said.

Simon took over. "You stole a baby. You owe a baby. It's a debt you have to pay my wife. You can pay that debt by giving her a baby."

"An eye for an eye, Azura," Hannah said. "That's *Teshuvah*."

"I don't understand." The ceiling seemed to lower. Azura scrunched down, curving her spine to fit.

"You must give us your baby as soon as it's born. It's what you owe. Your baby."

Azura clicked on "Leave meeting," slamming the monitor back into the wall.

A few minutes later, she began receiving a bombardment of emails. Some from Hannah. Some from Simon. Every few minutes.

You said you want to atone.

You owe us a baby.

Give back what you stole.

It's 'Teshuvah." Return a baby. To us.

She closed her email. What had she expected? Years of paying Hannah some enormous amount of money deducted from her meager income. Working for Hannah, doing odd jobs, in her free time after work. A heartfelt apology. A written account of what led to her crime. Of all the forms she thought atonement might take, she never imagined giving up her baby. She brought her knees as far up as possible, against her stomach, protecting Little Adam, as if he was about to be ripped from her womb.

She phoned Meg, her sponsor.

"Hello?" Meg had the gravelly voice of an aging alcoholic.

Azura sobbed. "It's me. I did Steps 8 and 9. I met with Hannah on zoom. She wants me to make amends by giving her my baby, Meg."

"What?"

Azura chocked out the words. "She says I owe her a baby because I stole hers. I can only atone if I give her mine."

"That's not the intent of Step 9. You don't give up a child for Step 9. That's bullshit. Just say you're sorry—that's all Step 9 requires, when there's no reasonable way of doing anything else."

A ping for a new email sounded. It appeared in a banner.

Face what you did. Simon has something to tell you about your mother. He will Zoom you at 6 p.m.

She read the email to Meg.

"You don't need to listen to him. Don't accept," she said.

Something about her mother? When the Zoom invite appeared just before 6, Azura almost declined before accepting. Simon's face hovered over her on the monitor.

"What's this about my mother. How would you have known her?" She would listen, quitting the meeting if she didn't like what she heard. She didn't owe this man anything.

"I used to be a member of the Woodland Cooperative, when she was pregnant with you. Did you know she stole a toddler named Calen?"

"She didn't steal Calen. She borrowed him. Later she adopted him." Simon had his facts wrong.

"She adopted him? Where are the court documents? Where's the bill from the lawyer? What's your proof?"

Her head hurt. She thought of her mother's last illness and death. She and Calen continued to live in the hollow tree her mother made into their home. Where would papers have been? Nothing existed there besides sleeping mats, a stove, and a few possessions. The closest thing to documents was the yellowing "Roots of the Woods," and that was a book, not legal papers.

Simon continued. "Your mother stole Calen from his parents, Jenny and Leo Berg. I was there when it happened. Jenny became hysterical when she woke up, and her little boy was missing. Leo tore through the forest looking for him. None of us believed that First Woman, your mother, our leader, would do such an awful thing. But she was gone, Calen was gone, Great Mother was gone, the dinghy was gone. Put two and two together. She stole him, Azura."

She pressed her throbbing temples with her fingers. "Why would she have done that?"

He stared at her, straight into the camera, unblinking.

"My best guess is that she thought we'd all die from the virus, except her, and she wanted a companion for you, a mate for you, when you were grown."

"Calen? A mate for me? My brother?"

"Two generations of baby theft. You owe us a baby, Azura."

She left the meeting without saying anything. The light hurt her eyes. Her head pounded. Simon lied. She needed to talk to her father right away, to find out what he knew. There was no way to contact him in the forest, except to go there in person, but she wasn't supposed to leave her room. She could be tracked by her cell phone or caught by patrols.

Desperate to get to the forest, she abandoned her phone, leaving it on the bed, put on a mask, and crawled out the door. The monitor was supposed to be for detecting alcohol or drugs, but it might also have tracking capability. And there was the risk of COVID-30. It was dangerous to touch anything. Virus droplets were everywhere. The buttons in elevators might be contaminated. The emergency stairway was safer if she didn't touch the bannisters. With furtive steps, she ascended to the lobby and left the building without getting caught.

The bus presented another obstacle. Safe distancing was impossible. She had to take the chance. Once at the state park, it was less likely she would be captured or contract the virus. She hoped to be able to return to her room after visiting her father. If the authorities discovered her absence, they might lock her out.

Her father prayed at the base of the waterfall. As usual, she endured his embrace before they talked.

"What can you tell me about my mother?"

"Your mother?" He sat on a log and looked at the rock face. "We had a chance encounter that produced you. It was over in minutes. I'm not proud of it. Right after our encounter, I began dating Hannah."

She sat on the rough log next to him. Her encounter with Larry had been similar, a onetime chance happening.

"Do you know anything about my brother, Calen? How she came to adopt him?"

He shook his head, continuing to gaze at the waterfall, seeing something that made sense only to him.

"What I found out much later was that your mother's name was Eva. She was about the age of a four-year-old girl with the same name who disappeared with her grandmother years before. It's one of those cold case crimes. The speculation in police circles is that your mother was that girl, stolen from her parents by her grandmother, your great-grandmother."

"Who told you that?" Her head hurt again.

"The police detective who investigated when you kidnapped Abe. After they charged you, he made the connection between your mother and the original Eva. Then they did a DNA on her remains."

"Oh My God, Dad. I'm in the middle of three generations of kidnapped children. And now Hannah wants my baby. She says I owe it to her."

Isaac's head snapped away from the waterfall. He looked squarely at his daughter.

"These are not biblical times. No firstborn has to be sacrificed to appease a Pharaoh or a god, or the Hebrew God — or Hannah. You don't owe anyone your baby."

"But, Dad. Three generations. What is *Teshuvah* for that?"

When she got back to her room, they had locked her out, as she feared. A bag hung on the doorknob. It contained her belongings, "Roots of the Woods," her phone, and a small key for unlocking the ankle monitor. She took it off and left it on the same doorknob. Now she was homeless.

The last bus to the state park took her back to the entrance. Instead of going in, she walked down the road to the next property and knocked on the steel door of the bunker. There was a grinding noise. Something needed oiling. When it opened. Larry stood there.

"I saw you coming through the periscope."

"You're unmasked."

"I'm vaccinated. Come in."

The inside of the bunker reminded her of a larger version of her room in government housing. Low ceilinged, confining, dark, grim.

"How did you get vaccinated? I didn't think anyone developed a vaccine for COVID-30."

"There isn't one — officially. I just know people who know people."

Larry. Old but still very attractive. Able to get whatever he wanted.

"Have you come to make a purchase?" Pharmaceutical dealing had many advantages during an outbreak.

"Oh, how I wish."

He smiled. "You liked Steel Wool. I remember."

"Yes, but I'm pregnant."

"Then I wouldn't advise it. I might have guessed. You have that pregnant woman glow." He always flirted.

"Larry, I have something to tell you and something to ask you."

"Better have a seat. Want a diet soda? Water?'

Azura told him he was the father of her unborn child. He didn't respond. A doubtful smile spread on his face. His shoulders rose in a perceptible shrug. She noticed, but it didn't matter what he thought. Then she told him what she learned about her mother from Simon. Larry had been in the Cooperative. What did he remember?

"Nothing about her earlier life. I knew Simon. He joined before me, when his wife died of COVID-19. We all ran from that virus. The Cooperative fell apart over taking in new members when we didn't have the resources for them. Your mother wanted us to re-camp across the lake where we'd be more secure. I don't know why, but she took the boy, Calen, and disappeared with him. She was pregnant with you. We trusted her. She turned out to be a piece of work."

"Thanks for not saying a 'bitch.'"

"I'm careful what I say to daughters about their mothers." He smiled, teasing.

She glanced around the bunker. There would be no bus service until the next day.

"I have nowhere to go. Can I sleep here for a night?"

"Sure. For a night."

The walls were reinforced concrete. Yet, it wasn't safe to be so near a source of Steel Wool. For her, it was a house of sticks, and Larry was the wolf.

On her phone, the banners kept appearing.

Give us what you owe.

Sign a termination of rights contract.

"Larry. There's something else." She told him about Hannah, about doing Steps 8 and 9, about Simon. She showed him the emails. He held her phone in his cunning hands and read the entire correspondence.

"Want my advice?"

"Yes."

"You feel you owe them, right?"

"Yes. That's the thing."

"You're young. You can have plenty of babies. But right now you're homeless and just out of Rehab. Your job will be gone. You might get the virus, if you're not very careful. You don't need a child right now."

"Are you saying what I think you're saying?"

"I'm saying Hannah and Simon can give a child a normal, privileged life. What can you give it? You won't even see it. To make ends meet, you'll have to work two jobs. By the time you pick it up from one of those government day-care centers, it'll be time for it to go to bed. It won't even know you."

"But it's my baby. My Little Adam. He's all I have."

Larry's shoulders raised again.

"Look, Azura. You have the upper hand. You can parlay this to your advantage. If you show me the contract Simon mentioned, I'll fix it so they'll support you now and maintain you for a while after the birth."

"I should sign a contract giving them my baby?"

As helpless tears bubbled up from deep within Azura, Larry had the excited gleam of someone who solves multiple problems with one smart move.

"You'll pay what you owe, but you'll make them pay to pay what you owe."

"What?"

"It's beautiful," he said. "Just leave everything to me."

The next morning, Azura left the bunker before Larry woke up. She stood outside, gazing at the trees across a field behind the entrance to Larry's residence. For the first time, she noticed brown discoloration among the pines. The forest was unhealthy. The town was riddled with virus. Neither were safe.

An idea came to her. Why didn't she think of it before? Perhaps she could find the Nathan sisters and her great grandmother, still in their cave, still caring for animals. If they were alive, Great Mother would be in her nineties and the sisters in their seventies. She'd lead them to the hollowed out tree on the other side of the lake, deep within the forest in an area of old growth, not infected, reachable by dinghy. Her childhood home. They'd help her with the delivery when her due date arrived. Living there would be another form of *Teshuvah*, a returning.

But if Adam was to have a future, would she have to steal a girl for him? It wouldn't be good for him to grow up without a companion. She might find one in her father's cooperative, a baby who had not yet been indoctrinated into the cult.

She hadn't been able to keep Abe safe. It occurred to her that he was the one who needed her amends, not Hannah. But how? That baby died. Maybe she should complete Steps 8 and 9 by preserving the next life, the one growing within her. If she remained hidden with the three older women, she could protect her child, or two children, or a colony who might be the only survivors in a dying world.

She found a spot in the meadow and pulled "The Book of Roots" out of her bag. It opened in her hands by itself to the last page, titled "Epilogue," containing a single sentence.

"She's waiting for you."

The grass beneath her smoldered. As she stamped it out, white smoke billowed around her, then gathered into a stream in front of her. It would lead her to Great Mother.

ABOUT THE AUTHOR

Carolyn Geduld is a mental health professional in Bloomington, Indiana. Her fiction has appeared in numerous literary journals and anthologies. Her first novel, *Take Me Out The Back*, was published by Black Rose Writing in August, 2020.

NOTE FROM THE AUTHOR

Word-of-mouth is crucial for any author to succeed. If you enjoyed *Who Shall Live*, please leave a review online—anywhere you are able. Even if it's just a sentence or two. It would make all the difference and would be very much appreciated.

Thanks!
Carolyn Geduld